4

Bottom Feeders

A Sylvia Avery Mystery

BOOK ONE

Jan Bono

Sandridge Publications
Long Beach, Washington

It's a mystery!
Jan Bono

First Printing, Fall, 2015

Printed in the United States of America
Gorham Printing, Centralia, WA 98531

Sandridge Publications
P.O. Box 278
Long Beach, WA   98631

http://www.JanBonoBooks.com

ISBN: 978-0-9906148-2-1

DEDICATED

to Rick

My best friend, traveling companion, tech guru,
and all-around good guy.
I am forever grateful for your constant encouragement,
support, kicks-in-the-backside, and love.
RIP, my Big Cuddle Bear.

OTHER BOOKS BY JAN BONO

Health and Fitness:

Back from Obesity:
My 252-pound Weight-loss Journey

Collections of humorous personal experience:

Through My Looking Glass: View from the Beach

Through My Looking Glass: Volume II

It's Christmas!
Forty-three stories and three one-act plays

Just Joshin'
A Year in the Life of a Not-so-ordinary
4th Grade Kid

Fiction:

Starfish
A Sylvia Avery Mystery, Book II

Romance 101:
Forty-two Sweet, Light, Delicious,
G-Rated Short Stories

Poetry Chapbooks:

Bar Talk and *Chasing Rainbows*

A number of Jan's books are now available as eBooks at Smashwords.com. Find them at:

http://www.smashwords.com/profile/view/JanBonoBooks

NORTH BEACH PENINSULA

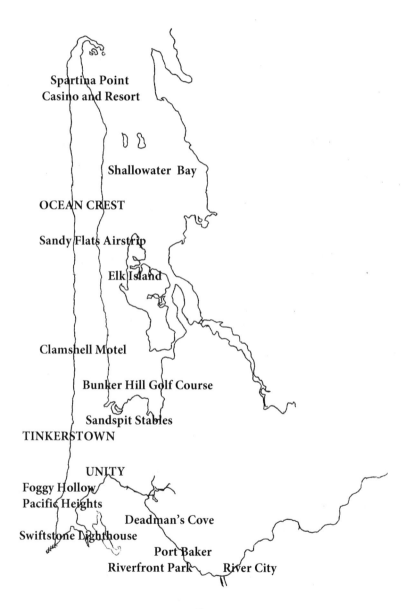

Spartina Point
Casino and Resort

Shallowater Bay

OCEAN CREST

Sandy Flats Airstrip

Elk Island

Clamshell Motel

Bunker Hill Golf Course

Sandspit Stables

TINKERSTOWN

UNITY

Foggy Hollow
Pacific Heights

Deadman's Cove

Swiftstone Lighthouse

Port Baker

Riverfront Park   River City

CHAPTER ONE

"Come on, Jimmy! Open up!" The sound of my impatient fingernails reported a machine gun rat-a-tat-tat against the window. It's a darn good thing my natural nails are strong, or the force of my rapping would have broken them all off.

The edge of the curtain quivered slightly, then Jimmy's scrawny arm snaked out to slide the pane back.

"Did anyone see you drive in?"

"Don't be so friggin' clandestine," I whispered. "I don't know why I can't just come in the front door of the motel office like everyone else."

"Can't risk it." Jimmy handed me a white plastic kitchen stepstool, which I unfolded and placed on the ground beside the wall.

I handed him my red high heels and climbed up the three short steps. He offered his hand, like a gallant knight come to rescue the fair maiden. Only it was I who was rescuing him. Again.

I had to shimmy my dress up nearly to my waist to straddle the windowsill. "If I ruin my pantyhose climbing in here, Jimmy, you're buying me two new pairs to make up for the inconvenience."

Jimmy just stood there, holding the shoes. Apparently the appearance of so much middle-aged bared leg climbing into his private domain rendered him speechless—or perhaps embarrassed—but I decided it was a compliment.

"Geez Jimmy, quit gawking. It's not like you haven't seen me in shorts before." I countered his gaping stare with a glare of my own, dropping down into the room with a soft thud. "Besides, I'm not your type."

"I, uh, couldn't decide where to put these." He flailed the high heels, one in each hand, like a kid trying to shake two bottles of catsup at the same time.

"I mean, uh, I keep all my sci-fi novels in alphabetical order on my bookshelves, and I don't know which shelf to put your shoes on. Should I file them under "R" for red, "S" for shoes, or "H" for high heels?"

"Why don't you file them under "D" for the dancing I won't be doing tonight because you have some sort of imagined emergency?" I exhaled noisily just to make him feel bad. "I knew I shouldn't have left my cell phone on."

"Come on, Sylvia," he countered. "It's not like you had a real date tonight."

"How many times have I told you—I don't need a man to be complete." I squinted my eyes at him. "I am a perfectly wonderful, autonomous woman. I am blessedly, not desperately, single." Holy crap, I was starting to sound like some kind of banner-waving feminist. I stopped speaking before I made a total fool of myself.

I leaned back out the low window and hauled in the stepstool. "I'm getting way too old for this kind of thing." I sighed loudly again, and slid the pane shut.

Jimmy looked at the floor. "I'm sorry I had to call you away from your fun tonight, Syl. I know you love your Friday nights out, but it *is* an emergency." He paused. "And you're probably the only one who can help me."

"Can, or will?" I sighed a third time for good measure, adjusted my skirt, and plopped down on the edge of his bed. "Let's hear it. Maybe I can solve your little problem and still get back to the Rusty Rudder for the last set."

"It's not that simple." Jimmy put my shoes down on top of his dresser and sat beside me. He pushed his black-framed glasses up with his middle finger, a habit he knows annoys me, leaned forward, and looked directly into my eyes.

"Sylvia," he began, "I know it's going to sound crazy, but I'm pretty sure somebody wants to kill me."

"Kill you? Oh, I can't imagine anyone wanting to do that..."

Jimmy ignored my obvious sarcasm and continued, "Well, you see, after I pulled out of the Cinco Amigos' parking lot tonight, this car behind me sped up like to pass."

"Mmmm," I interrupted. "That sounds good! I could sure go for some Chinese food right now. I love that place."

Tinkerstown is probably the only town in the world with a quality Chinese restaurant owned and operated by five Mexican friends who got fed up with working for minimum wage in the fish canneries.

"Sylvia!" Jimmy grabbed my arm. "Focus!"

I tried to pry his hands loose. "Jimmy! You're bruising me."

"Sorry." He put his hands back into his lap and folded them tightly in a gesture of constraint. "I need your undivided attention, Syl."

"Fine. No problem. I promise to hang onto your every word just as soon as you tell me if you've got any leftovers stashed in the fridge."

It was Jimmy's turn to sigh.

Jimmy Noble and I have been friends for a great many years. My name is Sylvia Lee Avery, and I'm a recent retiree from an area of what we used to call the Department of Health, Education and Welfare, or HEW. Somehow that morphed into the Department of Social and Health Services, or DSHS. We've gone through so many initials in the past 30 years I can't keep track of them all.

I spent the majority of my career with some derivation of CPS—Child Protective Services. Now I'm attempting to live on a moderate pension in the same small coastal community where I'd worked. Nevertheless, I'm thoroughly enjoying early retirement.

Jimmy, on the other hand, will never be able to retire from anything. For the past two decades he's been managing the 7-unit derelict Clamshell Motel. Even in its prime, say 50 or 60 years ago, the painted-over cinderblock construction had a grungy feel to it. It still has the bomb shelter logo, reminiscent of every cinderblock basement in the nuclear-scared 1960s, affixed to the side of the main unit. But Jimmy calls it home, and it provides him with a solid roof over his head. No pun intended.

Ignoring my quest for leftovers, he began again. "Okay. So this car comes up behind me, see, so I figured I wasn't moving fast enough to suit him, and I slowed down so he could pass. But then he just pulls alongside, and the guy in the passenger seat rolls down his window and sticks a gun out and waves it at me, real threatening-like." Jimmy looked at me like he expected me to say something, so I did.

"*And that's it?!* He just waved a gun in your direction and you think he wants to kill you?" I shook my head. "Jesus, Jimmy, it was probably just some big-city idiot with too much testosterone demonstrating his personal version of small-town road rage." I peered at him. "He didn't fire off any rounds or anything, did he?"

"No," admitted Jimmy. "He just sped off into the night.

But when I got home, there was this message on the motel answering machine—" He leaned over and picked up the phone receiver next to the bed. Then he pressed the speaker and voicemail buttons.

"Take that as a warning, spy-guy, and keep your Peeping Tom nose out of our business. Next time we see you hanging around where you don't belong, we're gonna make crab bait outta ya."

"You hear that, Syl?" Jimmy picked up a pillow and hugged it tight to his chest.   "Somebody wants to feed me to the crabs."

"HHhhmm..." I chewed on my lower lip. "I hate to admit it, Jimmy, but you may be right."

"You gotta help me, Syl." He blinked back tears. "Please." He swallowed hard and looked away. "I didn't know who else to call."

"How 'bout the police?"

I knew what his reply would be before the question left my lips. Jimmy had a reputation with the Local Leos for being somewhat of a hand-wringing worrywart. He'd called them so many times with imaginary 'emergencies' that they weren't likely to take him seriously about anything any more. According to a friend on the force, they privately refer to him as "Peter and the Invisible Wolf."

I softened. "Okay, Jimmy, what do you want me to do?"

Jimmy let out a huge rush of air. "Thank you, Syl. Thank you, thank you, thank you!" He opened his closet and pulled out an extra blanket. "You can sleep in here, and I'll take the couch."

"*What?!*" I scowled at him in disbelief, mindless of the wrinkles I was adding to my forehead. "You want me to stay *here* tonight?"

"Of course I do!" His head bobbed up and down. "You

don't think I want to stay here all by *myself*, do you?"

"Jimmy!" I placed my hands on my hips and gave him my best no-nonsense look. "I've put a lot of things on my bucket list since I retired, and protecting you all night from some crazed homicidal lunatic is definitely *not* on it!"

Jimmy stuck out his lower lip and looked at me pleadingly with his big, brown, cocker spaniel eyes. It might have been laughable, except for the fact that his face was so darn pale. Instinctively, I knew what was coming next.

"Didn't you promise Mom you'd always watch out for me?"

There it was—Jimmy's trump card. His mother, a former mentor and co-worker of mine, had succumbed to cancer early last year. Jimmy, her only child, was left a virtual orphan, his father having long since left the area with no forwarding address.

"Jimmy, that's not fair," I began half-heartedly.

He leaned down to give me a hug and I noticed the growing bald spot on the top of his head. The bald spot was pre-mature, but then, I thought wryly, so was Jimmy. He knew he had me, so what was the point of trying to wiggle out of this?

"Everything will look better in the morning," he said matter-of-factly, sidling for the door. "Isn't that what you've always told me? 'Few goblins survive the light of day.'" He nodded. "Yep, I remember you saying that, clear as..." He grinned for the first time since I'd arrived. "Clear as day."

I hated the way he was manipulating me, and also the fact that I feel so responsible for him, but I let him leave the room without further protest. I was thankful once again that my contacts are extended wear, and I disrobed and crawled into bed without even bothering to wash my face.

Several hours spent tossing and turning and I was more convinced than ever that agreeing to spend the night had been a bad idea. The bed, although here in his private quarters, was standard motel issue, and I ached for my pillow-topped mattress at home.

Vaguely, I could hear the sound of the TV coming from the other room. The red illuminated lights on the nightstand clock told me it was well after three.

I got up and rummaged through his closet. I don't mind sleeping in the nude, in fact I prefer it, but I wasn't about to make a trip to the bathroom sans clothing. I pulled out a baby blue terrycloth robe and tied it tightly around my waist before stepping out into the hall.

Pausing in the hallway for a moment, I thought I recognized the soundtrack of the movie Jimmy had on. I crept into the main living area and there he sat, fully dressed and obviously wide-awake. A small, huddled form cowering in an oversized black naugahyde vinyl recliner, he stared with a horrified expression at his enormous flat-screen HD TV. For a gay guy, Jimmy has absolutely no furniture fashion sense.

"Stephen King, Jimmy? *Seriously?*"

He jumped at the sound of my voice, spilling his calico cat Priscilla, who had been curled up in his lap, rudely onto the floor. "Sylvia! You scared me!"

"Turn off the TV, Jim. *Now.*" I was using my stern voice again, and this time it got his attention.

"Ah, Syl." He clicked the off the remote. "I couldn't sleep, and that was all that was on."

"You incessantly brag about having a satellite dish with hundreds of channels at your disposal, so don't give me that."

Jimmy shrugged. "You want some hot cocoa?"

"What I *want*," I said more harshly than I'd intended, "is to get some quality sleep, but that seems rather unlikely at this point."

"You wanna play cards?" he asked hopefully. "We could play cards until it gets light out."

By the time I'd finished in the bathroom, Jimmy had his portable poker table set up in the middle of the living room and was busy shuffling the deck. I sighed and held out my hand. "I'm dealing."

He relinquished the cards and started stacking colored chips in front of each of us. "Just a friendly game of poker," said Jimmy. "We'll play for chips."

"Like hell we will, " I replied. "Penny a point."

"But Syl— I— I don't want to take your money."

"Don't you worry about that," I replied, flipping a card in front of him. "And don't you dare give me that sweet and innocent puppy dog look again."

Daylight was in full force by the time we called it quits at the card table. I was up by a little over six dollars.

"Will you take a check?" he asked.

"I'll run you a tab," I generously replied, standing up and stretching. "Now put on some coffee while I go take a shower."

Jimmy crossed to the kitchen side of the room and dumped some kibbles into Priscilla's cat dish. He tugged on the window shade over the sink and it rolled up a few inches just as a big, black, shiny car pulled off the highway and into the motel driveway.

"Syl!" his voice came out in a squeaky whisper. "That's the car! Oh God, Syl, they've come to kill me!"

"Get down!" I commanded, following my own advice and ducking out of the line of sight from the parking lot. "Just stay on the floor."

I crept to the window on the side wall and peered cautiously through one of the slits between the panels of the still-closed Venetian blinds. The car made a big, looping turn in the gravel parking lot and pulled up near the office door. Someone in the passenger seat hoisted a large, bound, black trash bag out the car door, and the vehicle sped away, kicking up a plume of small rocks and dust before turning north on the highway.

"They're gone. You can get up now."

Jimmy remained prone on the kitchen linoleum, hugging the floor and murmuring The Lord's Prayer.

"I said, you can get up now."

Jimmy slowly got to his feet and peeked out the kitchen window. "You sure?"

"Yes, of course I'm sure." I hesitated before going on. "I'm going to skip the shower and just get dressed. I think it's time you called the police."

"But you said they're gone." He furrowed his brow. "Why should I call the police after the fact?"

"They're gone, alright, but they left us a little present."

"What kind of present?" Jimmy joined me at the living room window, pulled the drape back, and looked out. "Oh my God, Sylvia! It's a body! I just know it's a body!" his voice was high and squeaky again.

"Jimmy! For crying out loud!" I took him by the shoulders. "Come on, now, get ahold of yourself! We mustn't make assumptions. It might just be somebody illegally dumping off their garbage."

He collapsed into my arms and I held him while he took a few ragged breaths. It crossed my mind, not for the first time, that my promise to his dying mother to watch out for him should have had some limits put on it. The kid is in his late 30s—enough already!

After a few minutes, Jimmy looked up at me. "There's a dumpster at the other end of the parking lot."

"What?"

"If it were just someone dropping off their trash, they could have put it into the motel dumpster." He paused, then softly went on. "You don't think it's just garbage either, do you?"

"No, to be honest, I don't. So you need to make that call to the Sheriff's Office. I want an officer here before anybody—and I mean *anybody*— goes near that trash bag. Understand?"

Jimmy nodded and moved toward the phone while I went to pull on my clothes. I hoped it was still early enough that the dispatcher couldn't claim the department was too busy to respond to what he might think was just another of Jimmy's crank calls.

On second thought, perhaps I should have made the call myself. I desperately needed the comfort of having a deputy on the scene right away.

But it wasn't a deputy who pulled into the driveway just minutes later; it was the sheriff himself. I'd barely had time to zip up my dancing dress and run a comb through my hair before his patrol vehicle came blazing into the driveway.

Jimmy and I greeted him from the top of the motel office steps.

"What's this about finding a body?" Sheriff Donaldson hollered as he bolted from his vehicle.

I glared at Jimmy. "You reported finding a *body?*"

Jimmy hung his head. At least he had the good grace to show some humility in front of the sheriff. "I didn't think they'd come right away if I told them somebody dumped a trash bag by the door," he mumbled.

"You mean to tell me there's no body?" Sheriff Donaldson glowered at Jimmy.

"I think I said there *might* be a body." Jimmy looked up tentatively. "And now that you're here, Sheriff, you can check it out for yourself." He pointed to the oversized black plastic bag lying on its side between the stoop and the sheriff's car.

As if on cue, the bag settled slightly, and a red liquid substance leaked out onto the ground. Jimmy screamed and jumped back, the sheriff's eyebrows shot skyward, and I felt a sickening nausea wash over me. The air was suddenly filled with what I believed must be the smell of decaying flesh.

"Don't touch that bag!" barked Sheriff Donaldson in his most authoritative voice. Without taking his eyes off the red puddle forming, he pressed the radio button attached to the collar of his shirt.

"Dispatch, get ahold of the Coroner's Office right away. Tell the M.E. I need him and the meat wagon, at the Clamshell Motel. And I'm going to need both deputies on call out here too, stat."

The sheriff signed off and turned to his patrol vehicle, a brand new black and white Ford Police Interceptor SUV. Opening the back, he pulled out a thick roll of yellow crime scene tape. "Jimmy! Come help me with this!"

Jimmy rushed to step down the two steps of the stoop to the driveway and tripped over his own feet. He screamed again as he fell, landing face-first on top of the trash bag. The loose tie gave way and a considerable number of fish heads and guts burst out upon the ground.

Sheriff Donaldson's face and neck turned scarlet. He pressed his radio collar clip and spoke into it a second time. "Dispatch—false alarm. Cancel both those call-outs."

I held my breath. I'd known Sheriff Donaldson professionally for many years. He's a good guy, overall, but he's too conservative for my taste, and is generally known for always erring on the side of caution. Until now. What had possessed him to call in reinforcements before checking the contents of the bag was beyond me.

The sheriff's voice sounded far too calm for the rage I knew he must have felt. He returned the crime scene tape to his SUV, and closed the back hatch with a resounding bang. Then he turned to Jimmy, who had meanwhile gotten to his feet and was busily occupied wiping the fish guts off his clothing.

"It's against the law to call in a false report, Mr. Noble, and I've half a mind to lock you up for awhile so you can think about that fact."

"But— But I never said *for sure* it was a body!"

"Jimmy," I said, "why don't you go in and clean up while I apologize to the sheriff?" I held the door open for him and hurriedly waved him inside. Amazingly, he went without argument.

"Now, Carter," I began, employing my best eyelash-batting guile, "you know you don't have the jail space, or just cause, to take him in."

Sheriff Carter Donaldson looked closely at me for the first time since he'd arrived. He stroked his thick, salt-and-pepper mustache with his left hand, running his finger and thumb outward from the middle. He gave me a thorough up and down once-over while he thought about the wisdom behind my words.

Sheriff Donaldson is a good 6'4", and at 5'7", the only way I held my own was because I was still standing on the stoop, giving us more of a level playing field and making his obvious elevator-eyes appraisal of me not quite so intimidating.

As I suspected, when he finally spoke, it had nothing to do with arresting Jimmy. "Sylvia," he said, in a voice I'm sure he uses during interrogations, "would you mind telling me exactly what you are doing here at this time of the morning all dolled up like you're going out for a night on the town?"

No way was he going to make me blush.

"As if it's any of your business, Carter, Jimmy called me off the dance floor last night to come stay with him. He was genuinely frightened and I think this time there just might be something behind his paranoia."

"What makes you say that?"

"He received a definite death threat on his answering machine immediately after someone waved a gun at him from a big, black, shiny car. And then this morning, it's quite possible the same big, black, shiny car is responsible for dropping off these disgusting fish guts." I dramatically motioned with both hands to the bag still lying on the ground between us.

"So you think all three incidents are connected?"

"Sheriff," I said, placing my hands on my hips and speaking forcefully, "I'd bet anything on it."

Sheriff Donaldson smiled slyly, hooked his thumbs through his belt loops, and rocked back on his heels. "Oh, would you, now?"

His smirk deepened as he stood there leering at me. He stroked his mustache again and raised his eyebrows before he said, "Well then, Sylvia, if you're so all-fired sure, how 'bout you and I bet dinner on it?"

CHAPTER 2

Good grief and gravy! The old coot was hitting on me right in the middle of a serious, potentially crime-preventing conversation. Jimmy's life could be in danger this very minute and this stuffed shirt with a badge pinned to it was more interested in getting into my pants than protecting the people he was sworn to serve.

I wanted to do something dramatic, like spit at him, but it was the fear that Jimmy's life really could be at stake that made me bite my tongue and force a sweet smile before I opened my mouth.

"Why, Carter, I'd love to—"

I considered finishing the sentence with "stick it in your ear," but right at that moment, a freshly scrubbed Jimmy came bounding through the office door.

"Sheriff!" he blurted out. "I'm glad you're still here." He handed the sheriff a small, folded-over note. "I happened to see the license number of the car that drove through here this morning, and I just ran it through the motel's data base." Jimmy stood there looking pleased as punch.

"And?" prodded Sheriff Donaldson.

"And," Jimmy puffed out his chest and continued, "it's the same car that was registered here at the motel yesterday afternoon!"

Sheriff Donaldson squinted his eyes and peered at Jimmy. His rather prominent nose always reminded me of a parrot's beak, and the way he now silently turned his head this way and that while he was thinking made me want to ask if Polly wanted a cracker.

After a lengthy pause, the sheriff finally spoke. "The same car, you say?"

Jimmy breathed a sigh of relief and nodded. "I knew it looked familiar, but I'm not as good with makes and models as I am with numbers."

I was blown away by the fact that the sheriff had been able to put aside Jimmy's history of crying wolf, and the additional fact that just minutes ago he'd been personally embarrassed by an errant bag of fish guts, and was actually taking Jimmy's observation seriously. Maybe I'd been a little harsh in my previous estimation of Sheriff Do-right.

"And was the car this morning, the one registered here last night, also the same one in which someone threatened you with a gun?" the sheriff continued.

"I'm not sure," said Jimmy. "All I was looking at was a gun pointed out the window at me." He hung his head. "I didn't think to look at the license plate."

Jimmy's scowl deepened and he gnawed on his lower lip. "To be honest, I don't even remember if the guy who rented the room actually stayed here all night last night. I was more interested in getting home and eating and watching a movie. I'm sorry."

"But if he registered, and paid, why wouldn't he sleep here?" asked Sheriff D. "Does this happen often?"

"Um... sometimes," replied Jimmy. "Occasionally, someone will want to rent a room just for a couple hours, and since they pay the same for a full night or a partial night, I don't really mind. Especially if they pay in cash..."

"Oh. I see. Well, then..." Uncharacteristically, Sheriff D put a reassuring hand on Jimmy's shoulder. He cleared his throat and waved the note with the plate number on it in the air. "This gives us plenty to go on. You did just fine, son."

I gave the sheriff several dozen more brownie points for what seemed to be sincere compassion. Perhaps he wasn't such a pompous jerk after all.

Pressing his shoulder radio clip a third time, Sheriff Donaldson walked a short distance away while he called in the license number. We could still hear him, of course, but I think he thought he was being more professional by distancing himself.

"That's right," we heard him tell the dispatcher, "HR3 003. And just for good measure, I'd like a list of the registered owners for plate numbers five before and five after this one." The radio cackled and the sheriff smiled. "Just working on a hunch, that's all." Another short crackling pause, then, "Thanks."

Sheriff Donaldson rejoined us near the porch steps. "While you get this mess cleaned up, Jimmy," he said, pointing to the garbage bag, "I'm going to see if I can talk Sylvia into fixing me some coffee."

The bell on the door pinged as we entered the motel's lobby. It was a tiny room, barely big enough to hold a small counter and stool. A pegboard for the old-style room keys with huge plastic tags sporting the unit numbers hung on the wall. A phone, answering machine, registration book, memo pad, and ceramic cup holding pens sat on the counter.

It took us less than three strides to cross the small room and step through the inner door directly into the kitchen of Jimmy's private quarters. He'd made coffee after his call to the dispatcher this morning, and I got three cups down from the cupboard.

The sheriff didn't bother taking his hat off when he

came in. He just sat down at the end of the kitchen table like he owned the place. I refrained from comment and was in the process of pouring his coffee when his radio began crackling again. He stood and once again discretely moved a few feet away, this time onto the carpet in what Jimmy called his living room.

"Is that so?" the sheriff said. I couldn't understand a word coming through the radio, but he grinned from ear to ear. "Yep, that's all I need right now, thanks."

"Well?"

"Well, it just so happens that Harold Rodman the Third is the legal owner of the vehicle that registered here last night and dropped off Jimmy's surprise package this morning. He's also the owner of three other identical cars. Turns out he's got a small fleet of big, black, shiny cars."

Sheriff D lifted his cup to take a sip of coffee and I noticed his slight hand tremor. He noticed me noticing and hurriedly went on.

"The cars are all Lincolns, and their license plates are sequential, HR3 001 through 004." He smiled. "I should have figured it out myself—the HR3 stands for Harold Rodman the Third." He shook his head. "Talk about vanity plates."

"Uncle Harry owns those cars?" I couldn't believe my ears. "The biggest, baddest northwest coast mafia guy is now stooping so low as to harass Jimmy?"

"Alleged mafia guy," corrected the sheriff, sitting back down at the kitchen table and lifting his coffee cup to his lips.

"Alleged my ass," I retorted. "Anyone who knows anything about him knows that guy's connected to all things shady."

Sheriff Donaldson furrowed his brow and nodded

thoughtfully. "Ever since Rodman came to town and built the Spartina Point Casino and Resort, we've suspected he's using it as a cover for something much bigger." He sighed. "We just haven't been able to pin anything on him that will stick."

"Why not?"

"A couple months ago somebody registered a complaint with the gambling commission about possible violations at his casino. Naturally, we rounded up Rodman and hauled him into court."

"Naturally." I nodded.

"But then the petitioner suddenly withdrew the complaint." Sheriff Donaldson spread his hands in a gesture of hopelessness.

"And you think there was coercion on Uncle Harry's part?"

"The time before that we had a witness who would swear he saw one of the dealers using a marked deck." Sheriff D took another swig of his coffee. "Next thing you know, the witness is FTA."

"Failure to appear?"

"Right. No witness, no problem. At least not for Rodman."

At that moment, Jimmy bounded into the room. "What'd I miss?" He looked from me to the sheriff and back again. He froze in his tracks. "Uh-oh. You two don't look so happy."

"Can I take a look at your motel register for last night, Jim?"

"Sure thing, Sheriff." Jimmy retraced his two steps from the kitchen door into the motel lobby and immediately returned with the ledger. He sat at the kitchen table and opened it to the correct page. "Here you go." He pushed the book across the table.

I pulled up a third chair and peered over the sheriff's shoulder.

"Mr. John Smith," muttered Sheriff Donaldson.

"Not very original," I replied.

"He paid cash," Jimmy reminded us, pointing to a notation next to the name.

"And it looks like he stayed in Unit 4," I continued.

"That's right!" Jimmy was suddenly very animated. "I remember now! He insisted on the unit at the end of the row, the one closest to the dunes. Said he wanted to be able to hear the ocean in his room."

Sheriff Donaldson and I both laughed. The Clamshell Motel was built on a narrow piece of land between the highway and the ocean. Units 1 through 4 were arranged in a straight line, east to west. Across the driveway nearest the road was the motel office and Jimmy's living quarters. Then came Units 5 and 6. Unit 7, reserved for large family reunions or other groups, was upstairs above the motel office and rarely used.

While Unit 4 was indeed the closest to the ocean, the cinderblock construction made them all extremely soundproof.

Jimmy chewed on his lower lip some more. "You know, come to think of it, when I took the office trash to the dumpster last night I noticed he hadn't even left his window open, and it was a pretty nice night, too."

"Did you see or hear anything unusual last evening?" The sheriff reached in his uniform shirt pocket and pulled out a small, worn, spiral notebook and a stub of a pencil.

"Can't the Sheriff's Department afford iPads or Tablets or something a little more 21st century for you to take notes on?" I interrupted.

Sheriff D's neck started turning red again. "I prefer having my notebook right here in my pocket." He patted the star on his shirt, then muttered under his breath, "Never need to remember to recharge a paper and pencil."

I turned to retrieve the coffee carafe to refill the sheriff's cup so he wouldn't see the smirk on my face. No sense alienating him just when he was displaying a few attractively human characteristics.

Sheriff D flipped his notebook open and repeated his question to Jimmy. "Did you notice anything else you'd consider out of the ordinary when you went outside with the trash?"

"No..." Jimmy said slowly. "I was watching a Star Trek movie marathon. They were showing the first four movies back-to-back. I went out to the dumpster to empty the trash during a commercial, so I really wasn't out there very long." He paused like he was trying hard to remember something.

"I called in my take-out order about an hour later and went down to the restaurant to it pick up between the third and fourth movies. I was in a hurry, and didn't notice what cars were in the parking lot when I left. Coming home is when the guys in the car threatened me."

The sheriff scowled and said nothing, but I couldn't resist theorizing aloud.

"I'll bet Mr. John Smith saw you outside with the trash and thought you were spying on him," I said excitedly. "That's probably why they waved a gun at you."

Jimmy scowled and pushed his glasses up with his middle finger again. "Hey, wait a minute! It was someone in the passenger seat who had the gun, and John Smith registered only one person for that room! He was trying to gyp me out of the second guest fee!"

"I doubt something like that would have provoked such

a dire threat," said Sheriff D. "More likely, there was something much bigger coming down."

"That's it!" said Jimmy, slapping both his hands down on the table and jumping to his feet. "I'm out of here!" He ran to his bedroom and returned seconds later with an army surplus duffel bag. "I packed this last night, just in case I had to leave in a hurry."

Sheriff Donaldson's eyebrows shot skyward. "Just where do you think you're going? I need your help to get to the bottom of this."

"You can figure out what's going on while I'm on an extended European vacation." Jimmy tossed me the motel keys. "Please, Syl—" He looked at me pleadingly. "You've watched the motel for me before. Could you run things till I get back?"

"And when, exactly, will that be?" I asked, already regretting my involvement.

"When the coast is clear, and not a moment before!" Jimmy took his coat off a hook by the lobby door and draped it over his left arm. "Don't forget to feed Priscilla." He looked around to see what else he might need to tell me. "And please bring in the mail as soon as it arrives every day. The kids next door like to snoop through the boxes along the road if you don't bring it in before they get home from school."

"Have you reported that to the police?" asked Sheriff D. "Tampering with the mail is a Federal crime."

"U.S. Code Title 18, Section 1705," said Jimmy without missing a beat. "I got the Label 33 sticker from the Postal Inspection Service and stuck it on my mailbox, but the kids ripped that off, too."

It always amazes me how much specific and detailed information Jimmy retains in that head of his. He's like some kind of savant or something. I never know what obscure and usually relevant fact he's going to rattle off.

He jerked opened the outer door. "And Syl— if anyone comes looking for me, tell them I've left the country!"

Jimmy flung the last sentence over his shoulder as he bolted from the building. He hopped into his ancient split pea green Ford Pinto and roared out of the drive. I looked at the sheriff and shrugged. "Now what?"

"Now it looks like we've a bit of a mystery to solve," he said. "There's no actual evidence, thus far, that a crime has been, or will be, committed, other than possible fraud for not registering a second guest."

"I doubt Jimmy will be eager to press charges over that."

"We still need to cover all the bases." Sheriff D looked at his watch. "What time does the motel maid come in?"

"Sometime between 10 and 11," I replied. "Check-out is at 11, and she rides the transit." I got up and reached for the phone on the kitchen counter. Jimmy has phones in every room of his 900 square foot apartment, plus the one in the motel office. "I'll call Felicity Michaels to see if she can get over here right away."

Sheriff Donaldson frowned. "Is she the maid?"

I sighed. "No, Carter, she's a teacher at the high school."

"Then why do we need her?"

"Do you happen to speak Spanish, Sheriff?"

"I'm afraid not."

"Well, neither do I, but Felicity is fluent in it. Lupé, Jimmy's motel maid, doesn't speak English very well, and I figure we could probably use some help communicating."

"Good plan."

"We're lucky it's Saturday," I continued. "I just hope I can catch her at home."

Felicity primarily teaches English, but recently picked

up a couple history classes when Walter Winston retired after nearly 40 years in the classroom. Both of them worked with me on several occasions when social services were called to step in as an advocate for a minor. Walter gladly gave 100% for his students, and Felicity is showing the same dedication to her career, much to the detriment of any social life.

These days, Walter follows Felicity around a lot, as his wife apparently married him for better or for worse, but not for retirement. She moved out a few months after Walter completed his last day at school, leaving him at loose ends until he became a volunteer teaching mentor. He says it makes him feel useful again.

So I wasn't at all surprised when Felicity's gray Toyota Camry wheeled into the driveway with Walter riding in the passenger seat. Lupé arrived via the transit bus while we were all still in the parking lot making introductions.

Lupé's dark eyes darted back and forth between us as she trudged up the drive in her heavy skirt, and she anxiously began wringing her hands at the sight of the sheriff. But Lupé held firm as Felicity asked her, in Spanish, if she had noticed anything out of the ordinary around Unit 4 as she'd finished up work Friday afternoon.

"No clean!" Lupé adamantly shook her head. Then she went on in Spanish, rapidly and with many hand gestures and facial expressions, punctuating her speech with more determined head bobbing. The only thing I heard that made any sense to me was "mucho dinero."

Felicity touched Lupé's arm and spoke calmly. Then she repeated to us, "I told her she's not in any kind of trouble."

"Trouble?" asked the sheriff. "Why'd she think she was in trouble?"

"Apparently Lupé was told by the man who rented Unit

4 that he was renting it for the entire month and wouldn't need her maid services. He gave her a big tip not to come near his room," said Felicity.

"Uh-oh," I interjected. "Jimmy never, ever, rents by the month." I retreated to the motel office and came out with the back-up key to Unit 4. "The receipt was for one night only," I told them. I looked from face to face. "So—who wants to go in first?"

Sheriff Donaldson took the key from my hand and instructed everyone to just stay put. So naturally we all trotted right along behind him as he crossed the parking lot, and gathered close as he put the key into the lock.

"What part of 'stay put' do you all not understand?" He glowered at us.

"No habla ingles," said Lupé.

The rest of us did our best to look as sweet and innocent as Lupé did while quietly standing our ground.

The sheriff sighed and swung open the door. "What the—"

A short, high-pitched squeal escaped Felicity. "Oh my God!" she exclaimed as her hand flew to her mouth.

"Ditto!" said Walter, equally aghast.

Lupé made the sign of the cross, fell to her knees and once again began speaking rapidly in Spanish, her intelligible words punctuated by sobs.

For one of the very few times in my entire life, I was rendered completely speechless. I thought I felt a hot flash coming on, but more likely it was nausea gripping my insides so tight I could hardly breathe.

In the main room, two kitchenette-type chairs were overturned, broken pieces of a ceramic lamp littered the floor, and the picture over the bed hung at a rakish angle. Dark red stains blotched the modest indoor-outdoor carpet. The door to the bathroom was ajar, and it looked like the shower curtain had been torn from the rod. There were no towels anywhere in either room.

"Well, kiddies," said Sheriff Donaldson, pushing his hat back on his head, "it looks like what we have ourselves here is a definite crime scene."

Felicity took Lupé by the arm to help her to her feet, but the poor woman stayed where she was, and continued to wail nonstop in Spanish, her hands tightly clasping a metal cross necklace with beads strung on it, her head bowed.

"What the devil is she saying?" asked Walter.

"She's reciting the 23rd Psalm," Felicity replied matter-of-factly. "Yea though I walk through the valley of the shadow of death—"

Sheriff Donaldson took a step back and firmly closed the door. "Nobody goes inside until the investigators are finished with the room." He walked briskly to his Interceptor and got out the "Do Not Cross" yellow tape for the second time that morning. He tied one end to the planter box beneath the office window and strung it across the driveway, effectively cutting off access to every unit.

"I've called for the Crime Scene and K-9 Units," he told us. "Meanwhile, I'll need to run the fingerprints of each of you. For exclusion, of course."

"Of course." I nodded. "Walter and Felicity and I already have our fingerprints on file with the state."

The sheriff's face puckered up rather prune-like. "And why's that, exactly?"

"Walter and Felicity were printed when they began working for the public school system, and mine were taken when I signed on with DSHS."

"Oh, of course." Sheriff Donaldson seemed genuinely disappointed in my response. He turned to Felicity, and inclined his head toward Lupé, who was still muttering. "Can you explain to her that I'll need to take her fingerprints?"

Felicity crouched down and made eye contact with the still-kneeling Lupé. She began speaking slowly and carefully in Spanish. I've no idea what was said, but suddenly Lupé sprang to her feet, clutched both hands to her heart and began running hell bent for salvation down the driveway, mumbling incoherently as she went. She turned south at the highway and kept right on going.

Sheriff Donaldson pursed his lips, rolled his eyes, and expelled one large breath before speaking directly to Felicity. "Did you, by chance, happen to mention to her that I do not work for immigration?"

Felicity shot a quick glance at me before replying. "No, sir, we didn't get quite that far in the conversation. As soon as I said 'fingerprints' she began screaming that she wasn't going to work for anyone who didn't trust her."

"Who didn't trust her?" I interjected.

Felicity looked taken aback by my harsh tone.

"Felix…" I consciously softened my voice and called her by her nickname. "Jimmy adores Lupé. He's never had anything but praise to say about her work."

"I think she thought she was being accused of stealing." Felicity sighed. "At any rate, she won't be coming back. She quit."

"Quit?!"

"She said she wasn't cleaning up no bloody messes for any girly friend of her boss. She said anyone who thought no more of her than to think she was guilty of being a light-fingered petty thief would have to do the laundry himself. Or something like that. I'm really not too sure about the translation." Felicity shrugged. "She was speaking so fast I couldn't catch it all."

"It's likely she's an illegal," said the sheriff. "We'll just wait and see what the CSI team comes up with before I spend any taxpayers' dollars trying to track her down."

None of this was how I imagined I'd be spending my early Saturday afternoon. After a quick sniff around the room, the police dogs, who'd arrived during the Lupé debacle, were taken outside. The only thing they seemed genuinely interested in was chasing Priscilla up the scraggly pine next to the motel office.

Walter decided it was about time to head for home, but Felicity said she wanted to stay a little longer to watch the techs at work in Unit 4. Fine by me. I told her I'd drop Walter off at his place if she'd keep half an eye on the office for me. I didn't expect anyone to cross the crime scene tape for a chance to stay in this particular motel, but you never know.

I was in desperate need of a change of clothes. A gal can only wear a red dancing dress and heels for so many days in a row before she starts getting offers on the street.

Before we left, Sheriff Donaldson cautioned us about not starting any rumors in the community. "Y'all just keep this under your hats" were his exact words. "We don't want to jump the gun and have people start thinking we're not moving fast enough to solve this murder."

"Murder?" I looked over at Walter as we walked across the parking lot to my car. "Who said anything about a murder?"

CHAPTER 3

I dropped Walter off and swung by my house on Sandspit Road to change my clothes and pick up my toothbrush and eye shadow. I can do without a lot of things, but eye shadow is not one of them. I just don't feel dressed unless I have some on.

It felt good to get out of that sparkly red dress and into a comfortable pair of jeans, a light pullover sweater, and a pair of tennis shoes. Sweaters are my all-weather standby. Here on the North Beach Peninsula it's never too warm or too cold, so my entire wardrobe is pretty much an all-season affair.

An hour later I returned to the Clamshell with enough clean underwear and clothes to get me through at least a day or two. I was pleased to see the parking lot held just Felicity's Toyota and one white Dodge van from the crime lab parked next to Unit 4.

Felix was standing next to the scraggly pine tree by the office with an open can of tuna, trying to coax Priscilla down from the safety of her perch.

"You ever see a cat refuse tuna?" she asked as I got out of my car.

"You ever see a cat carcass up in a tree?" I countered.

Felicity scowled. "What's that suppose to mean?"

"It means she'll come down when she's hungry."

"I just don't want her catching her rhinestone collar on a tree branch and hanging herself up there," said Felix. "Not on my watch!"

I sat on the bench near the office door. "I'm assuming the dogs didn't find anything, or they'd still be here."

Felix sat down next to me. "No bodies, but the sheriff was quick to point out there's a lot of dune area out there to bury a corpse in." She shuddered. "You don't think—"

"I try not to," I interrupted, smiling at her. We sat in companionable silence for a few moments. Miss Priss, curious as to why we were just sitting there, made her way back down the tree trunk and headed straight for the tuna still in Felicity's hand.

"What did I tell you?" I watched as Felicity handfed Priscilla a few bites of fish.

"The sheriff says you can go ahead and turn the 'Vacancy' sign back on."

"Swell." I sighed. "Now all I need is a new motel maid." I shot a glance at Felix. "You know any high school kids looking for a part-time job?"

She frowned. "That's kind of a sore subject with me right now."

"Why so?"

"The kids aren't waiting till summer to get their summer jobs this year. They're already picking up part-time work down at the port docks, breakfast diners and up on the north end at the Spartina Point Casino and Resort. Some of my more ambitious kids are working two jobs every weekend—early mornings at the port and evenings at the casino. Apparently the tourist season started early this year."

"And that's a problem?"

"The kids are falling asleep in class, not doing their homework, and if they're not careful, they'll have to take summer school to make up credits required for graduation."

Priscilla head-butted Felicity's hand and she placed what was left of the can of tuna on the ground beside the bench. "It's a big problem, Syl, and it keeps getting worse. The kids see the immediate money and not the big picture. Education needs to be their top priority right now or they'll be stuck working in menial jobs the rest of their lives."

She took a deep breath. "Aren't you glad you asked?"

"I didn't realize it had become such a big deal."

"It *is* a big deal. Competition is fierce for summer employment, so the kids start looking for work earlier each year. Some of them have been working year 'round since the new casino was finished." Felix looked off toward the dunes. "I realize the tourists are good for our coastal economy, but there must be some way to encourage the kids to stay interested in school."

I kept my mouth closed. Teachers have always been tops in my book, and I wished I could think of a way to help. Besides, of course, not hiring a student to fill in the current opening I had for a motel maid.

"The dropout rate is over 25% now," Felix continued. "Some of the kids are leaving just months before graduation because they don't see the value of having a high school diploma when they can already have a paycheck in their hand."

The door to Unit 4 opened and two men carrying tool caddies appeared. They loaded their gear into the rear of the van. "All clear," the man getting into the driver's seat called out. "We've got everything we need."

"I thought you were going to watch them gather evidence," I said.

Felix smiled. "Turns out photographing the room and putting little pieces of hair and fiber into tiny little plastic bags and meticulously labeling them isn't nearly as interesting as it seems on TV." She shrugged. "Besides, they were both married."

We laughed and Felicity leaned over to pick up the now-empty tuna can. We stood to go inside, taking Priscilla with us. The first thing we both noticed as we entered the motel office was the blinking red light on the answering machine.

"Oh no!" said Felicity, genuinely upset. "You left me here to keep an eye on the motel and I missed a call that might have been a reservation."

"Don't worry about it," I replied, reaching for memo pad before pressing the message button. "If they want a reservation, they'll leave a number."

A harsh male voice blared from the machine. "I told you to mind your own business, spy-guy. Now you went and got the cops involved. I wouldn't close my eyes when I go to bed tonight if I was you."

"If I *were* you," said Felix under her breath. "Why don't people use good grammar any more? His sentence is clearly in the subjunctive mood. He should have said *were* not *was*."

"Felicity! Snap out of it!" I picked up the receiver and dialed 911.

"What is the nature of your emergency?" asked the operator.

"This is Sylvia Avery," I said. "Tell Sheriff Donaldson I desperately need him to meet me at the Sandy Bottom Coffee Cup right away." Then I hung up.

Felicity was staring at me with a puckered brow. "Syl, as close as we are, I still can't read your mind. Why are you meeting the sheriff at the coffee shop?"

I unplugged the answering machine cords from the wall

jack and the power strip and started wrapping them around the base. "Obviously, we can't have the sheriff come out here again, so I'll have to take this message to him. And since I don't want anyone to see my car at the police station, the coffee shop will have to do."

Felicity nodded. "Okay, I get that. But I'm not staying here alone. I'm going home." She picked up her car keys and headed for the door. "Call me after you talk to the sheriff. I want to know what he thinks about that message."

I hadn't even had time to turn the 'Vacancy' sign back on, so I only had to put Jimmy's nonspecific "Back in an Hour" sign in the window, lock the door, and be on my way. It was only a short, three-mile drive south to Tinkerstown, but today it seemed to take forever.

Sheriff Donaldson stood up when I entered the Sandy Bottom. He wore a big, silly grin, his hat was off, and his hair was combed. I'd always wondered if he was bald under that hat; I'd never seen him with it off before.

"Sylvia!" he greeted me with an unexpected bear hug. "I'm so glad you called!"

He'd apparently drenched himself with Stetson cologne. It suddenly dawned on me that the delusional old fart thought this was a date! I backed up and shoved the answering machine hard against his chest. He hung onto it with both hands, looking dumbfounded by my behavior.

"Carter! I'm here on business. Strictly business!"

He looked rather dismayed, no doubt about it.

"But—" Sheriff D fumbled for the right words to save face—the face that at this minute glowed a deep crimson, a color that was getting to be the norm rather than the exception with him. "But Syl—"

Deciding to gently let him off the hook, I calmly sat down. He mirrored my movement and sat in the chair he'd previously occupied across from me. The barista, who happened to be one of the two women owners of the Sandy Bottom, chose that moment to bring our coffees to the table.

"I swear, you're my only two regulars who drink plain old coffee these days," said Bim, as she placed the steaming cups in front of us. "Of course," she said aside to me, "since it's afternoon, yours is decaf."

"You're a peach, Bim," I replied.

"Just holler when you need a refill," she said, returning to her post behind the counter.

I sniffed the delicious aroma emitting from my cup and took a small sip. "Mmmmm..."

The sheriff had used the interruption to regain some of his composure. He, too, sipped at his coffee, but he didn't look at me.

I lowered my voice and leaned in. "Carter, I'm sorry you misunderstood my message. The dispatcher probably left out the part about me having some new evidence." I hoped he wouldn't catch too much hell later for my fib.

"Evidence. Yes, of course." He looked down at the answering machine sitting in his lap and quickly shifted gears. "What have we here?"

There's nothing the matter with my memory, despite the way I had just covered my backside. I repeated the message on Jimmy's answering machine verbatim.

The sheriff's eyebrows rose an inch or more. Now his eyes met mine and held them. "This is serious."

"Serious? You're damn right it's serious! I'm the one who's staying at the Clamshell while Jimmy's on some kind of escape hiatus!" I heard my voice go up about an octave, but couldn't control my mounting hysteria. "I'm the one who'll be trying to sleep there tonight with my eyes open!"

Sheriff Donaldson reached across the table and put his right hand over my left one. The gesture was unbelievably comforting, and I surprised myself by not pulling away.

"Would it make you feel better if an officer of the law stayed at the motel tonight?" he said, never taking his eyes off mine.

"Carter, the parking lot can be seen from the highway. That's why I called to ask you to meet me here. What do you think this guy will do if he drives by and sees a cop car in the lot all night?" I shook my head. "I'm in trouble enough."

"What if the officer was undercover?"

"Like it's in the county budget to pay an undercover cop to babysit me?"

"Syl, please, let me finish." Sheriff D took a deep breath. "What if the undercover officer was *off duty* and he just so happened to check into the Clamshell for a few days?"

"Yeah, right, Carter. The Clamshell's no five-star resort, you know." I smiled for the first time since hearing the recording. "Heck, it's not even a one-star." I paused and lifted my coffee cup to my lips with my right hand. I took a small sip and set the cup back down. "So just who you gonna sucker into voluntarily staying there?"

"I thought I would."

Abruptly, I jerked my hand away.

The sheriff's face turned scarlet again. Cripes, this was happening so often, he might as well be in menopause too.

"I'll stay out in one of the units, of course," he blustered. "I wasn't implying any undue intimacy would be happening between us."

I fought the urge to tell him where he could shove his cockamamie idea. After all, his offer was extremely generous, even gallant. And I really would feel safer with him sleeping just across the driveway. So for once, I kept my acerbic tongue in check.

"Thank you, Carter. I'd appreciate that."

Sheriff D beamed, and I swear his chest puffed out a good four or five inches. He looked at his watch. "I'll pick up my go bag, switch vehicles, and follow you out there."

"Now? It's only a little after 3 o'clock."

He smiled. "I set my own hours—one of the perks of being the boss. And besides, it's Saturday, and I've already put in enough 12 hour days this month to merit an early day today."

"But what about the evidence on the answering machine? Can you copy it or something? I need to take it back to the motel."

He considered the machine still resting in his lap. "This is a really old one," he mused. He pressed a button on it and the cassette popped out. He smiled, took the tape and slid it into his shirt pocket. "Jimmy keep blank cassettes at the motel?"

"Yes. I believe they're in his desk drawer."

"Problem solved."

I arrived back at the Clamshell just a half hour later, the sheriff's blue Chevy pickup pulled in so close behind me I could have been towing it.

Not that I'd ever hitch anything behind my shiny, new Mustang convertible. This car was my one frivolous expenditure when I retired. I considered it a well-deserved present to myself for surviving a full 30 years working for the state, since they don't give out gold watches or anything anymore.

I went all-out and got the customized chameleon paint job that looks green from one angle and purple from the other. The vanity plate reads "SYLLEE," which is actually a nickname of mine, but maybe it's a statement about buying this excessively extravagant car, too. I don't care; I love it.

We parked in the lot side-by-side. This time there was only one other car parked out there: Walter's. He was sitting on the bench by the door, slouched down with his collar turned up and his hands in his pockets, looking none-to-pleased to see me arrive with the sheriff in tow, so to speak.

"Hey, Walter! What are you doing here?"

"Felicity called me," he replied, "and I didn't want you to be alone out here tonight, so..." He stood and pointed to a small brown suitcase on the ground beside him. "I thought I'd check in for a few nights."

Sheriff Donaldson had retrieved his duffel bag from the bed of his pick-up and now approached us. "Well, well," he said, quickly taking in the situation, "looks like Syl's going to have two gentlemen friends here looking after her tonight. Lucky girl."

I swear I could see the testosterone flowing down the driveway. I sighed, shook my head, and rolled my eyes.

"Come on in; I'll get you both room keys." It was pointless to argue with either one of these wannabe knights in shining armor, so why bother trying?

The four units across the driveway have only one double bed each, while Units 5 and 6, next to the office, are larger, set up for several occupants at a time, or families of up to six, complete with a kitchenette. Unit 7, upstairs, can hold even more. While the men wrote their names and license plate numbers in the register, I planned my strategy.

Since Unit 4 was currently offline, I put the sheriff in Unit 3 and Walter in Unit 1. That put both of them across the driveway from the motel office, and I figured neither one of them would be brazen enough to try anything dumb tonight, for fear of being observed by the other one. I couldn't decide if I felt safer, or more like totally annoyed, by their presence.

"Here you go." I handed them their respective keys, then guided them out the door, pulling it shut tight behind us. The "Back in an Hour" sign was still in the window. "So, you boys go right ahead and get settled in. I've got some errands to run, but I won't be long." I blew a generic air kiss in their direction and hopped back into my car. No way was I going to stick around and be witness to their pissing match.

I'll bet anything they were still standing in the parking lot with their mouths hanging open as I pulled out onto the highway, but I didn't dare look back. I was too afraid they'd see my ear-to-ear grin.

This time it didn't seem quite so far into Tinkerstown. I wheeled into the Rusty Rudder's parking lot and pulled my car into the farthest space from the door. I always parked in this spot because A, I can use the exercise and walking a few more yards gives me a sense of accomplishment, and B, my car is far less likely to be hit by some dancing fool at night pulling in or out of the parking lot when my car is this far from the entrance.

Rich Morgan, owner of Captain Morgan's Deep Sea Charters in Unity, was the only one I recognized sitting at the bar. He sat huddled over a beer, eyes fixed on the TV screen above. He wore his perpetual black baseball cap, embroidered with the name of his charter business, but otherwise, you'd never guess he fished for a living. He cleaned up real good.

Rich was alone, and since I preferred not to be, I slid onto the swivel stool next to him and tapped him on the shoulder.

"Hey, stranger!" His eyes lit up and he greeted me with a big smile. "Long time no see! What's new with you? Can I buy you a beer?"

I returned his smile. "It *has* been a long time! And absolutely you can buy me a soda, but if you really want to know what's new, it's going to cost you an early dinner."

Rich's smile got even wider. He immediately picked up his beer glass and stood up, turning toward the bar's small dining room. "Then I guess we better get us a table."

I'd been joking when I'd suggested he buy me dinner, but now I realized my stomach was screaming for food. Since coffee doesn't count, the only nourishment I'd had all day was a few crackers and some cheese I'd snagged when I'd gone home to change clothes.

Rich lifted two menus from a pile on the corner of the bar as we passed by. There was no one eating dinner this early, so we had our pick of tables. He raised his eyebrows in an unspoken question and I led us to a table by the window. When he handed me a menu and held my chair, I almost laughed.

"You looking for a part-time job, Rich?"

"I might soon have to be," he said, settling onto the wooden chair across from me. "The way the state set the fish limits this year, I may as well close down. The cost of fuel is so high I have to have a full boat to go out, and the tourists don't want to pay what we need to charge them if they only get to bring home one measly fish."

"HHhhmm.... I see your point." I was too busy salivating over the menu to be paying much attention.

The waitperson, a sweet young thing who couldn't be more than 17, approached the table, set down two glasses of water, and offered to take our order. Her nametag said

"Lyndi." I assumed this was one of the high school students Felicity had told me about, working her weekends away. Under "Coastal Favorites" I spotted a pretty fair-sounding spinach salad. I read the description aloud to Rich. "Baby spinach, mandarin oranges, dried cranberries, pecans and red onion in a vinaigrette dressing with your choice of goat cheese or Bleu cheese crumble."

Rich squinted at me. "Is that all you're having?"

"A gal has to watch her figure, you know."

Rich lowered his voice and leaned in over the table. "You can leave your figure watching to me," he said, drool practically dripping off his chin.

I simply ignored his remark. Lyndi was the one who blushed. She looked down at her order pad and began scribbling furiously. "One spinach salad." Her eyes met mine. "You want that with the Bleu cheese or goat crumble?"

Rich snorted in his beer. "Goat crumble?!"

I sighed, wondering just how many beers he'd already had. "It's goat *cheese* crumble, Rich. Goat *cheese.*" To Lyndi I said, "Goat crumble will be just fine. And a diet soda, please."

Rich ordered a steak, "so rare that if you take it to the vet, it'll get well," and Lyndi laughed uproariously at his description. Either she was hoping for a big tip, or she was so young she hadn't heard that line a thousand times before.

Rich and I settled into amicable conversation over dinner. Disregarding the sheriff's edict to keep it quiet, I told him, in great theatrical detail, the highlights of my day. Rich listened attentively, urging me to continue with thought-provoking questions.

It finally dawned on me I was sharing much more than

was probably prudent. I concluded with "you'll keep this all to yourself, of course," and promptly clamped my mouth shut.

"Of course." He grinned. "You're a good talker, and I'm a good listener. We make the perfect couple."

Rich reached across the table and put his calloused hand over mine. There seemed to be a lot of that going on today. This time I didn't hesitate in quickly pulling it back.

Then he leaned in to whisper, as if we weren't still the only ones in the dining area, "I've always liked you, Syl. Whaddya say you and I—"

"Oh geez! Would you look at the time!" I abruptly stood up, wiped my mouth with my napkin and dropped it on the table. "Sorry, Rich. The motel's been closed up most of the day, and I still have units to be rented. Thanks for dinner." I was getting good at not looking back as I beat a second hasty retreat in as many hours.

What's with guys these days, anyway? They buy you dinner, or even a cup of coffee, and they suddenly start thinking they might be able to get a little. Is it suddenly socially acceptable to be a horndog, or am I wearing some kind of sign saying since I'm now in I'm in my 50s, I'm desperate?

I was still musing these and other sociological questions when I wheeled back into the Clamshell parking lot. To my dismay, a big, black, shiny car was already parked in my spot. License plate HR3 004.

CHAPTER 4

I carefully parked on the other side of the sheriff's Chevy pickup and slowly got out of my Mustang. I had my self-defense pepper spray from the glove box clenched tightly in my fist. Trying to act nonchalant, I casually turned my head to see if the sheriff was watching. His drapes were pulled shut, as were Walters.

The driver's door of the big, black, shiny car swung open just as I put the key into the office door.

"Hello there!"

I swallowed hard, plastered a fake smile on my face, and turned to face the man. He didn't look too scary. Maybe 5'10" and 165 pounds. If I had to, I thought I could take him—with the help of my pepper spray. "Hello. Are you looking for a room for tonight?"

"Yes I am. Your sign says no vacancy, but I was hoping if I waited until someone returned, there might be a room available after all."

Of all the gin joints in all the world— Why this particular motel? But I'd promised Jimmy I'd fill in for him, so I knew what I had to do.

"You're in luck," I said, going inside and putting the registration counter between us. "It just so happens I do have several units available. Will there be anyone staying with you? Any pets?"

"Nope. Just me today. I'm here on business."

I discretely slid the pepper spray into my jeans pocket

as I turned to take the key down from the wall rack for Unit 2. I nodded toward the guest book. "If you'll just fill out the form there in front of you, we can get you all taken care of."

"We?" The man looked around the tiny office, then tried to peer through the windowed, but curtained, door into the living quarters. "Is that the Queen's 'we,' or is someone else inside?"

I stood there mute. Improvisation usually came much easier to me, but then, I'd never wondered if anyone in the audience was one of Uncle Harry's hired thugs. For the life of me, I couldn't come up with anything to say.

"Where's Jimmy?" the man continued with a charming smile. "That nice young man who's always been so helpful. Where's he tonight?"

"You've stayed here before, then?"

"Many times." He nodded. "I'm in sales. The boss gives me a nice car to drive to impress the clients, and a cushy expense account." He lowered his voice conspiratorially. "I collect the same amount no matter where I sleep, so I stay here and pocket the difference." He smiled, exposing a perfect row of bright white teeth. "You won't tell him, will you?"

I couldn't help myself; I smiled back. "That's exactly what *I'd* do."

"So then, where's Jimmy?"

His question brought me abruptly back to the possible danger at hand. "Jimmy's on holiday. He took a lengthy leave of absence and pointed his car toward Europe." I felt my face flush. "Metaphorically speaking, of course."

The man nodded thoughtfully. "That's probably for the best."

"Why do you say that?"

"Let's just say that the last time I saw him he looked like

he could use an extended vacation." He picked up the key and turned toward the door. "I just hope, for his sake, he stays away long enough to put some color back into his cheeks."

I'd never heard someone's well-wishes sound like a threat before. I watched him while he retrieved a small valise from his car and entered Unit 2. He was sure traveling light. I copied down his information from the registration book and quietly let myself out.

Sheriff Donaldson opened his door before I even knocked. His laptop was open on the bed, and his 9mm was lying next to it. I handed him the man's registration.

"Robert Jones," read Sheriff D. "Another original name."

"Goes right along with last night's John Smith, doesn't it?" I sat in the chair next to the small vanity.

The sheriff sat back down on the bed. "It wasn't necessary to run his plates. That car is one of the four registered to Rodman."

"Lincoln Continentals, right?" I wanted to impress him with my car knowledge, but it backfired. No pun intended.

"Lincoln Continentals were discontinued in 2002." The sheriff absentmindedly scratched his head. "Rodman's cars are all Lincoln Town Cars. They run about 50 grand each. Only get about 16 miles to the gallon."

There were two quick raps on the door, thankfully saving me from having to eat any more humble pie.

Walter came right on in without waiting for an invitation, a pair of binoculars dangling from his neck. "Nice work, Syl."

"Nice work?" I looked from Walter to Sheriff D and back again. "I don't understand."

Walter beamed. "After you left, the sheriff and I settled

our, uh, differences, and created a joint plan of action. Good thing we did, too. That Lincoln Town Car drove up just after we started surveillance in our separate rooms."

Swell. So everybody knew more about cars than I did, with the possible exception of Jimmy, who was not here to embarrass himself.

"Old Betsy and I were keeping a mighty close eye on things from here." Sheriff D patted the Glock sitting next to him on the bed.

"*Seriously?* You named your Glock after Davey Crockett's rifle?"

The sheriff opened his mouth to reply, but Walter couldn't wait to put in his two cents worth. "I read lips," he said hurriedly, "so the sheriff outfitted me with binoculars to make sure you didn't talk yourself into a corner."

"We were both watching you the entire time," added Sheriff D.

"You were as safe as if you were in your father's arms," Walter chimed in.

I didn't bother to tell them my father's arms, when he was alive, hadn't been the sanctuary they assumed it was. I simply waited until they were finished patting themselves on the back, then said matter-of-factly, "I knew you were watching."

Furrowed brows greeted my statement.

"How?" they said in unison.

I smiled. "Nobody, but nobody, pulls the drapes completely shut in these units until after nightfall." I motioned to the two-bulb pole lamp in the corner. "It's just too dark in these units unless you let in the available daylight."

Deflated, but not defeated, the men graciously acknowledged my superior powers of observation. Or at least that's the way I see it. Again, no pun intended.

Then with Walter's unbidden assistance, I related my entire conversation with the renter in Unit 2 to the sheriff. We all agreed there was nothing to be done about Mr. Robert Jones for the time being. He hadn't done anything illegal—yet.

"Meanwhile," said Sheriff Donaldson, opening a bookmarked webpage on his laptop, "I've been doing a little research into the very interesting business dealings of one Harold Rodman the Third here on the North Beach Peninsula."

There was that slight tremor in the sheriff's hand again as he manipulated the touch pad, and I knew it wasn't from nervousness. I scooted my chair nearer the bed and Walter stood close behind me, peering over my shoulder.

"See here," said the sheriff, pointing to a detailed map of the south end of the peninsula. "His corporation, Rodman Enterprises, has purchased every single parcel of available land up on Pacific Bluff."

"A lot of folks refer to that area as Poker Bluff," interjected Walter.

"That's right," I agreed. "As in, it's a real gamble whether the housing development up there is going to stay put or come washing down into the drink."

Sheriff Donaldson scrutinized the colored elevation graphics. "How much of the hillside has trees left on it?"

"Hardly any," I answered. "At least that's what I've heard. Haven't gone up there yet myself to have a look. The developers were more interested in how many condos with ocean views they could cram in than in preserving the natural wilderness beauty and they neglected to leave part of the area in heavy vegetation to keep the hillside stabilized."

"Pacific Bluff," read Walter from the screen, "an elite, gated community where the only thing we overlook is the beautiful Pacific Ocean."

I snorted my disgust.

"Rodman is a relative newcomer here," Sheriff D mused, "from southern California, or maybe Nevada. Rumor has it he has family in the area and bought up the land at Spartina Point during one of his visits."

"Spartina Point is on the north end," Walter said thoughtfully. "So what's with all this interest in housing on the south end?"

"That's what I'd like to know," replied the sheriff.

I reached over to Sheriff D's laptop and scrolled down the page.

Walter whistled when he saw the figures attached to the condos being built on speculation. "That's more than I made in my last five years of teaching—combined—and before taxes!"

"I suppose he thinks he's going to make a killing in real estate, then," said the sheriff.

"Maybe not," I suggested. "I heard there was a problem up there with getting water from Unity's reservoir. It could be Uncle Harry's looking to lose money on purpose. You know, some kind of big corporation tax write-off."

"Or maybe he's just a legitimate businessman," offered forever-optimistic Walter. "Could be he's willing to invest in the future of the North Beach Peninsula and is providing upscale housing to attract upscale residents to our area."

Sheriff Donaldson and I both stared at him.

"Or not." Walter shrugged and looked sheepish.

We heard a car pull into the driveway and Walter pulled back the curtains to look. "It's Felicity."

She parked on the far end nearest the dunes and got

out. Walter had the door open and quickly motioned for her to join us in the sheriff's room.

"What's going on here?" Her voice was high-pitched and came out in a squeaky rush. "Is everyone okay? Who owns that Lincoln out there? Did the bad guys return to the scene of the crime?" She was trembling all over.

Walter put his hands reassuringly on her shoulders. "Take a breath, Felix."

She took several gulps of air in rapid succession. Then she choked out, "Okay— When I left here a couple hours ago, Syl was going to meet with Sheriff D at the Sandy Bottom. I called Walter to let him know about the new phone threat, and that's the last I've heard from any of you. Can you imagine what I've been going through?"

Felix looked directly at me, raised an eyebrow, and put her hands on her hips. "Syl, where's the motel answering machine?"

"It's, uh, still in my trunk."

"I thought as much." Felix pursed her lips and turned to Walter. "Why isn't your cell phone on?"

"I can answer that," interrupted the sheriff. "I told him to turn it off while we were doing surveillance. Couldn't risk it ringing."

"Harrumph," said Felix, not willing to let it go. Addressing both Walter and me, she continued, "Look you two. I care what happens to you. I don't think it was very considerate to keep me out of the loop. You knew I'd worry." For a moment I thought she might cry.

"I'm truly sorry, Felix." And I was.

Walter put a reassuring arm around her. "I'm sorry, too. You're right. We could have called to let you know what was going on."

Sheriff Donaldson peeked out the window. "It's almost

dark."

Nothing gets by him.

He looked at Walter. "You want the first watch, or the second?"

"First," Walter replied without hesitation. "I'm too wired to get right to sleep tonight anyway."

"Alright then," said Sheriff D, "you can keep an eye on things until 3. I'll set my alarm and watch from then until my deputy comes to relieve me at 8."

"Sounds good." Walter set the binoculars on the vanity. "I guess I won't be needing these any more."

"Let's all get back to our own rooms now and get a good night's sleep," the sheriff continued in his official sheriff voice, as if just by saying it authoritatively he had the power to make it happen.

Felicity nodded. "I brought my gym bag with everything I need in it." She turned again to look me in the eye. "I'm staying on Jimmy's couch. It's Saturday, there's no school tomorrow, and I'm not about to leave you alone out here.

The expressions on the men's faces were priceless.

Felix held up her hand to stop them from protesting. "You two can sleep in your own cozy little bungalows, and I'll be the one on the inside. No arguments."

For someone who was on the verge of tears just moments ago, Felix sure found her backbone in one heck of a hurry.

We walked as quietly as possible back across the driveway to retrieve the gym bag from her car, Jimmy's answering machine from mine, and past the line of cars to the office.

Jimmy would have been amazed to see all the vehicles at the Clamshell that night. Although there was only one paying customer, I'll bet it was the first time there'd been five vehicles parked in the lot all at one time this spring.

I pulled another blanket and a pillow out of Jimmy's linen closet and together Felix and I started making up the couch.

"You don't have to stay, you know," I began. "You could go home and spend the night in your own comfortable bed. I wouldn't think any less of you, and I promise I'll call you right away if anything happens."

"Syl... " Felicity gave me one of her best teacher looks— one eyebrow up, and one down, and glared at me over the top of her glasses. She really should patent that look. It's scary. "I'm staying, and that's that. But I'm calling dibs on the first shower tomorrow morning."

I smiled. "So you've heard about Jimmy's irrationally small hot water tank, huh?" I tossed her pillow at her. "We'll just see who's first in the bathroom, Missy!"

Felix grabbed the pillow with both hands, made a threatening gesture with it, then burst out laughing. "I guess we can't have a real pillow fight with only one pillow!"

It was good to hear her laugh. "Everything will look better in the morning," I told her, painfully aware that Jimmy had been right—I use that phrase far too often.

I headed for the bedroom. "Good night, Felicity."

"Good night Syl. Sweet dreams. Don't let the bed bugs bite."

I closed the bedroom door, hoping against hope that bed bugs would be the only thing any of us would have to worry about this night.

Attribute it to the fact exhaustion wiped out all the adrenalin of the past 24 hours, but I actually slept until the sun was just coming up. I'm not sure what it was that woke me. It might have been the smell of coffee, or the sound of the shower running in the bathroom.

Damn! I'd have to wait at least 30 minutes after Felix was finished in there for the water heater to recover. But at least she'd made coffee.

I pulled on the pink and purple jogging suit I'd brought from home and laced up my tennis shoes. I don't jog, but I liked the feeling of the material on my skin. When the sales gal told me how good I looked in the outfit, I'd bought several in different colors just to wear on weekends.

Good thing I'd pulled something on. Sheriff Donaldson already sat at the kitchen table, typing on his laptop and enjoying his first cup of joe. He looked up from the screen as I entered the room.

"My, don't you look tousled this fine morning," he said much too cheerily.

"If that's supposed to be a compliment, it falls way short."

He laughed. "I guess you're not a morning person."

I peered at the clock next to the coffeemaker. "If it were still winter, this would be the middle of the night." I poured myself a cup and sat down at the small, rectangular, gray formica-topped table. "What you working on?"

Sheriff D turned his laptop so I could see the screen. He'd organized his notes into a pretty impressive summary. Included were specific details about Jimmy's drive-by threat on Friday night, Uncle Harry's car fleet, the two answering machine messages, the arrival of the fish guts, the trashing of Unit 4, and finally, everything we knew thus far about both Rodman Enterprises and Mr. Robert Jones.

"Speaking of our motel guest..." I rose to look out the window.

"He's gone," said the sheriff.

"*Gone?!*" I turned to stare at him. "What do you mean, *gone?*"

"He pulled out over an hour ago."

"It's awfully early to go making sales calls on a Sunday, isn't it?"

The sheriff smiled. "Buoy 10 Bakery, the Sandy Bottom, and the Sea Biscuit all open at 5 seven days a week."

At the mention of the Sea Biscuit Breakfast House, my stomach started rumbling. I looked hopefully toward the bathroom, but apparently Felix was intent upon using every drop of hot water in the place. It would be a while before I'd be presentable enough to go into town to eat.

I remained standing by the window, sipping coffee. "Carter, did you bring any of your evidence bags?"

The sheriff looked up and frowned. "Yes, there're some in my pickup. Why?"

"Well, don't you think we'd better go see if Mr. Jones left anything suspicious in Unit 2 we need to collect?"

Sheriff D laughed. "Syl, you watch too many TV crime shows. Jones didn't leave anything behind but rumpled sheets and a few towels on the floor."

Unfortunately, the sheriff was right. The only thing in the trashcan by the vanity was yesterday's newspaper, folded back to the editorial page. I got on my hands and knees to look under the bed, but all I found were a few resident dust bunnies.

I stood up and wiped my hands on one of the unused hand towels. "If Lupé hadn't quit, I'd be tempted to fire her." I sighed. "But now I guess I'll have to clean these units myself."

A marked patrol car pulled into the drive and parked in the spot nearest the office—the one recently vacated by Mr.

Jones. From the window in Unit 2, I watched as a uniformed deputy about 15 years my junior stepped out and self-consciously adjusted his utility vest. He had dark hair and a tanned complexion. I guessed he was about 5'10" or maybe 5'11" if you didn't count the two-inch heels on his worn cowboy boots, which I was sure were not standard police issue.

Sheriff D opened the door. "Freddy! Over here!"

Felix, fresh from her lengthy shower, came out of the office and joined us. First name introductions were made all around, then the sheriff excused himself to go home to shower and change into this work clothes. Although he'd been up since 3 a.m., it was time for him to report for official duty. I didn't envy his schedule.

"Well, I guess I'll get started," I said, accepting the fact I'd have to play the part of motel maid, at least for today.

Felix and Freddy trailed along behind me as I went to the laundry room for cleaning supplies. "Would one of you mind grabbing the linens over there on the shelf?" I smiled as Felix quickly moved to do so.

"And Freddy," I said, resisting the urge to bat my eyes, "would you mind bringing the vacuum along?" I hoped Felicity wouldn't call me on my variation of the 'Tom Sawyer whitewashing the fence' routine.

While Felicity sprayed the bathtub/shower in Unit 2 with disinfectant, I stripped the bed. Freddy, probably feeling foolish just standing there watching us work, grabbed the clean sheets and flipped the fitted one open. I took one side, and together we made up the bed in nothing flat.

Then I went after those long-term dust bunnies with a vengeance. I was almost finished when I caught Freddy eyeing my behind as I vacuumed under the bed.

Instead of being embarrassed by me catching him, he had the gall to throw a pick-up line at me. "Is it hot in here, or is it just you?"

"Oh for crying out loud!" I admonished him. "Does that old line ever actually work on anybody?"

"I honestly don't know," Freddy admitted. "But I was sure hoping it would work on you."

I could hear Felix softly chuckling in the bathroom.

I took a deep breath. "I appreciate the sentiment, Freddy, but it just so happens that I could have a son your age. That is, if I'd had any children."

"No kids?" asked Freddy. "That must be why you've still got such a great figure."

Felix snorted and burst into a fit of laughter.

"Look, Freddy, I know you've been assigned to keep me safe today, and I appreciate it, I really do. But if you want to keep your job," I said sternly, "you're going to have to quit trying to hit on me. Got it?"

Freddy grinned. He really was kind of cute, adorable dimples and all. "Got it. Yes, ma'am. No worries, ma'am. Won't happen again, ma'am."

The 'ma'am' was a bit much, and I knew he was laying it on thick for effect. Nevertheless, I had more important things to think about just then than some star-struck kid falling into puppy love, or even just into bed, with me.

"So," I said, just to change the subject, "is your full name Frederick?"

"Yep," Freddy replied, nodding. "That it is."

"Then why not go by Fred or Rick?"

Freddy grinned. "I tried to use Fred, but the kids at school called me Fred Flintstone, or Fred the Red, and I hated it."

"Fred the Red?" I queried.

"I'm an eighth Native American," Freddy explained. "And one of the racial slurs for Native Americans is Redskins. Hence, Fred the Red."

"Kids can be so cruel," verified Felix.

"And since my dad's name is Richard," continued Freddy with his practiced explanation, "Rick sounded too much the same. So I've always gone by Freddy."

We finished Unit 2 in no time at all, the place totally spic and span and ready for the next renter. Walter was still sleeping in Unit 1, and the sheriff was going to come back to Unit 3 this evening, and didn't expect maid service. So that only left Unit 4.

"Oh no you don't—" Felix balked as I started down the driveway. "You're not going to finagle me into helping you clean up that bloody crime scene."

Freddy's ears perked up. "Crime scene? Sheriff Donaldson told me I had bodyguard duty, but he didn't tell me anything about a crime scene."

CHAPTER 5

Felicity returned to the motel office, but Freddy wanted to see the room on the end for himself. I gave him a quick recitation of the events leading up to his arrival while we walked to Unit 4. I slid the key in the lock, but hesitated before opening the door.

"I— I'm not sure what condition the crime techs left the room in."

"They usually bag and tag any evidence, but don't do any cleaning." Freddy studied my face for a moment. "You don't have to do this right now, you know. It sounds like you've had quite a time of it the past two days."

I appreciated his concern, but shook my head. "Eventually, it has to be faced, and there's no time like the present."

Freddy was right about the techs not doing any cleaning. Even though I'd seen it before, it was still a pretty gruesome sight, and my stomach went into a hard knot at the thought of tackling the cleanup.

Freddy surveyed the scene and nodded thoughtfully. "No offense, Sylvia, but I think you're going to need to hire a professional cleaner for this one."

A professional cleaner? Now why hadn't I thought of that? "You mean there are actually people who will happily tackle a mess like this?"

"Well, maybe not 'happily'," said Freddy, "but yes, there are several local businesses the department uses who specialize in these kinds of dirty jobs."

"And do you happen to know of a company I can call on a Sunday morning?" The day suddenly seemed a whole lot sunnier.

"You bet," replied Freddy, "but it's going to cost you."

I smiled. "No problem. I have full access to the motel's finances. Jimmy put me on all the accounts right after his mother died."

"That's not what I meant." Freddy grinned from ear to ear. "You're going to have to agree to have breakfast with me in exchange for the name of the cleaning service."

I locked the unit door and we started back to the office in silence, dropping off the cleaning supplies and vacuum on the way. With my hand on the motel office door, I finally responded to Freddy. "About this breakfast—can Felix come with us?"

"Sure," said Freddy, nodding happily. "Why not?"

"And..." I asked, using my best sweet-and-innocent voice, "do we get to ride in the patrol car?"

"Yes, of course. We'll have to take the cruiser, anyway, since I'm officially on duty." His brow furrowed. "But why do you ask?"

I smiled. "I want Felicity to have to ride in the backseat like a common criminal. She stole all the hot water this morning, and I want her to pay!"

We laughed companionably and entered the living quarters.

"What about Walter?" Felix asked when we told her we were all going out to breakfast.

"Let him sleep," I replied. "He was up half the night. We'll make it up to him another time."

I took the world's quickest shower, even though now there was enough hot water for a decent soak, and changed into my standard jeans and sweater attire while Freddy called and arranged for the cleaners to come take care of Unit 4 first thing Monday morning.

In no time we were on our way. Red-faced, Felicity ducked down in the backseat, hoping none of her high school students would see her riding back there.

"This isn't a Crown Victoria, is it?" I asked Freddy, feeling a little self-conscious riding around with him and trying to make small talk.

"It's the new Police Interceptor," Freddy proudly boasted. "It's 25% more fuel-efficient than our old Crown Vics.

I really wasn't the one to be talking about fuel efficiency, me with my gorgeous, but gas-guzzling, Mustang, so I abruptly changed the subject.

"Can I turn on the siren and the flashing blue lights?" I asked, knowing full well the answer would be 'no.' But my question got the desired effect from the passenger hiding in the rear seat.

"Don't you dare!" exclaimed Felix. "Freddy, please, please don't let her do it!"

"But I'm hungry," I replied, with all the feigned innocence I could muster. "I just want us to get there a little faster."

The Sea Biscuit Breakfast House serves nothing but breakfast, 5 a.m. to 1 p.m., and they do it better than any place I've ever eaten.

The young woman who showed us to our seats was Lorrie, one of Felicity's honor students. "Ms. Michaels!" she gushed. "I'm so happy to see you here!"

None of us bothered with a menu; we knew it all by heart. Felix and I often frequented the place, and, apparently, Freddy ate here a lot too. Lorrie quickly wrote down our order and scurried off to the kitchen.

Felicity shook her head. "I don't think my students realize I have a life outside the classroom." She sighed. "And sometimes I'm afraid they're right."

Lorrie returned with two coffee carafes and filled our cups. The one she used to fill my cup was decaf. I feel like I'm apologizing whenever I explain that no one really wants to see me wired on caffeine, and the two cups I'd already had at the motel was my self-imposed daily limit.

Felicity couldn't resist 'talking shop' with Lorrie, and asked her how many hours a week she was working now. Lorrie told her not to worry, she'd have her term paper finished and turned in days before it was due.

"It's Kasey who needs a swift kick in the behind," said Lorrie. "He used to only work weekends as a deckhand for Captain Morgan, but now he's making fish deliveries up to Spartina Point a couple times a week." She paused, then shrugged. "He's making really good money, lots more than I am, but I miss spending time with him."

"Don't you make good tips here?" I asked, not wanting to be left completely out of the conversation.

"Well, yeah, I do, but I saw Kasey's paycheck last week, and it was a doozy. Captain Morgan pays him gas and mileage on top of his hourly wage for those deliveries, and of course he gets a share of the tips from the tourists when he deckhands."

The kitchen bell dinged, and Lorrie left to retrieve our food.

"I used to deckhand for him," volunteered Freddy, "but I got fired because I get so seasick." He took a sip of coffee. "Even thought I'd inherit the charter boat one day."

Our breakfast arrived before I could ask him to explain his statement, and there was no more talk of deckhands or charter boats or summer jobs as we dug into the plates of wonderful food set before us.

As we finished our amazing omelets and light-as-air biscuits, the three of us speculated on who might have been in Unit 4 Friday night, and what might have happened.

I was pretty sure someone had been taken there against his or her will, and Felicity suggested 'the victim,' as we referred to the unwilling guest, may have arrived at the motel in the trunk of the big, black, shiny car Jimmy had checked in. But had he or she arrived in the afternoon, or later in the evening?

Since Jimmy had been distracted watching the Star Trek marathon, it was doubtful he had heard the car's comings and goings over the television volume. And we all agreed Mr. John Smith must have gone out at least once, most likely for dinner.

In no time at all, Freddy was completely up to speed with the investigation thus far, and had a few ideas of his own he wanted to check out.

"What do you say we take a quick run up to Pacific Bluff?" he asked, after he paid the bill for all three of us, despite Felicity's protest.

"Sounds good to me," I readily agreed.

"Sounds like I'll be spending more time in the backseat of a patrol car to me," grumbled Felix.

It was a short 10-minute drive, which wound around the hilly southern end of the North Beach Peninsula. This wasn't an area of the peninsula I personally frequented— wild and rustic, a popular destination for tourists who liked to camp—and I honestly couldn't remember the last time I'd driven this scenic loop.

From Unity, there were two ways to get to Poker Bluff, as the road started in town and circled the whole outcropping. Freddy turned right at the intersection, and we broke out of the trees near the northwestern crest of the hill.

"Oh my god," whispered Felix, looking out the side window.

My sentiments exactly.

Freddy stopped the cruiser right in the middle of the road while each of us solemnly took in an almost incomprehensible scene.

Where once was a lush, green, heavily-forested hillside, hardly a blade of grass now stood. The entire area had been savagely clear-cut and bulldozed. A few recently-paved roads, complete with sidewalks, meandered here and there across the hilltop, ending in bulbous cul-de-sacs. Three-foot high phone and cable posts dotted the landscape, marking proposed future driveways.

Numerous cement pads had been poured, but only a half-dozen condos were under construction, their skeletal frameworks barely begun. Idle heavy machinery stood waiting out the weekend. There were no sounds of hammers this day.

The palpable silence enveloped us, and I honestly felt like I might lose my breakfast.

"Where will all the deer go to live?" said Felicity in a tiny little voice. "I saw them everywhere up here when I went hiking last summer."

Freddy cleared his throat, put the car in gear, and eased it on up and over to the south side of the development. Here, several condos were nearing completion and an "Open House" sign was stuck in the dirt near the entry of a three-story unit. A big, black, shiny Lincoln was parked in the driveway.

I gasped, only it sounded more like an inhaled shriek.

Felicity ducked down behind the seat again.

"It's okay, Syl— you're in a patrol car, remember?" said Freddy, not unkindly.

"You wanna hide back here with me?" asked Felix without lifting her head.

Brash as all get-out, Freddy pulled right in behind the vehicle and jotted down the license plate number. Deliberately taking his time, he slowly turned the cruiser around and we headed back down the hill.

My breathing returned to normal almost as soon as we cleared the open wrought-iron gate at the bottom.

"I wonder who's driving that one?" Freddy mused aloud. "You say Jimmy didn't get the plate number of the vehicle he encountered Friday night, but we've got the numbers off the one delivering fish guts, which is the same one that stayed in Unit 4 at the Clamshell Friday night: HR3 003.

"The one Robert Jones was driving last night was 004, and now this one is 002."

"Are you assuming Friday night's gun-waving threat was, or wasn't, made from one of the cars we've already identified?" I asked.

"That it was," Freddy replied. "I already know Uncle Harry drives one of them himself, and since I doubt it's him out here working the real estate sales office today, let's assume he drives 001."

"That makes sense," I agreed. "The boss drives car number one, and unless he does his own dirty work, the gun-waver had to be in number two, three, or four."

"Using the process of elimination, since number two is back there up on the hill, and Jones was in number four, it's logical that number 3, the one Jimmy checked in, was responsible for the gun-waving."

"The gun-waving *and* the fish guts," I reminded him.

"Is it enough for a warrant?" asked Felicity, popping her head back over the seat.

"It's plenty to put out an APB for HR3 003," said Freddy, using his police lingo. Then he scowled. "But at this point, I doubt the car will be all that easy to find."

We lapsed into thoughtful reverie as Freddy continued to drive us through Tinkerstown and back up the peninsula.

"Well," said Felicity, breaking the silence, "I think the whole Poker Bluff development is a front. Sure there's a great view, but nobody I know could ever afford such a place."

I agreed. "He'll go bust in a few months when he can't pre-sell enough units to make wages."

"So it really could be just a tax write-off," said Freddy. He shrugged. "Oh, well. Nevertheless, I, for one, am extremely glad we drove up there this morning to check things out."

"Why is that?" Felix asked.

Freddy caught her eye in the rearview mirror and grinned. "It allowed me to spend more quality time this morning with your good friend Sylvia. Maybe soon she'll admit how worldly wise and devilishly handsome I am and start thinking I'm not too young for her after all."

"I'm right here! I can hear you, you know!" I shook my head and looked out the window, hoping neither one of them could see my cheeks flush.

Freddy started humming some song I vaguely recognized from some classic movie. I'm sure it was supposed to have some deep, poignant meaning concerning our relationship, but I chose to ignore it.

Oh good god! I gasped to myself. My blush intensified, if that was possible, when I realized I'd used the words

'Freddy' and 'relationship' in the same thought. I continued to stare out the window in silence the remaining few minutes it took us to return to the Clamshell, preparing to use the "Menopausal Hot Flash" card if either of them noticed my red face.

As I'd expected, Walter's car was gone, so the only vehicles left in the lot were Felicity's Camry and my Mustang.

"That's some 'Stang you got there, Sylvia."

"Thanks." I smiled.

"It's so 90s," Freddy continued, "and it's so... so... *you!*"

"You just met me," I said, getting out and leaning back in the door. "So how would you know?"

Freddy grinned. "I know a lot about you already," he replied. "I'm a trained observer, you know. That's why the sheriff assigned me to bodyguard duty."

I had no comeback for that, but thankfully, he remained in the cruiser to radio his report to the sheriff while Felicity and I went inside.

"You really ought to give him a chance," Felix began as soon as the inner office door closed behind us.

"He's a good decade and a half younger than I am," I reminded her. "A lot closer to your age than mine."

Felix shrugged. "He's obviously into you, and he's probably somewhere in his 40s, and you're in your 50s. So what's the problem?"

"I'm not looking for a relationship right now," I hedged.

"Of course not," replied Felicity. "A guy who's smart, cute, and definitely interested in getting to know you better comes knocking on your door, and you're suddenly not in the mood." She glowered at me. "I think you have commitment issues."

I laughed. "I'd venture a guess that 'commitment' is

close to the last thing on Freddy's mind," I said pointedly.

"What is it you always tell me?" Felicity looked at the ceiling, pretending to be searching her memory banks. I knew damn well what she was going to say next, so I said it with her.

"No contempt prior to investigation."

Felix laughed and started gathering her things together. "You really should consider following that advice."

"You going somewhere?" I asked, abruptly changing the subject.

Felicity reached for the blankets on the couch. I grabbed one end of the top one and together we started folding.

"I've got to get home and finish up my lesson plans. Walter's going to be my substitute for the week while I'm out on an authentic Lewis and Clark camping reenactment trip with my honor history students," said Felix, beaming. "Isn't that great?"

"The fact that Walter's going to substitute for you, or the fact that you're willingly going camping with a whole class of hormonally-challenged teenagers?"

"Well, now that you put it that way, both." Felix laughed again. "But I was really referring to Walter covering my other classes."

I shook my head. "I'm surprised he's now substituting after he's already done 40 years in the classroom."

"Thirty-eight," corrected Felicity. "And he's doing it for me as a personal favor." She batted her eyelashes. "I shamelessly begged."

"So when are you leaving on this reenactment thing?"

"This afternoon, actually," said Felicity. She put her pillow on top of the folded blankets at the end of the couch. "The kids are gathering at the school at 2 o'clock."

I was sure this adventure wasn't in Felicity's teaching

contract, but nobody was holding a gun to her head. "Well... have a good time!"

"Oh, we will! We're going to boil sea water to get salt and render some lard to make candles and even tan a hide one of the parents saved for us when they butchered a cow!"

It didn't sound like my idea of a good time, but I kept my mouth shut. No sense raining on her parade, but speaking of rain— I looked through the kitchen window at the darkening sky.

"You taking umbrellas?"

"It rained all but three or four days the entire time Lewis and Clark were here along the coast," she replied. "We'll be fine."

I walked her to the door. Freddy was heading in just as Felicity was heading out. Swell. With Walter gone, that meant I was going to be left alone with Freddy all afternoon. Not that being left with Freddy *and* Walter would have been any more desirable, but there was relative safety in numbers.

"Tootle-loo." Felix wiggled her fingers at us as she drove away.

If I could have reached her, I swear I would have wiped that silly grin off her face.

I looked at Freddy. He looked at me. We stood there, both of us silently appraising the situation.

"Well," he finally said, "are you going to invite me in?"

"Are you housebroken?" I took a deep breath and stepped back, no longer blocking his passage through the door.

He grinned, but I noticed he didn't answer the question.

We walked through the office and into the living quarters. Freddy immediately crossed the kitchen linoleum and went on in to the carpeted living room area. Like a bloodhound, he located the TV remote and clicked on the 52-inch screen.

"What kind of movies does Jimmy have?" His dimples deepened. "I'll even watch a chick-flick if I have to."

I took the remote from him and flipped to one of the dozens of Jimmy's sports channels. "The Mariners are playing this afternoon. You have the choice of either watching the game with me or not. Take it or leave it. Make up your mind right now, cause I'm making popcorn, and I need to know if I'll need one or two bowls."

Baseball is the only professional sport I follow, and even then I'm not what anyone would call a fanatic. I do know all the players' names, but I usually catch only a game or two a week. Sunday afternoons, though, are sacred.

"Geez, Syl, you sure drive a hard bargain." Freddy plopped down in Jimmy's recliner. "Who's pitchin'?"

"A new guy from the Dominican Republic."

"Good deal," said Freddy. "He threw a hundred mile an hour fastball his last time out."

I had to admit it was nice to have someone to watch the game with who knew a little something about the sport. It turned out that Freddy actually knew a great deal about it, and I found myself having a really good time, despite my former misgivings.

Too bad the game wasn't more exciting, though. By the 7th inning stretch, the score was 10-2, and the 10 did not belong to Seattle.

A sharp rap on the office door startled me awake. I looked sheepishly from the couch to Freddy in the recliner. It was obvious he'd also been caught dozing.

"G'mornin' beautiful," he whispered huskily.

I made a face at him as I dumped Priscilla off my lap

and struggled groggily to my feet. The rapping on the door grew more insistent. "Coming!" I loudly called out.

Freddy snorted.

"You behave yourself," I hissed.

Running my fingers quickly through my short hair, I made my way across the room and opened the inner door. Sheriff Donaldson stood outside the office in his off-duty clothes, his laptop tucked under one arm. He looked genuinely concerned.

"Everything okay?" he asked as soon as I unlocked and opened the outer door. He looked past me to Freddy, who was now standing in his stocking feet before the open refrigerator door, surveying the contents.

"Everything's fine, sheriff," said Freddy. "No worries." Then to me he said, "You got any orange juice, Syl? I always like to enjoy a big glass of orange juice right after I wake up, don't you?"

Sheriff Donaldson looked quickly from me to Freddy and back again.

"It's not what you think," I said quickly. "We were both watching the ball game and eating popcorn, and—"

"Ah, Syl, give it a break," said Freddy. "We slept together, plain and simple."

Thankfully, the sheriff was used to Freddy's suggestive remarks, and he wasn't so easily duped. But I could see he was bothered by the fact that Freddy and I had so easily become this comfortable with each other.

He came in and set his laptop on the kitchen table. "Thanks for the call this morning, Deputy. After your report on your visit to Pacific Bluff, I dug a little deeper into Rodman's business history." He turned on the machine and we waited while it booted up.

"And?" I prompted, eager to find out what he'd learned.

"And," said Sheriff D, sitting down and also making himself right at home, "it turns out he has quite a shady history with the law in other states."

"But Uncle Harry's never served any time, has he?" asked Freddy.

"Deputy Morgan," said the sheriff, sitting up straight and officious in his chair and glowering at Freddy, "kindly refrain from referring to a 'person of interest' in an ongoing investigation in such familiar terms. It's neither dignified nor deserving of your position."

It was quite a slap-down, and I'm pretty sure it had been done to both impress me and reinstate Sheriff Donaldson's authority. But Freddy floored us both by immediately trumping the sheriff's hand.

"Harold Rodman the Third really *is* my uncle," he said softly. "He's my dad's half-brother; they had the same mother."

Hold everything! Had the sheriff really just called Freddy 'Deputy Morgan'? I felt my eyebrows skyrocket upward as I turned quickly to Freddy. "Who, exactly, is your dad?"

"Richard Morgan," he said matter-of-factly. "Captain Morgan to most people. He owns the charter business I was telling you about at breakfast. The one I thought I'd eventually inherit, until my father decided not to leave it to his seasick-prone son."

The dots finally connected, and I sat down heavily on a vacant kitchen chair. Last night I'd had dinner with the father, and this morning I'd had breakfast with the son.

Felicity was going to love this—if I ever decided to tell her about it.

CHAPTER 6

I waited until Freddy left to tell the sheriff about my dinner conversation with Rich Morgan, emphasizing the fact that I now suspected the good captain might have been using me to get insider information about the case.

"Honestly, Carter, I had no idea he and Rodman were brothers."

"Half-brothers," corrected the sheriff.

"Whatever."

Once again, Sheriff Donaldson proved to be a whole lot quicker than I'd given him credit for. He tipped his head to one side and eyed me warily for several moments before he spoke. "So you're dating both Freddy *and* his father?"

"Let's just focus on the case, Carter." I turned to get a soda from the fridge, hoping the blast of cool air would help ease the heat I felt creeping up my neck. Without turning around, I held up a can of diet cola. "Want one?"

"What. I. Want," said Sheriff D, practically spitting out each word, "is for you to explain to me exactly why you found it necessary to go spilling your guts to one of your boyfriends just hours after I told you to keep it under your hat."

I whirled around, sure that venom dripped from my bared fangs.

Carter's face, naturally ruddy anyway, had turned dark red, lending emphasis to his disapproval. More than just his hand was trembling now. He looked as though he wanted to pick me up and squeeze me until my head popped off. And judging by his angry glare, I was pretty sure he was quite capable of doing just that.

I was truly remorseful for having disclosed so much to Rich, but I was backed against a wall. I hunkered down into preservation mode, and figured my best defense was a good offense.

"He's *not* my boyfriend, and I did *not* spill my guts to him!" I took a hefty swig from the pop can, and set it down on the table with a resounding bang. "And besides, how could I have possibly known Rich was related to Uncle Harry? *You* didn't even know that!" I folded my arms across my chest and glared at him.

Surprisingly, Sheriff D stopped his sputtering long enough to consider my statement before speaking. His face softened, and he blew out a lungful of animosity, his cheeks puffing and then deflating as he did so. "You're absolutely right, Syl."

What did he mean, *I was right*? Why wasn't he still taking my head off? What was the old fart up to? Didn't he realize he had me dead to rights for screwing with the case? Wasn't he going to continue to admonish me for not keeping my big mouth shut?

Confusion tumbled around in my head, bombarding my brain with dozens of questions, but the best I could muster was a weak "Huh?"

"I've been looking exclusively into Rodman's business dealings." He sighed. "I forgot all about any familial connections. I dropped the ball when I didn't follow up on those previously alleged relatives he has in the area."

"They aren't so 'alleged' any more, are they?" I said icily. I knew I was pressing my luck, and should be grateful he wasn't arresting me for obstructing justice, or some such legal-sounding thing.

"But you still shouldn't have blabbed so much to Rich Morgan."

"I realize that now, Carter, and I'm sorry." I did my best to look humbled. "I've known Rich for years, and consider him a good friend. But we're not all that close—Heck, I didn't even know he had a son..." I shook my head, letting my words trail off.

"Freddy's been away for over 20 years," said Sheriff D. "Did a stint in the military right out of high school. I just hired him a few months ago." He shrugged, paused, seemed to think about saying more, but looked toward the fridge. "If you're still offering, I'll take that soda now."

I got up to get him one. For once, I kept my feminist beliefs to myself and didn't say a word about how I wasn't his slave, or how his legs weren't broken, or how he damn well could get his own damn pop. Instead, I focused on being grateful we'd avoided a serious breach in our friendship.

"What we have to do now is figure out if whatever happened in Unit 4 is in any way connected to Morgan. *Richard* Morgan." The sheriff sighed and took a drink from the pop can. "I'm afraid this could put Freddy in a really uncomfortable position."

I agreed. "It is if Rich is actually involved. I'm pretty sure Freddy wouldn't cotton to have to arrest his own father."

"What about his uncle?"

"Technically, we don't have any proof yet that Uncle Harry has done anything illegal, do we?"

The sheriff smiled. "You ever watch NCIS?

"Yeah, doesn't everybody?" I tilted my head, searching for the connection. Finding none, I asked, "But what's that got to do with this?"

"Leroy Jethro Gibbs isn't the only one who knows when his gut is telling him something. Right now I'd bet a year's pay that Rodman had someone killed in Unit 4 last week. I don't know who, I don't know why, I just know."

"I can't argue with you, Sheriff; I feel exactly the same way."

"What we need now," said Sheriff D, "is someone on the inside at Spartina Point."

"Carter," I said, smiling for the first time since Freddy had left, "It just so happens I know someone who has worked there ever since they opened. Someone who majored in water cooler gossip." I got up to get my purse and car keys. "Someone I know we can trust."

At first, I didn't think the sheriff was going to let me out of his sight, even though I assured him I was only going to visit a girlfriend, nothing more.

"It would be great if you could stay here," I said, concluding my argument by throwing in a purposefully distracting element. "The cat could use the company."

Sheriff D looked over at Priscilla, napping on the back of Jimmy's recliner. "What's the cat got to do with it?"

"Priscilla's been alone most of the day. She's not used to that."

"So you want me to cat sit?"

My ploy was working perfectly. I should have majored in miscommunications. He was now more focused on Priscilla than what I might, or might not, ger myself into when I left the motel.

"And if you stay here in the office, I can keep the 'Vacancy' sign up, and it will look like business as usual around here."

It took me all of two minutes to show him what he

needed to do in the unlikely event someone wandered in on a Sunday night needing a room.

"Syl..." Sheriff D took me by the shoulders, and for one horrifying moment I thought he was going to try to kiss me. "Please try to stay out of trouble."

"No worries, Sheriff." I wiggled out from under his grasp. "I'll only be gone an hour or so."

"Not if you obey the speed limit," he said. "Spartina Point is a good 25 minutes from here, so that's a full hour of travel time alone. And knowing how you like to talk..."

I made a face at him. "Your point, Carter?"

He looked at his watch. "Promise to check in with me if you're going to be gone longer than, say, two and a half hours."

I pulled my cell phone out of my pocket and waved it at him. "And I promise to call right away if there's anything you need to know before I get back."

"Is it turned on?"

I pointedly flipped the switch with my thumb. "It is now."

That seemed to satisfy him, so I crammed the phone back into my jeans and escaped to my car.

As soon as I pulled out of the lot, I pressed the button to put the convertible top down. It was late afternoon, and the air really wasn't quite warm enough to open it up, but for once it wasn't raining. I know people think I'm nuts for buying a convertible in this climate, but sometimes I just need the feel of the wind rushing by to clear the cobwebs between my ears, and this was one of those times.

Sheriff Donaldson was right; it took me close to half an hour to reach my destination, only taking the car out of cruise control long enough to pass through the tiny town of Ocean Crest.

It was disconcerting to drive through the familiar and relatively undeveloped area behind the main ocean dunes and then suddenly arrive at such a high-class resort area. It had pretty much the same affect on me as the housing project on Poker Bluff. And oddly enough, the same man was responsible for both.

I don't know how Uncle Harry got away with filling in so much wetland at the north end of the peninsula. Rumor had it he'd made some kind of swamp swap with the environmental watchdogs and traded other land parcels to be left au naturel. I vaguely remembered the newspaper coverage of the story a couple years ago.

Spartina Point Casino and Resort was built in record time, and opened for business late last summer. Tourism boomed, and the county unemployment rate dropped. The main building sported a decent-sized casino parlor on the first floor, complete with blackjack and craps tables, a roulette wheel, and plenty of slot machines.

There was also a fairly upscale restaurant, gift shop, multi-screen TV sports lounge, piano bar, and two reception halls. The larger hall was used for concerts and conventions while the smaller one rented out for private parties.

Above the actual casino was a small but posh hotel, complete with indoor pool. What was most striking about the building was its exterior. It was built to look like a miniature medieval castle, including turrets at each corner with Rodman family crest banners flying high in the breeze above. A mock drawbridge crossed a decent-sized moat for entrance to the building from the main parking lot.

Uncle Harry had installed a helipad behind the casino for himself and his VIP guests. The resort was surrounded on three sides by a sanctioned nine-hole golf course.

My friend Mercedes plays piano and sings in the lounge most weekends and for special events. She's never told me her last name, and I suspect Mercedes is not her real first name, but she's otherwise a straight-up gal I can always trust to have my back.

Before getting the regular gig at the casino, she lived like a gypsy, residing in her motorhome in the parking lot of whatever bar hired her to sing that weekend. Old habits are hard to break, and her motorhome was now parked as discretely as possible in the far corner of the secondary resort lot. I'll bet Uncle Harry just *loved* that.

I parked beside her trailer and put the convertible top up. Weather around here changes only slightly quicker than the fishing quotas. I got out and pounded on the motorhome door.

"If the trailer's a-rockin', don't come a-knockin'," she called out.

"Mercedes! It's Sylvia! Lemme in!"

The door opened a crack and she peered out at me. "You alone?"

"Same as you are."

She laughed at that and pushed the door open. "Didn't want nobody to see me without my make-up on. A girl's got to protect her public image, you know, even on her days off."

I climbed up the metal stairs and stooped to give what she called her 'five foot two inch frame without heels,' a hug. "Merc, it's been too long."

"Right," she replied, motioning for me to sit down on the half-sized burnt orange tweed couch. "I haven't seen you since you made that hasty departure from the dance floor a couple months back. Never seen anybody kick off their heels and sprint out the door like that in all my years of playing piano bars." She sat opposite me in a matching swivel-rocker. "What was that all about, hhmmm?"

"Long story, ancient history, and not why I'm here."

"Hey, I understand if you don't want to talk about it. That guy you were with was genuinely butt-ugly."

"I wasn't *with* him, and you know it."

"Uh-huh, whatever you say, girlfriend." She grinned. "So why *are* you here? I know you didn't come all this way to see my new henna tattoo." Mercedes pulled the collar of her hot fuchsia pink jogging suit down to show me the artwork just above her right breast.

"Love you?" I questioned the inscription.

"Hey, temporary tattoos last lots longer than most of my relationships. I'm not about to ink some guy's name on me when he may be up and gone the next week."

"So there's still no one special, Merc?"

"They're all special!" She laughed. "Just ask 'em!" Then she turned serious. "I've been married four times, and I've learned my lesson. I'm an entertainer, and entertainers have groupies, not husbands." She abruptly stopped talking and looked around like she'd lost something.

"Brutus! Where are you, Brutus? Come here, boy!"

I know my brow furrowed, darn it, and I'm trying so hard not to attract any more wrinkles than I already have. "You got a dog?"

"You betcha!" She beamed. "A dog is loyal, and trustworthy, and if you get him neutered, he won't have any reason to run out on you."

I wouldn't dream of arguing with logic like that. "And... you've misplaced him?"

Mercedes stood and climbed up on the couch next to me on her knees to peer over the back of it. "There's my good boy," she cooed. She reached down and hoisted 'Brutus' up and over the couch back and straight into my lap.

'Brutus' looked like some kind of strange cross between a basset, a little German Shorthair Pointer, and a dachshund.

"He's a little shy at first," explained Mercedes.

I patted the top of his head, and his tail wagged tentatively. "I thought you didn't want to be responsible for a pet." I tilted my head thoughtfully. "And didn't you tell me just a few months ago you had no room for an animal in here?"

"I got him for protection."

Mercedes' cell phone suddenly rang. Brutus yelped, jumped off my lap, and scampered back behind the couch.

"Some protection."

Merc pulled her cell phone from the left side of her bra and checked the incoming number. "Telemarketers." She hit the ignore button and returned the phone to its usual location. "So where were we?"

I brought her up to speed on everything that had transpired since Jimmy's desperate call Friday night as quickly as I could. I breathlessly concluded my recitation with "and now we need your help."

Mercedes had been listening with rapt attention. Not once had she interrupted me. Now she spoke softly under her breath as she exhaled. "Hay-soose."

We've been friends long enough for me to know that what Merc had whispered was the closest thing to swearing in her entire vocabulary.

"Yes," I agreed, and repeated what she'd said in English. "Jesus."

"Uncle Harry is a no good bum," said Mercedes. "I shouldn't complain, him giving me this steady job and all, but I see things going on that just aren't right."

I brightened. "That's just what the sheriff and I are counting on, Merc."

"I'm all over it." Mercedes sprang up from her chair and Brutus, who had tentatively poked his head out from behind the couch, scurried back out of sight. "Just give me a couple minutes to make myself presentable, and we'll go check a few things out, up close and personal."

I was sure Sheriff Donaldson would understand why I'd decided there was no time like the present to do some internal casino reconnaissance. He'd only admonished me to stay out of trouble, not stay out of the casino.

Twenty minutes later, Mercedes entered the living area and twirled around. "So whaddya think?"

Since I wanted her help, I didn't dare tell her what I really thought. She was decked out from head to toe in mauve sequins. Her touring cap, her shoes, her over-sized dangly earrings—everything glittered and sparkled. Clutched in her hand was a matching drawstring purse.

"Does, uh, your, uh, fingernail polish, uh, glow in the dark?" I finally managed to stammer out.

"It sure does! I always wear it! Different colors to match my outfits, of course. It's quick-drying, thank goodness! Looks pretty on the keyboard in the dim light of the piano bar. You like it? I'll give you some." She started back down the hall.

"No!" I heard my voice involuntarily go up an octave. "I'm sure you'll be attracting enough attention all by yourself."

"Harrumph." Mercedes sat back down in her swivel chair. "I can see you're less than enthused by my chosen ensemble."

"To be honest, Merc, it's just not something I'd personally wear while breaking and entering."

"Don't you get it?" She sighed. "This is what my public expects me to wear. They'd know something was up right off if they saw me in black sweats and a dark stocking cap. We'll be hiding in plain sight, just like that old TV show, get it?"

Unfortunately, I could see some merit in what she was saying. I stood up. "Alright then, let's go." I put my hand on the exit door.

"Wait! We need to wear gloves so we don't leave any fingerprints!" Mercedes headed back down the hall. "Don't you *ever* watch television?"

She returned moments later with a couple pair of latex doctor examination gloves. Purple. She handed me a pair. "One size fits all."

"Don't tell me you have latex gloves to match every outfit?"

"Nah, just got lucky this time," Merc replied. "And I only have these cause I dated a proctologist for a week or two. He was a little kinky; liked to do it in his examination room. Figured I had to get something worthwhile out of the relationship."

I stared at the gloves in my hand, horrified.

"Don't worry," said Mercedes matter-of-factly, "these ones haven't been used."

She tucked her pair into her handbag and I stuck mine in my back pocket.

It had gotten dark in the time it had taken Mercedes to change her clothes. We left the overflow lot where her motorhome was parked and started making our way across the crowded main parking area. The external lights illuminated the place like it was the middle of the day, so it was easy to see where we were going.

Even on a Sunday night, the place was comfortably full.

Next to the handicap spaces near the door, in spaces marked "Reserved," were three big, black, shiny Lincoln *Town Cars* with license plates: RH3 001, 002, and 004. RH3 003 was, of course, missing.

I snapped a picture of the group of them with my cell phone, making sure the license plates were clearly visible. I was sure there was enough light from the lamps around the moat for the sheriff and me to read the numbers later. We might not need this information, but you never know.

RH3 004 was the car Bob Jones had been driving. The 002 was the car we'd seen up at Poker Bluff earlier this afternoon. Assuming Freddy was right, Uncle Harry drove 001. If we ever managed to catch up with him, Mr. John Smith, with the missing 003 car, had quite a bit of explaining to do.

"Whatcha taking pictures of these cars for?" asked Mercedes.

"Do you know who drives them?"

"Number one belongs to Uncle Harry. I don't know about the others. When I come to work there's usually two or three of these look-alike cars parked here. I honestly never give them no mind," said Merc.

"On Friday and Saturday nights, and sometimes for special occasions, there's valet service," she continued. "But I haven't convinced them yet they need to come pick me up when it's raining."

She started across the mock drawbridge ahead of me. I caught up with her when she stopped in the center of the walkway to dig around in her handbag. Finding a couple coins, she tossed them into the moat. "For luck," she whispered.

She looked at my hands. "Where's your purse?"

"In the car trunk. I don't like to carry it around with

me."

"Then where's your gun?"

"Also in the trunk."

"What in Hay-soose's name is your gun doing in your trunk?"

I shrugged. "I'm not planning on needing it tonight."

"Well, I got mine right here," she patted her sequined bag. "Never leave home without it."

This was news to me, so I asked to see it. When she pulled out her .22 caliber pistol, I started to laugh. It was pink.

"Hey, what're you laughing at? It's for protection."

"So's Brutus, but I don't think either one of them would garner you much respect from any bad guys."

She smiled widely. "That's okay," she said, tucking the gun back into her purse and marching resolutely toward the casino entrance. "Sometimes respect is not exactly the thing a girl is going for."

I followed her through the door without further comment.

The relative silence of the world outside that door was in stark contrast to the assault of ringing bells and flashing lights inside.

Mercedes set a brisk pace through the main room, purposefully not turning her head to gawk at all the whirling slot machines. Unlike me. I was instantly mesmerized by them and wanted nothing more than to stop and play the slots for a little while. I was both disappointed and thankful I'd left my money in the car.

I followed Mercedes out through the double swinging doors on the far side of the room. As soon as the doors closed behind, it was eerily quiet again. She smiled. "Ain't soundproofing grand?"

We walked down the short hall to the registration desk. "The old man in today?" Merc asked the young man at the hotel counter.

The clerk nodded. "Holing up in his usual room, 552. Must be some kind of big pow-wow going on up there today. He told me to hold his calls until further notice."

"Yeah, well he's probably just up there screwing his Flavor of the Month and doesn't want to get distracted."

They both laughed, then Mercedes abruptly changed the subject. "I got some laundry to do," she began. "Any chance you've got a spare keycard today?"

"Sure thing, Merc." The clerk handed her a keycard and she quickly tucked it into her bra. "Thanks, Ralph, you're a peach."

Ralph grinned. "Anything for you, Mercedes."

"I'll remember you said that, darlin'," she smiled and blew him an air kiss as we walked to the elevator.

"Laundry?" I asked as we waited for the elevator to return to the ground floor. The casino hotel was rumored to have the slowest lift west of the Mississippi.

"It's one of the perks of working here," said Merc. "On days when there aren't too many hotel guests, the staff can use the machines to do our personal laundry—for free."

"But I don't see—"

"Shhhush." Mercedes put her finger to her lips just before the elevator doors opened. A happy crowd of gamblers stepped out and bustled toward the excitement of the slot machines.

We stepped inside and Merc waited for the doors to close before she spoke. "It's a master key card," she said quietly. "All the maids have them."

The full impact of her statement hit me like a punch in the nose.

CHAPTER 7

Mercedes pressed the elevator button for the fifth floor. "Uncle Harry calls the fifth floor the penthouse." She laughed. "It's his own little joke. Penta means five, like in pentagon and pentagram—get it?"

She reached inside her bra and produced a tissue to wipe her fingerprints off the fifth floor button. "Can't be too careful."

I finally found my voice. "What else you got tucked in there?"

"Just my cell," said Merc. "I carry my police whistle, gun, and condoms in my purse." She grinned at my expression. "A girl can't carry too much protection these days, you know what I mean?"

I fervently hoped I didn't know what she meant, but I decided now was a really good time to change the subject.

"I wonder why Uncle Harry only built five stories high?"

Mercedes had the answer. "Oh, that's a real sore subject with Uncle Harry," she began. "Ed, the building maintenance supervisor, told me all about it. Uncle Harry's original plans called for the building to be twice as high, but the Coast Guard squelched that. Told him there was some county ordinance or federal mandate or something on the official books somewhere about tall buildings along the coastline endangering their rescue helicopters.

"Apparently there are strict laws about such things, and

no matter how mad he got, or who he called, or how much he was willing to pay for a variance, he couldn't get anybody to budge." Merc smiled. "There were lots of side bets made by the staff as to how far up in the government he could go to pull strings, but in the end, he couldn't pay off anybody high enough to make an exception to the law."

"That must have really pissed him off."

Mercedes laughed. "That's why he hung those huge Rodman family crest banners on flagpoles atop the turrets. There's no law about how high *flagpoles* can extend beyond the actual building. He refers to them as his middle-fingered salute to the Coast Guard."

We exited on the fifth floor without running into any other hotel guests. "They wouldn't notice us anyway," mused Mercedes. "Nobody ever sees the hired help. It's kind of sad, really. It's like we're all invisible."

I rolled my eyes, a bad habit I'm trying to break, but Merc didn't see me do it. I'm pretty sure it doesn't count if nobody sees you do it.

The plush carpet absorbed whatever sounds our shoes might have made in the hallway. Nevertheless, we tiptoed past Room 552 without talking. Mercedes put on her purple latex gloves before she inserted the keycard into the door of the Room 554.

"What about the security cameras?" I whispered, also pulling on my gloves. "Isn't somebody watching us right now?"

"No cameras in the hallways," Merc replied. "They're in the casino, the restaurant, the bar, and the parking lot, but not in the bathrooms or the halls. Guess they don't care whose wife is sneaking around with whose husband inside the hotel."

The blinking red light flashed green and the latch

released. Mercedes turned the handle and we quickly stepped into the room.

"It's not really breaking and entering if we have a keycard, is it?" she giggled. "I bet a good attorney could get us off on a technicality."

I hoped against hope we'd never have reason to test that theory.

Mercedes went straight to the mini-bar and returned with two empty glasses. She handed one to me. "You do know how to use this to listen in on the people in the next room, don't you?"

We crept to the living room side of the unit, to the wall separating the two suites. Mercedes carefully placed the open end of her glass against it. Then she pressed her ear against the bottom of the glass. I did the same. I'd seen this trick done in the movies dozens of times, but had never had an opportunity to try it myself.

Too bad we weren't making a movie. I squinted my eyes tight shut, barely able to make out a few words now and then. Words like 'I'm telling you,' and 'make it right.' The biggest phrase I could understand was 'put on your trunks.' But I couldn't piece together anything that sounded intelligible.

I had my ear pressed so hard against the glass bottom I thought my ear would go permanently numb. I was just about to tell Mercedes I'd had enough when her cell phone started buzzing.

"Brrrrrrr..... Brrrrrrr..... Brrrrrrr..... Brrrrrrr."

Mercedes grabbed the phone from the left side of her bra and switched it off. She grinned at me and whispered, "Good thing I had it set on vibrate, huh?"

First, I put my finger to my lips, scowled meaningfully at her, and shook my head. Second, I reached into my pocket and turned my own cell phone off. Third, I looked on the floor to see if I'd left a puddle.

Mercedes motioned for me to join her in the suite's bedroom. "Could you hear anything?" she asked.

I related to her the partial phrases I thought I'd heard. To my list she added, 'hold down,' 'going swimming,' and 'deep shit,' pardon the language.

"You heard them say 'pardon the language'?"

"No, I said 'pardon the language,' cause I wanted to repeat exactly what I'd heard, but I didn't want you to think I normally talked like that. Them cuss words are not part of my normal vernacular."

I mentally added up what we'd heard, and knew we didn't have near enough to go on, but that minor fact didn't keep Mercedes from jumping to conclusions.

"Know what I think?" said Merc.

I've never professed to be a mind reader, but I didn't think she'd fully appreciate my sarcasm just now, so I kept my mouth shut.

"I think somebody's gonna be drowned in the casino swimming pool. Uh-huh, I'm sure that's it."

I wanted to laugh and tell her she'd seen way too many movies, but another part of me was afraid she might be right.

"You got any friends here in Security, Merc?"

Mercedes nodded thoughtfully. "Of course. Why?"

"I'm thinking it may be time to get the professionals on board."

"No way!" she replied. "We'd have to admit where we got our information and I'd end up losing my laundry rights." Her head shook vehemently.

This gal was really putting my resolution to stop eye rolling to the test. I took a deep breath. "You got any other ideas?"

"As a matter of fact, I do." She put our eavesdropping tools into the suite's sink and headed for the door. "Follow me."

Merc's master card key got us into the resort's Lost and Found. There, she picked out a swimsuit roughly my size, and proceeded to the women's poolside locker room on the second floor. Three-hundred fifty-nine days a year, give or take a day or two, peninsula weather doesn't favor swimming in an outdoor pool, even if it's heated. Uncle Harry, although from someplace a lot warmer, had done his homework when he built the casino pool and spa inside.

"I don't see why you can't join me in there," I said, as I pulled my sweater off over my head.

"I just had my hair done at the Cute Me Up Salon." Mercedes patted the sides of her newly-coiffed platinum blonde hair. "And if I dunk it in a chlorine-filled pool before the color's set, my hairdresser will absolutely kill me."

"Poor choice of words," I said, sliding out of my pants and pulling on quite possibly the world's most unflattering one-piece floral bathing suit.

"Eeeuw." Mercedes made a face at me. "Go get into the water quick, before anyone has time to see you in that suit."

"And just what will you be doing while I'm paddling around in there waiting to stop anyone from being held under the water?"

"I'll be back in half an hour. I'm going to go talk to the bartender in the main lounge," said Merc. "Hairdressers and bartenders, you know—they hear it all."

I pulled a clean towel from the shelves by the door. "Speaking of hairdressers, would you mind telling me who you go to?"

"I told you—the Cute Me Up Salon."

"That's a where, not a who."

"Okay, okay, don't go getting all syntactically technical on me... My hairdresser's one of the 'L' gals... Lacie or Liz, I get them mixed up." Merc turned her head and looked quizzically at me.

"Thinking of going blonde, are you?"

"Not if I can't go swimming for fear my hair will turn green," I tossed right back. "I'm happy with my own natural chestnut color, it goes perfectly with my hazel eyes, thank you very much, but I do want to keep the gray from taking over."

Merc grinned. "Dating younger men these days, Sylvia?"

I froze halfway out the door leading to the pool. "Who told you that?"

"You going all Cougar on me?" she teased.

"We're not dating!"

Mercedes tried to look all sweet and innocent. "Word gets around," she replied, "and when it does, I can't help it if I'm there to hear it." She tootled her fingers as she headed out the other exit. "Hairdressers, bartenders, and piano playing lounge singers, deary."

I took Mercedes' advice and got into the pool right away. From there, since I still had my contacts in, I could watch both locker room doors, plus the entrance leading from the hotel hallway.

Five children were roughhousing in the shallow end, their mothers fully dressed and engaged in animated conversation in lounge chairs near the sauna. A young couple, with eyes only for each other, were in the hot tub. An elderly woman was attempting to swim laps, but having a tough time dodging the children at the shallow end when she made her turn.

Nothing too exciting, but what did I expect early evening on a Sunday? I paddled over to a duck-shaped water toy and pulled the floatation ring over my head. I bobbed around in the pool for the better part of my half hour. For variety, I treaded water furiously for a few minutes, then alternately kicked softly to catch my breath.

The children and their mothers left, the couple in love left, the old woman doing laps left, but nobody new, either potential murderer or murderee, arrived.

My fingers had begun to look like little wrinkled raisins. When did Mercedes say she'd be back? What if Uncle Harry had discovered we'd been eavesdropping on him? What if something had happened to Merc and she wasn't *ever* coming back? What if my whole body looked like a giant prune by the time I emerged from the pool?

I was able to work myself up into a frantic state in no time. I climbed the pool steps and was just toweling off when I heard someone trying to get my attention.

"Pssssst— Hey, lady— Over here."

A shady-looking character was standing in the doorway, one foot still outside in the hall. "Lady, if you don't mind—" he waved a paper cocktail coaster at me and held out a pen. "I'd shore like your auddograph, Ms. Williams." He looked a little embarrassed. And drunk. "Your mudder was one hell of schwimmer."

"Huh?" My usual witty repartee was apparently stalled—or waterlogged.

"Ms. Williams, over here!" Mercedes called from door of the women's locker room. She was obviously trying to control her laughter.

"Pull-ease! Ms. Will-ams! Juss one little auddograph bah-fore you go!"

I glared at Merc and draped the towel over my shoulders. Then I surprised myself by striding boldly over to the autograph hound. I took his pen and wrote 'All the Best' followed by an almost indecipherable attempt to write 'E. Williams.'

The man squinted at his paper. "E?"

"Esther junior," I replied, and ducked into the Women Only locker room to shower and dress. I couldn't wait to get my hands on Mercedes.

She stood just out of reach, openly laughing at me while I stripped off my suit. "Not funny," I told her. "Definitely not funny."

"Everybody in the bar sure thought so."

I stepped into the shower. "You told everybody in the bar that Esther Williams' daughter was swimming in the pool here today?"

"Didn't have to." She raised her voice so I could hear it over the sound of the running water. "They could see you for themselves." I shut off the water and she tossed me one of the skimpy white pool towels.

"What, exactly, are you talking about?"

Mercedes put a little more distance between us before she answered. "In the wall behind the first floor lounge is a big picture window that mimics an aquarium."

"Mimics?" I hoped Merc wasn't going to say exactly what I heard her say next.

"Everyone in the bar has been watching you paddle around in your little ducky inner tube for the past hour. The bartender loves you; you've drawn quite a crowd."

I threw my soggy towel at her. "Mercedes! Why didn't you tell me?!"

"Would you have gone in the pool if you had known 15 or 20 guys were going to be staring at your bright white legs beneath the water?"

"Hell no!"

"That's why I didn't tell you."

I pulled on my sweater and jeans without saying a word. Not only had my undercover work been a bust, but now my underwater legs had become a new source of embarrassment. I wondered if there'd been anyone in the bar I knew.

"By the way," hollered Merc, leading the way back through the maze of slot machines, "you might want to consider getting a membership to the new gym in Tinkerstown. They'd be happy to help you get rid of those jiggly thighs of yours."

Mercedes literally burst through the outer doors of the casino, and started running, if you could call it that in those 3-inch lavender stilettos of hers. She didn't stand a chance—I was wearing my tennies.

I took a couple quick strides and caught her by the collar. Whirling her around to face me I said, "I'm in a lot better shape than you are, little miss Lipo Queen. You wouldn't last two minutes on a treadmill."

Mercedes looked at me like she thought I might punch her. "Don't mess up my face," she begged, holding her hands in a defensive manner and cowering. "My face is my fortune. They don't hire ugly entertainment."

The fact that she feared me was enough. I let her go and put my hands on my hips in the Wonder Woman power stance. "Admit you need to work out a lot more than I do."

Merc tentatively smiled. "Bender and Stretch is having a two for one membership drive," she offered. "We could go together."

"Bender and Stretch? Sounds more like a law firm than a fitness center."

Mercedes broke into a genuine grin. "In our case, that would be Bender, Stretch and Fart, y'all."

I tried not to laugh, but she knew she had me. "Speak for yourself."

Together we turned and walked arm in arm back through the maze of cars. A steady drizzle was beginning to fall, and by the time we returned to her motorhome, we were both plenty damp. It didn't bother me any, my hair was already wet, but Mercedes was mumbling the whole way about ruining her new 'do.'

We hadn't learned a darn thing. All our clandestine undercover work had been for naught. Disappointed, I bid her goodnight and got into my car to head back down the North Beach Peninsula, grateful I had put the car top up.

I'd driven this road thousands of times, so after I passed through Ocean Crest, the only real town between Tinkerstown and the casino, it wasn't long before the rhythmic slap of the windshield wipers and constant speed held by the cruise control lulled me into a less-than-observant state.

Headlights on high beam behind me alerted me to sit up and pay attention. My speed was set at 50 mph, so I knew I hadn't been unconsciously holding up traffic, but this guy, or gal, was apparently in a great hurry to get somewhere.

But what kind of a jerk would roar right up behind me without dimming the headlights? Good grief and gravy! I tapped my brakes in the hopes the driver would back off a little. If anything, he, or she, edged closer. *Damn!*

Annoyed, I slowed the car and edged over toward the side of the road to let the car pass. The driver also slowed down and edged over. All my senses went on red alert. Was I purposely being stalked? I knew better than to stop.

I pulled back into the center of the lane and returned to 50 mph. The car behind me also sped up, and now lightly tapped my back bumper. *What the hell?* Was the driver drunk? With one hand, I pulled my cell phone out of my pocket. I turned it back on and fumbled to dial 911. Another damn! No cell reception between the towns!

The car pulled out and came around as if to pass, but instead, only pulled even with me. I could tell the car was big and black and shiny, and I didn't care if it was a Lincoln or not. I didn't wait to see what would happen next as the passenger window started down. I slammed on the brakes and pulled hard to the right. As I said, I know the road well, and now was a good opportunity for me to level the playing field.

As soon as I was stopped, I threw the car into park, jumped out and ran around to the trunk. I'd already popped the lid, so I quickly lifted it up and grabbed for my gun. The big, black, shiny car hadn't expected my sudden stop, and by the time it pulled off the highway, it was several car lengths ahead of me.

The weight of the gun in my hand was reassuring, but I hoped I wouldn't need to fire it. That hope, however, was short-lived.

"Ka-pow! Ka-ping!" What the heck? "Ka-pow! Ka-ping! Ka-pow! Ka-ping!" They'd shot three times in my directions, and all three bullets had struck my open trunk lid, which now served as an inadvertent shield. They'd hit my Mustang! My gorgeous green and purple chameleon custom paint job had been violated! Screw them! Screw them and the car they rode in on! Enough was enough!

"Son-of-a-bitch!" I shrieked like some kind of American ninja warrior. It was one thing to shoot at me, but totally another thing to pockmark my car with bullet holes.

Without thinking, I stepped out from behind the back of the car, holding my Glock 19 in both hands for stability, struck the same stance I used at the firing range, and emptied the entire magazine.

"Ka-pow! Ka-pow! Ka-pow! Ka-pow! Ka-pow! Ka-pow! Ka-pow! Ka-pow! Ka-pow! Ka-pow! Ka-pow! Ka-pow! Ka-pow! Ka-pow! Ka-pow! Ka-pow! Click." I smiled. Ok, so maybe firing all 15 rounds in the magazine, plus the one in the pipe, was a bit of overkill, but lordy, it felt so good!

The big, black, shiny car streaked off into the night, spewing gravel and leaving me with a sense of complete empowerment, and a feeling a lot less vulnerable. I didn't know if I'd actually hit anything, but my offensive actions ought to make them think twice before messing with me, or my Mustang, ever again.

I was still standing there in the rain, soaked to the skin but feeling pretty cocky, when the very next vehicle traveling southbound pulled off the highway behind me. And there I stood, like the fabled deer in the headlights, lamely holding an empty gun.

I made the vehicle out to be a heavy-duty, white pickup truck, a four-wheel drive vehicle with extra lights mounted on the top. The headlights all but blinded me, but I could tell it definitely wasn't one of the sheriff's beach fleet.

When the driver's door swung open, I lifted my weapon and struck my 'Charlie's Angels' pose one again. Whoever it was couldn't have known I was out of ammo. Maybe I could bluff my way out of this.

"Sylvia! Don't shoot!" Captain Morgan emerged from the headlights and walked toward me. I dropped my gun on the pavement and collapsed into his arms, all the starch in my knees suddenly turning to warm Jell-O.

"There, there," Rich cooed, stroking my wet hair, which

was getting wetter by the minute. "It's alright Syl," he said, when I briefly told him what had happened. "You're safe now."

I wanted to believe him. I wanted to wake up and have the past two days be just another one of my crazy bad dreams. I clung to him as a drowning man, or in this case a drowning woman, clings to a life ring. With the rain coming down harder now, it crossed my mind that both of us really could stand right there and drown if we opened our mouths and looked skyward. I'd read somewhere that turkeys did this all the time.

It was a funny visual image, and I started giggling uncontrollably at the thought of the next day's newspaper headline: 'Couple perishes in freak drowning accident.'

The thought of the two of us being a couple made me laugh even harder.

"Syl! Syl! Get ahold of yourself," Rich admonished me.

I stopped laughing, but for a few minutes longer I hung onto him for dear life. Several cars passed us without stopping, and I finally tilted my head and looked up. Rich studied my face for a few seconds, then he asked, "Is the sheriff still staying out at the Clamshell with you?"

"Yes."

"Then I'll follow you there," said Rich. "I have to get up early tomorrow morning to take a charter group out, so I won't stop, but at least I can make sure you get there without any more trouble tonight."

He picked up my gun and put it back into my trunk, closing the lid securely. Then he helped me get behind the wheel, leaned in and gave me a quick kiss on the cheek. "Drive safely."

True to his word, Captain Morgan, my unlikely hero in a white pickup truck, flashed his headlights twice as I pulled into the Clamshell lot and drove on by.

I parked next to Sheriff D's pickup and got shakily out of my war-torn Mustang. Under the big office security light, I could see the extent of the damage to the trunk lid. My shaking body filled with rage.

"Somebody's damn sure gonna pay!"

I strode angrily across the parking lot, through the motel office door, and on into the living quarters. The sheriff looked up from his laptop at a soaking wet female rat with pure fire in her eyes.

"What the—" he began, but I cut him off.

CHAPTER 8

"Where the hell were *YOU*?" I demanded. I glowered at him, put my hands on my hips and stomped my foot for emphasis. And then I burst into tears. Not exactly the indignant impression I wanted to make.

Sheriff D got up from the table, took two steps to the couch, grabbed one of Felicity's nicely folded blankets, returned to the kitchen side of the room, and wrapped it tightly around me. He sat me down in the chair he'd just vacated at the table, and turned on Jimmy's teakettle.

It took half an hour and a huge mug of hot cocoa for me to relate the story of my harried trip home from my visit with Mercedes. Twice.

The first time through, my teeth were still chattering and my voice was too high for Sheriff Donaldson to make much sense of it. At his insistence, I went through it with him again, mile by mile, coming down the highway in the dark an hour earlier. He asked copious questions, ferreting out details, jotting it all down in his little pocket notepad.

I had purposely left out what Mercedes and I had done while I was with her, and began the story where I left the parking lot. The earlier tale could wait for another time, or not at all. I also didn't mention my encounter with Rich Morgan, but I'm not sure why I kept that part to myself.

Sheriff D tapped his pencil on his notepad. "Why was your gun in the trunk, again?"

I chewed on my lower lip for a moment before

answering. "Because I don't have a concealed weapons permit."

"They're called 'CPLs'—Concealed Pistol Licenses," said the sheriff.

"Yeah, whatever."

He frowned. "I would have sworn I saw your name on the list of those who completed the firearms safety course."

"It was, and I did." My hands were still tightly wrapped around the mug in front of me, even though it was empty. I wanted another cup of cocoa, but knew the caffeine in the chocolate wasn't a good idea if I wanted to get any sleep later.

Sheriff Donaldson could tell my mind was drifting. He repeated his question in a slightly sterner tone. "You passed the course, so why haven't you—"

"Because I haven't filled out the paperwork yet, that's why!" I could feel my cheeks grow hot, and knew it wasn't hormone-induced. At least a part of me was warming up.

"I'd be happy to expedite the paperwork for you."

"No, thank you, Carter. I don't want any special favors."

"But Syl— You *are* special to me."

I gave him my absolute, all-time best glower.

Wisely, the sheriff didn't pursue the subject. I stood, pulled the blanket securely around me, and walked to the kitchen window. "Look, Carter, I may be a bit lackadaisical about filling out the permit forms, but at least I'm not breaking any laws if I keep an unloaded weapon in the trunk."

Sheriff Donaldson cleared his throat. "I'll send one of my deputies out to police for brass and look for other evidence along that section of highway first thing in the morning."

I nodded, but remained staring out into the night. The

rain ran down the pane, making everything outside look a little blurry, but I could still make out our two vehicles parked side by side. "I'll bet my trunk's leaking."

"We can take care of that first thing in the morning as well," said Sheriff D. "Put a little duct tape over it, and it'll look good as new."

I knew he was trying to be practical, helpful, even considerate, but at that moment I figured it was a good thing my gun was still in the car. And empty. I turned and glared at him once more. "If you think for one damn minute I'm going to be seen around town with duct tape patches on my car—"

"Chill, Syl. It'll only be temporary. Just until you can take in to get it fixed."

"My insurance company is going to love this." I yawned and changed the subject.
"Since I don't see any other cars out there, may I assume nobody checked into the motel while I was away?"

"Nope, nobody even stopped to inquire." The sheriff tilted his head this way and that, looking intensely at me, still wrapped inside the blanket. "Would you feel safer tonight if I slept here in the apartment with you?"

Absolutely not! I wanted to shout, but managed to hold my tongue. "I think you'll sleep much better over there in a real bed instead of being over here *on the couch,*" I said pointedly. "At least I know I will," I said under my breath.

"Huh?"

I chuckled, but concluded our conversation on a more professional tone. "You'll be right across the driveway, Sheriff. Thank you for your generous offer, but I'll be fine. Really."

He opened the fridge and pulled out a can of diet soda. "If you don't mind," he said, "I think I'll just take one of these back to my room with me."

People were getting awfully familiar with Jimmy's fridge.

I bid the sheriff goodnight and locked the outer and inner office doors after him. A girl can't be too careful, I reasoned.

Discarding the damp blanket on one of the kitchen chairs, I walked down the short hall to the bathroom and stripped off my still-wet clothing. A hot shower was going to feel really good.

The toilet seat had been left up. Okay, the sheriff had been babysitting the motel for hours. No problem. At some point he must have had to pee. That was certainly reasonable. I tried to shake the uncomfortable feeling that washed over me. Nothing else seemed to be amiss, but the hair on the back of my neck said otherwise.

Now naked, and very vulnerable, I tiptoed toward the bedroom to retrieve Jimmy's commandeered blue bathrobe. From the doorway I saw wet footprints just inside the sliding window—the very window I had climbed through just two nights ago.

Silently, I reached for the bathrobe lying across the vanity chair. I slipped it on and headed for the outer doors, quietly grabbing my car keys off the kitchen counter. Outside, I was dismayed to discover how tender my bare feet were. Navigating the gravel driveway hurt like hell, but I was a woman on a mission.

I retrieved my gun from the trunk of the Mustang and quickly pressed the lid back down just hard enough for it to latch. There was still the little problem of having no ammunition, but if worse came to worst, I was pretty sure I could clobber the intruder over the head with my weapon and break his freakin' skull. My indignant rage at having my car, not to mention my personal security, violated, had returned with a vengeance.

I was so incensed by the idea that someone had the gall to think they could intimidate me that it didn't even occur to me to go get Sheriff Donaldson, right over there in Unit 3 across the parking lot. It just never entered my mind.

Reentering the living quarters, I quietly crept from the kitchen, around the hall corner, and past the bedroom entry. There was only one place in the apartment where I thought an adult person could successfully hide. I stood in the hall outside the linen closet, and pulled back the slide in my empty gun.

It's amazing how loud the metallic click of a cocking gun sounds in a quiet hallway. Then I accessed my most authoritative voice, the one I usually reserve for dealing with telemarketers, and barked, "Alright you measly scum, show yourself!"

Instantly, I heard a sniffle and a whimper from inside the closet, then, "Please don't shoot!" That was the second time tonight someone had implored me not to shoot. An odd sense of pride washed over me. I kind of *liked* being considered a ferocious, gun-toting, serious threat.

The door slowly opened and a man stepped out, his hands shaking in the air high above his head.

I lowered my weapon. "*Jimmy!* Oh, for crying out loud!"

"I'm so sorry, Syl," Jimmy began, his hands still raised.

I reached over and pulled his right hand down with my left one. He lowered the other one on his own. Still holding his hand, I led him to the living room, where we sat together on the couch. I set my Glock down on the coffee table.

"Jimmy, you could have gotten yourself shot."

"Maybe..." His voice faltered a little. "...but maybe not."

"Why do you say that?"

"I heard say you'd shot up all your ammo. So unless you had time to borrow some from Sheriff D," he motioned to the Glock, "that gun's empty."

I scowled at him. "Just how long were you in the closet? And where's your car?"

"I ditched the Pinto in the public parking lot over behind the Sandy Bottom," Jimmy began. "It's always full of tourist's cars downtown, and I didn't think anyone would think to look for it there."

"How'd you get home?"

"I took the bus. Nobody's going to look for a guy on the peninsula who owns a car to be riding the bus."

"Well, yeah, I guess you're right." I squinted at him. "So where have you been holed up since yesterday morning?"

He sighed. "I don't even have a passport, so I couldn't go too far."

I almost laughed. Almost. "But you're still not answering my question."

"Okay, well, let's see..." He pushed his glasses up with his middle finger and looked at the ceiling as if his recent itinerary might be written up there. "I left here and went down to the port in Unity. I was thinking maybe I could find a place to hide out in one of the boats with a cabin on it."

"Jimmy! That's breaking and entering!" The irony of my statement did not escape me; I was a fine one to talk about B & E.

"Most of those boats aren't even locked up," he rationalized, "and I wasn't going to hurt anything. I'll bet some of the owners would pay me to be their boat sitter."

"Boat sitter?"

"Yeah, you know, like a house sitter, only on a boat." He beamed. "There could be a whole, untapped market there."

"Jimmy—" I said sternly, "you'd be getting paid to keep other people from doing exactly what you were planning to do. How hypocritical is *that*?"

"Well, anyway, I didn't find anything I liked, so I just went and hung out at 'Can't Fathom It' until they closed at 2 a.m."

"That place is such a dive."

"Tell me about it." Jimmy got up and went to the refrigerator on the kitchen side of the room. He swung open the door. "Hey! Where'd all my soda go?"

I didn't have the heart to tell him how, in just two days, his living quarters had become the peninsula's version of Grand Central Station. "So what'd you do after the bar closed?" I prompted.

He got a can of warm soda from his stash under the sink and plopped back down beside me. He popped the top of the can and slurped the foam as it fizzed up. "I didn't want to put any of my friends at risk, so I just slept there in my car." "You mean 'slept it off' don't you?"

"I was scared, Syl." He hung his head. "I still am."

I lamely patted his hand, trying to comfort him. "Don't feel bad, Jimmy, there's definitely some bad guys out there, no doubt about it. Maybe just staying here and lying low is the best thing to do."

Priscilla jumped up in Jimmy's lap and head-butted his hand, shamelessly demanding he pet her. He absentmindedly scratched under her chin. She stretched out her neck and closed her eyes, lost in the bliss of the moment.

"See? Miss Priss thinks you ought to stay right here, too." For a few minutes we sat in companionable semi-silence, Priscilla's loud, contented purring the only sound in the room.

"So what did you do all day today?" I finally asked him.

"For a while I just drove around," said Jimmy. "I figured it was harder for them to find a moving target."

I smiled. Jimmy watches more cop shows than anyone I know. "And then?"

"And then Bim and Geri let me help out at the Sandy Bottom. I stayed in the back room all afternoon and even learned how to roast coffee beans."

"Ah, yes, a skill that's in hot demand these days."

Jimmy scowled. "You making fun of me, Syl? Please don't make fun of me. I'm at wit's end."

He looked it, too, but I hadn't heard his whole story yet. "So how'd you end up in your own linen closet?"

"When I got off the bus at the highway, I came around back and climbed through the window in case the front entrance was being watched," Jimmy replied. "I didn't want anyone keeping an eye on the place to know I was back."

"The closet, Jim..."

"Your car was gone, and I didn't know the pickup belonged to Sheriff Donaldson. I didn't think anyone was here, so I went in and used the bathroom."

"So it *was* you who left the toilet seat up!"

"Guilty," said Jimmy. "But it's *my* toilet seat, remember?"

I said nothing.

"So anyways, I headed for the kitchen to get a soda and I saw someone sleeping in my recliner. I couldn't tell who it was. I just saw the back of someone's head and a right arm dangling over the side of the chair, so right away I knew it was a guy, and I knew he was asleep."

"And so you hid in the linen closet?"

"I didn't know who it was, Syl, but I knew sooner or later you'd come back and I wanted to be able to listen in, in case it was a bad guy and you were in trouble."

"Why Jimmy, that's almost sweet of you," I said a bit sarcastically. "Then why didn't you come out when you heard it was the sheriff?"

"I was embarrassed," said Jimmy, and then he grinned a genuine grin. "And it wouldn't look so good if Sheriff Donaldson realized I could have gotten the drop on him."

"Smart thinking." Sheriff D's world-class ego was a well-documented fact around the county. "Ok, Jimmy, you're off the hook, but you're not getting your bed back tonight. I need a hot shower, then I'm definitely going to collapse into that lumpy bed of yours and sleep for as much of tomorrow morning as I can get away with."

"No problem," said Jimmy. "The couch will be just fine."

I stood up to leave the room.

"And Syl—"

"Yes?"

"Thanks for not making any jokes about me coming out of the closet."

"It was a supreme effort, believe me."

Unfortunately, I didn't get nearly as much sleep as I'd planned on. Images of big, black, shiny cars squealed around inside my eyelids every time I closed my eyes. Too early on Monday morning, I decided to get up, get showered, get dressed, and put on some much-needed coffee.

Oblivious to the world, and also to the noise I made as I rummaged around his kitchen, Jimmy slept on, with Priscilla sprawled out comfortably across his chest.

I took a couple sips of coffee, then spread a dish towel

out on the counter next to the sink. Every time I fire my gun, I make sure to clean it right away. I took it all apart, laying the pieces out in a simple pattern to help me remember how to put it back together again, just like I'd been taught.

In my firearms class, I'd also learned that Dawn dishwashing liquid works about as well as any pricey gun cleaner. Suits me. The ammo for this thing is expensive enough, especially if I run around emptying my clip at every opportunity.

Satisfied with my cleaning job, I rinsed off my Glock and dried it as best I could. Then I went into Jimmy's bathroom in search of his portable hairdryer. Gun maintenance 101: It is essential that the gun parts be completely dry before reassembling.

Sheriff Donaldson's tap on the outer door interrupted my thorough dryer job. I let him in, handed him an empty cup, and pointed to the coffeemaker. Then I returned to the task at hand. Another half a minute and I had all the individual parts dry as a bone. I flipped off the hairdryer and unplugged the cord.

Meanwhile, Sheriff D had poured himself some coffee and now sat at the kitchen table. "Good girl, Sylvia," he said. "As long as you keep your piece clean, it'll be there for you when you need it, just like a good friend."

He handed me a box of ammunition. "Of course, you need to keep it loaded." He took a swig from his cup. "MMmm, good coffee."

"Did somebody say coffee?" Jimmy raised his head from the couch.

The sound of Jimmy's voice gave the sheriff a start. "When did you get here?"

"A little after you went to your room," I quickly offered,

"and I didn't think his arrival was reason enough to wake you." I got out Jimmy's cooking oil to lubricate my gun. This was the most time I'd spent in a kitchen in months.

Jimmy set Priscilla on the floor and got to his feet. He stretched and yawned and then padded over to the kitchen side of the room. Likewise, Priscilla stretched and yawned and went to stand meaningfully next to her food bowl in the kitchen.

"Yeah, yeah," said Jimmy, pouring her a generous helping of generic kibbles. Then he opened the fridge and just stood there. "HHhhmm...." he said at last, "if I were going to be sticking around, I'd say it was time to do a little grocery shopping."

"What do you mean you're not sticking around?" I could feel my hackles rising, whatever hackles are. "You think I've got nothing better to do than babysit this poor excuse of a motel for you?"

"But Syl..." Jimmy gave me the puppy dog eyes.

"But Syl nothing!" I snapped. By this time I had my Glock almost back together and considered putting a bullet in the chamber so I could threaten him.

"But Syl," suggested Sheriff D, "we need to keep him out of sight. We don't know for sure if Robert Jones relayed the message to Harold Rodman about Jimmy being in Europe. Jimmy's life could still be in danger."

"Bob Jones was here?" Jimmy's face lit up. "That guy has some of the greatest traveling salesman jokes—"

"Jimmy," said the sheriff, "Robert Jones works for Rodman. It's likely that being a salesman is only his cover story."

If I'd looked 'crestfallen' up in the dictionary right then, I'm sure I'd have seen a picture of Jimmy.

"So this guy's one of Uncle Harry's henchmen?" he

asked, looking from the sheriff to me and back again.

"That's a definite possibility," said Sheriff Donaldson.

"I'm such a dufus," said Jimmy. "I thought the guy really liked visiting with me. He acted so friendly."

"The Clamshell is halfway up the North Beach Peninsula," continued the sheriff. "It's more likely this Jones fellow was just scoping the place out, getting to know a little about your routine here, maybe looking for a nondescript place to hole up if necessary."

Without another word, Jimmy sat down across from Sheriff Donaldson. I wrapped the cord around the blow-dryer handle, set it on the counter next to my sparkling clean and well-oiled Glock, and joined them at the table.

"So what am I going to do?" Jimmy asked.

Sheriff D and I exchanged a glance. I'm not at all sure what he was thinking, but I did know for sure what I thought.

"You're going to stay put," I began, "and I'm going to go home this morning, pick up my mail, water my plants, and gather a suitcase of clothes together."

"But you'll be back?"

"Yes, Jimmy, I'll be back. I promise I'm going to stick it out with you until we get this whole thing settled." I inhaled deeply and met the sheriff's eyes again. "Sheriff Donaldson will stay right here till I return."

"And in the meantime," said Sheriff D to Jimmy, "you and I can go over everything we know, or think we know, about this case. You might have remembered something since Friday night that will help us solve this investigation and get everything, and everybody, back to normal."

"Gee, thanks, you two." Jimmy's eyes gleamed with genuine gratitude and his tense shoulders relaxed. He mustered up enough bravado to say convincingly, "I love it when a plan comes together."

I drained the last of my coffee and set the cup in the sink. Outside the rain was really coming down. The sheriff walked up behind me and placed his hands on my shoulders. I stiffened slightly, but stood absolutely still.

Sheriff D leaned down and put his lips close to my right ear. "Don't be mad, Syl," he began in a soft voice. "But early this morning I took some photos of the bullet holes in your trunk. You can use them for your insurance claim and I needed them for the investigation."

His mustache tickled my ear and I wanted to laugh, jerk away, or both, but managed to hold my ground.

"And...?"

"And then I covered the holes with duct tape," he continued, "so the bare metal edges won't rust and the trunk won't leak until you can get it fixed."

I seriously did not know if I was going to punch him or kiss him. I'd been dreading dealing with this whole situation, and he'd bought me a little time. "Thank you, Carter," I said, and I meant it.

Then I artfully wiggled out from under his grasp without turning to face him, and gathered my purse, keys and cell phone. "And Carter," I said, "a cleaning service is coming to clean Unit 4. Please let them in for me."

Sheriff D agreed and I picked up my sparkling clean gun, the box of ammo, and headed for the door. I don't often wear a jacket, rain or not, and today was no different.

I quickly puddle-hopped to my Mustang and took a look at Sheriff D's handiwork. The three pieces of duct tape he put on my trunk lid had been cut to resemble little silver daisies. I returned my Glock to the trunk, and softly closed the lid with a lump in my throat and a very soft spot in my heart for Carter Donaldson.

Glancing toward the kitchen window, I waved and gave the sheriff a big 'thumbs up.' Then I slid behind the wheel and headed for home.

Home. The word had a very nice sound to it, and I longed to take a quick nap in the sanctity and security of my own personal space.

CHAPTER 9

I live on the 'back side' of the North Beach Peninsula; the tourists stay mainly along the oceanfront. Crossing from front to back roads never fails to give me a sense of peace and tranquility. This morning I especially appreciated the effect.

By the time I turned north on Sandspit Road, my outlook had improved considerably. I looked forward to getting home and spending a few minutes in quiet solitude without worrying about big, black, shiny cars or potential bad guys.

My home is my sanctuary, nestled deep in the quiet of the trees. Although Shallowater Bay is only a few hundred yards away to the east, I live on the west side of the road. My only view is of the grassy cleared area in front of my beach bungalow, which, as often as not, goes unmowed for months at a time.

With a deep sigh of relief, I turned off Sandspit and into my driveway. I rounded the final brush-covered curve, and— *what the?!*

I slammed hard on the brakes, feeling like one of the three bears returning home and discovering there'd been an intruder, or in this case, intruders, plural. And holy mother of Goldilocks, they were still here!

A least a dozen cars were parked helter-skelter all over the grassy area in front of the house and several small tents dotted the landscape.

The first thing that entered my head was that "Mr. X," my former husband, had returned with an assortment of his unemployed, ne'er-do-well hoodlum friends and was staking a claim on the property by utilizing 'squatter's rights.'

The second thing that came to mind was that, as far as I knew, my former spouse was still safely tucked away in an out-of-state jail. When the initial panic cleared, I recognized the gray Toyota Camry parked nearest the garage. *Felicity!*

I abandoned my car right where it was and stormed inside. There were high school students with sleeping bags everywhere. They sprawled on the couch, the loveseat, in the recliner, on air mattresses, and right in the middle of the carpeted floor in my living room. A few were still sleeping, but several were reading or typing on their laptops.

"Where's Ms. Michaels?"

The girl sitting in my recliner looked up from her Sudoku puzzle book and answered first. "She's out back on your covered deck. Your Iditarod chair is her command post."

I sighed pointedly. "You mean my *Adirondack* chair?"

"Yeah, whatever."

I hate it when my sarcasm goes totally wasted.

Working my way through the house, I stepped over nearly a dozen sleeping bags and almost as many bodies. Backpacks and tennis shoes made it even more difficult to navigate the room without tripping myself up. I couldn't wait to get my hands on Felix.

Felicity's eyebrows shot up a quarter mile when I walked out onto the deck. "Syl! Oh my goodness! What a surprise! I thought you were going to be gone all week!"

"Obviously." I gave her a disapproving look, pulled a picnic table bench over close to her, and sat down.

"Look, Felix, you're my best friend," I said between clenched teeth. "I gave you my house key for emergencies, not so you could host high school frat parties while I'm away."

She closed the lid of the PC on her lap. "Believe me, Syl, it *was* an emergency."

"Sure it was." I blew out of big breath of pent-up air. "You and Jimmy are full of them." Then I paused to consider Felicity's haggard look and uncombed hair. I took another breath and calmed myself. "Ok, Felix— I'm listening."

"When we gathered at the school yesterday afternoon to go on our Lewis and Clark camping reenactment, both parent chaperones were no-shows. I didn't want to disappoint my honor students, but I couldn't see myself managing to ride herd on this many kids without being in a contained area."

"How many are there?"

"Eighteen. Twenty signed up, but Lorrie is working at the Sea Biscuit this morning and will join us later, and I have no idea where the other one is."

"And you figured you could all just camp here this week, and no one would be the wiser?" I glowered at her, but not quite as harshly as I might have.

"I was going to tell you," Felicity replied, "at the very first opportunity. But the kids were already complaining about the rain, and I just needed to get the week with them started on a more positive note."

"Complaining about the rain, huh?" Despite how much I wanted Felicity to suffer a little more of my ire before I forgave her, I smiled. "What a bunch of wusses. They

119

wouldn't have lasted 10 minutes with the real Corps of Discovery."

"Tell me about it," Felicity said softly.

"Did you tell them it rained all but four days of the entire four months the Corps spent in our area?"

"Sometimes I forget you majored in history," Felix interjected wryly.

"So for the sake of realism," I blithely continued, "shouldn't the kids at least be outside?" I thoroughly enjoyed watching her squirm.

"I get it, I get it," said Felicity, holding up her hands in surrender. "This reenactment is a sham, a travesty of the truth, a miscarriage of history!" She peered at me, assessing the current level of my displeasure. "Will that appease you, or do I have to sacrifice one of the female students to regain your favor?"

"If that's as close as you're going to manage for an apology, I accept it."

We lapsed into a comfortable silence for a moment, then Felix spoke again. "So what brings you home so bright and early this soggy spring morning?"

"Jimmy has returned from the world's shortest European vacation ever," I began. Then I quickly brought her up to speed on what she'd missed since yesterday afternoon, again leaving out the parts about attempting to spy on Uncle Harry in his hotel, my very public appearance in the resort's bar aquarium, and the knight in a shining white pickup.

Felix sat listening with rapt attention. "Oh God, Syl, I'd wet my pants if someone shot at me!"

"Believe me, it was an experience I don't care to repeat!"

Felicity set her laptop on the picnic table, along with the blanket she'd had covering her legs. She stood up and gave me a hug. "Truce?"

"Only if there's still some coffee in my cupboard."

"We'll just have to go see about that." She turned and led the way to my kitchen.

Not only was there no coffee to be found, but two boys were standing by the stove, watching open pots of water boil on every burner. Felicity reached around them and turned all four dials from 'High' to 'Off.'"

"But Ms. Michaels!" protested the taller of the two boys. "We're in charge of the salt cairn, and it's too darn nasty outside to start a campfire."

"You're using my stove and sauce pans to boil saltwater down to salt?"

"Well, it's not really saltwater," explained the shorter boy. "We had to improvise."

Occasionally, I like to make homemade ice cream using an old-fashioned hand-cranked machine. The empty rock salt bag on the counter told me all I needed to know.

"Look," I began, "I'm pretty sure I'm not insured against my house burning down while recreating a salt cairn."

"It's okay," the taller boy spoke again. "We found a fire extinguisher in your broom closet. We'll make sure nothing gets out of control."

My level tone of voice belied the anger rekindling inside me. "I'm quite sure Ms. Michaels will understand if you don't complete your assigned task." I turned to Felicity. "Won't you, Ms. Michaels?"

She nodded and told the shorter student to go check on the progress of the hide tanning committee out in my woodshed.

"Ms. Avery," she said in her practiced teacher voice, "I'd like you to meet Kasey Walker. He's the young man Lorrie spoke so highly of at breakfast yesterday."

Kasey dipped his head slightly. "Nice to meet you, Ms. Avery. Sorry about the rock salt." He solemnly shook my hand.

Well, well. Kasey Walker, almost all grown up. Years ago, Kasey'd been one of 'my' kids, assigned to me for representation in court as his child advocate. Obviously, he didn't recognize me, or my name, and I never break confidentiality if it's not life determining, so I pretended we'd never met.

"Kasey's twin brother, Keith, is the other one who hasn't arrived yet," continued Felicity.

Ah yes, Keith. The calmer and usually more conscientious of the two young hellions.

"I tried to call him on your land line," Kasey said to me, "I hope that's alright. None of our cell phones work out here."

Cell coverage is a mixed bag on the peninsula. Some services work better on the north end, and some on the south, but none at all covered the area where my house is situated. I raised an eyebrow. "Keith has a local number, I assume?"

"Oh yes ma'am," Kasey hurriedly assured me. "There won't be any long distance charges on your phone because of me."

"We're becoming quite concerned." Felicity reached up to ruffle the tall young man's hair. "Kasey asked Keith to take a delivery for him from Captain Morgan up to the Spartina Point resort last Friday night, and nobody's heard from him since."

I didn't dare make eye contact with Felicity right then. I was pretty sure we were thinking the same thing, and I sure didn't like the way the vague trail of dots seemed to be connecting.

"Why didn't you make the delivery yourself?" I asked Kasey, hoping it sounded like I was just making conversation and not conducting an official inquiry.

Kasey looked at his feet and blushed. It was refreshing to think there were still some things that could make a 17-year-old boy uncomfortable around adults.

"I, uh, had a date with Lorrie that night," Kasey began, "and, uh, if I'd had to go all the way up to the casino with that fish, I wouldn't have made it back in time for the movie."

"Since Kasey and Lorrie both have full-time school and part time jobs," put in Felicity, "it isn't easy for them to juggle their schedules."

I thought it was kind of cute the way Felicity was trying to rescue Kasey from the hole he was digging himself.

"Kasey, what did you mean when you said you were supposed to take 'that fish' to the casino?" I asked, still trying to make my question sound like nothing more than polite chit-chat.

"Well, most of the time Captain Morgan just hires me to run some fresh fish filets up to the restaurant at Spartina Point. You know, usually salmon or rock cod." He paused, then continued more to himself than to us, "And I sure don't mind the extra money."

"What about last Friday?" I prodded him. "Were you transporting filets then, too?"

"No Ma'am. Every so often Captain Morgan gets a special order from the restaurant. Then he gets some crab or a live sturgeon from one of the commercial fishermen he knows and pays me to transport whatever it is to the casino in my pickup."

I frowned in thought. "And you deliver this crab or live

sturgeon to the restaurant kitchen?"

"The crab, yes, the sturgeon, no. All I have to do when I get there with a sturgeon is unload it directly into the moat."

"The moat?"

"Maybe the chefs just go get a fish from the moat whenever they need one," offered Felix. "Maybe when it says 'fresh sturgeon' on the menu, they really mean it."

"I don't think they ever eat these fish," said Kasey. "Captain Morgan told me the moat is stocked with sturgeon because there are laws against using alligators."

"*Alligators?!*" Felix and I said simultaneously.

Kasey chuckled. "Sturgeon are the closest legal thing to alligators we've got around here, and I guess the owner of the resort wants the moat to look authentic."

Felicity and I exchanged a puzzled glance. She shrugged. "It takes all kinds."

Kasey asked Felicity if he could go join the candle-making group in the garage and she informed him she had nixed the hot-wax candle making in favor of stitching together moccasins. Then she sent him on his way.

"So what do you think?" Felix asked me as soon as Kasey left the kitchen.

"I think it's *possible* Keith either went partying with friends this weekend and is still too hung over to make an appearance here, or that when he saw the weather outside this morning he decided to ditch the whole experience."

Felicity nodded. "I hope you're right."

I hoped I was right, too. I didn't want to think about any other scenario just now, especially scenarios that included men in big, black, shiny cars, whether they be Lincoln Town Cars or any other make and model.

I opened my refrigerator and stood staring at the

contents. Or maybe I should say the lack of contents. The only things left were just traces of the usual condiments: a lonely half jar of mayonnaise, one of mustard, and a squirt bottle of catsup. The relish jar was also there, but empty, and I was damn sure I hadn't put the jar back in the fridge with nothing in it.

"What happened to my yogurt and cheese and milk and— and everything else?"

Felicity gave me a palms-up 'search me' attempt at innocence.

"Didn't you guys think about bringing food along?"

"I had no idea teenagers had such voracious appetites," said Felix. "By midnight last night it looked like we'd be living out the week on marshmallows."

"Marshmallows? *Seriously?*" I raised my eyebrows. "And just how many bags of marshmallows did Lewis and Clark bring along on their journey in 1805?"

"Point taken," said Felicity, "but the kids still have to eat."

"Eat what?"

At least she had the decency to look chagrinned before responding. "I think we can survive on peanut butter and jelly for lunch, and Walter will be bringing us a half dozen pizzas after school gets out."

"You asked Walter to bring you pizza?" I echoed unnecessarily.

"I'm sure the kids would have called in an order last night, but there's that problem with cell phone coverage, you know."

"And, once again, may I remind you that Lewis and Clark did not have pizza delivered?"

Felix expelled a deep breath. "We ran out of pemmican and elk jerky right off. And it's enough of a trial for them to be without access to Facebook. At this point Syl, I just want Friday to arrive without a mutiny."

I took pity on her and reluctantly agreed to let them have the run of the house until the end of the week, on the condition they replaced anything that got broken and thoroughly policed the grounds before they left.

"I don't want to find the slightest trace of them ever having been here by Saturday morning."

"Agreed!" said Felicity.

I walked down the hall to my bedroom with Felix trotting along at my heels. My bed was rumpled and unmade. Turning around, I pursed my lips and glared at her. "And just who's been sleeping in my bed?"

"Come on, Syl, you have to have more faith in me." She put her hands on her hips. "This room is totally off-limits to the students. I'm the only one who is allowed in here for any reason. Violators of that rule will be sent home immediately."

"You pinky swear?"

Felix grinned. "I pinky swear." We hooked little fingers in a childhood pledge.

I got out a large suitcase. I threw in another sweat suit, several changes of underwear, and a decent dress with pantyhose and heels. I didn't know what all to anticipate this week, but I wanted to be prepared for anything.

I'd already picked up my makeup Saturday afternoon, but Jimmy's industrial strength dandruff shampoo was making my hair stand out in all directions, so I stuck in some extra shampoo and a few other toiletries.

In no time at all, I zipped up the suitcase and wheeled it toward the front door. Ok," I said to Felicity, "I think that'll do me."

My living room was still strewn with sleeping bags,

pillows, iPods and iPads. The kids, however, all seemed to be attending to their various Corps of Discovery tasks in either the garage or the woodshed. Maybe they were learning a few things about roughing it in the wilderness after all.

I gave Felicity another hug at the door and wished her well. I was almost to my car, still parked halfway up the driveway, when she called out to me.

"Wait!" she hollered. "You're almost out of toilet paper!"

"But Ms. Michaels," I called out, getting into my newly-decaled flower-powered Mustang, "I'm pretty sure Lewis and Clark didn't *HAVE* toilet paper!"

I was still chuckling about Felicity's plight when I arrived back at the Clamshell, but the first thing I did when I entered the motel office was pick up the telephone.

"Would you please tell Mr. Winston that Ms. Michaels would appreciate him bringing a generous supply of TP to the reenactment along with the pizza this afternoon?" I asked the high school secretary. She laughed and assured me she would give him the message personally. I guess I'm not as heartless as I lead people to believe.

In the living quarters I discovered Jimmy and Sheriff Donaldson at the kitchen table playing cards. Jimmy's hair was bleached white-blonde.

"Who's winning?" I asked nonchalantly.

"The sheriff's up about three bucks," said the blonde Boy George Jimmy.

"Three fifty-five," replied Sheriff D.

I grinned. "Jimmy, Jimmy, Jimmy, when are you going to learn?"

He folded the cards in his hand and threw them on the table. "I'm out."

"Three sixty," said the sheriff with a smile. He gathered up all the cards and put the deck back into its box.

"So," I said, pulling up a chair to join them at the table, "what's with the hair?" I was speaking to Sheriff Donaldson, but inclining my head toward Jimmy.

"Don't you dare talk about me like I'm not here!" said an indignant Jimmy. He shoved his glasses up with his middle finger and glared at me. "I decided to change my appearance so those creeps in the big, black, shiny cars can't find me."

"Okay, sure, I get it. Good idea, Jimmy. No one will ever notice an albino man walking around Tinkerstown. You'll blend right in."

Sheriff Donaldson stood up. "It' about time I changed into my uniform and got back out on the streets. I don't think anyone's going to return to the scene of the alleged crime, whatever it is, so I won't be staying out here tonight." He smirked. "I guess you two will just have to look out for each other."

Swell.

"Feel free to call me on my cell if anything comes up." Sheriff D handed me his business card with his personal number written on the back of it. "Or, if you just want to see me." Then he winked!

Good grief and gravy, the old coot actually winked at me! What was I going to have to do to get the point across that I was definitely not interested?

"Meanwhile," he continued more solemnly, "I'm going to get on down to the port in Unity and see what connections, business or otherwise, I can find between Harry Rodman and Rich Morgan."

"*OH!*" I put my hand over my mouth. I'd been so distracted by Jimmy's new hair color I'd forgotten to tell the sheriff about Kasey's fish delivery service.

Sheriff D appeared to listen attentively.

"Very interesting," he said when I finally finished. "So Felicity just used her key to your place and moved in a whole class of high school students without bothering to ask your permission? Do you want to press charges?"

"For crying out loud, Carter!" I scowled at him. "Of course not! How could you think such a thing? You missed the whole point of what I was trying to tell you!"

Sheriff Donaldson had been standing by the door the entire time I'd been talking. Now he came back and sat down at the table in the chair he'd recently vacated. He leaned forward and spoke softly. "Sylvia," he said, "believe it or not, I heard you. Since I arrived here Saturday morning in response to Jimmy's 911 call, I've heard every single word you've said, and I've also heard every single word you haven't said."

The sheriff sat still and looked me squarely in the eye. The room became eerily quiet. Even Jimmy kept his mouth closed. I couldn't decide if it would be better to look away or wait to see who blinked first. I was afraid it would be me.

Priscilla decided at that moment to jump onto Sheriff Donaldson's lap. He gently lifted her up and set her down on the floor, then looked back to me. "So tell me, Sylvia Lee Avery, just what did you and your friend Mercedes hope to accomplish with your little visit to the casino hotel last night?"

For a moment I considered telling him I had no idea what he was talking about, but on second thought that seemed like a pretty dumb idea, and I'd already had enough dumb ideas in the past couple days to last me a while.

"We didn't find out anything of interest," I began, "so I just didn't bother to mention we'd gone into the resort." I didn't ask how he knew what we'd done; I refused to give him the satisfaction.

"And if you'll recall," I continued, my voice rising as I suddenly became more than a little irritated with him, "I was nearly run off the road and then shot at on my way home. I had other things on my mind than my hotel reconnaissance with Mercedes by the time I arrived."

"I totally understand," said Sheriff Donaldson, with just a smidgen of arrogance. "And I assume that's why you also failed to tell me that Rich Morgan had been in the next vehicle on the scene?"

"What's that got to do with anything?" I asked belligerently. "Rich just happened by and—"

"He just happened by?" interrupted Sheriff D, shaking his head in disbelief. "Do you honestly believe he just happened by, Sylvia?" He harrumphed. "That's one hell of a coincidence, don't you think?"

CHAPTER 10

Confused, I tried to figure out what Sheriff Donaldson was getting at. I looked at Jimmy, but apparently he was also clueless.

The sheriff continued, "And what lame excuse did Captain Morgan give for not coming inside with you when you got back here?"

"He said he had to get up early in the morning to take a charter group out, and..." I paused. My face grew hot as I realized exactly what the sheriff was going to think of the rest of my statement. "...and I told him you were still staying here at the motel."

"Sylvia." Sheriff Donaldson pursed his lips and shook his head. "When are you going to learn?" He sighed, leaned back in his chair and stared at the ceiling. "You know, I almost hate to be the one to tell you this—"

"Oh for Chrissake, Carter, just spit it out!"

"Okay, fine," he said harshly, bringing his chair back down and scowling at me. "I'll do just that. According to the Washington Department of Fish and Wildlife, the spring Chinook salmon fishery is currently closed, and won't reopen for another two weeks."

The silence hung in the air like an all-day coastal fog as the meaning behind his statement sunk in.

"Holy shit," said Jimmy under his breath.

Holy shit indeed.

The three of us still sat without moving, each

contemplating all the various possible ramifications of Sheriff Donaldson's pronouncement, when the motel phone rang.

"Aaaaahh!" Jimmy shrieked. He put his hands over his head in a defensive manner and slid off his chair, cowering under the table.

"Some protection you'll be later tonight," I muttered. I got up to go answer the telephone myself, actually grateful for the interruption.

"Clamshell Motel, how may we help you?" I said in my most pleasant professional voice. I hoped using the word "we" would persuade any potential bad guys that I was not a poor, defenseless, woman, out here running the motel all by myself.

"Sylvia!" said Freddy enthusiastically. "I've been thinking about you all night!"

"Uh-huh," I replied, turning my back to the gentlemen eavesdroppers at the kitchen table.

"Have you missed me, too?" Freddy went on.

There was no safe way for me to answer his question directly. "May I help you?" I said noncommittally.

"Oh, I get it," said Freddy, "you're not alone."

"That's right."

"So you did miss me," he said coyly, "but you can't say it in front of anyone."

Right this minute, I couldn't honestly say how I felt about him. He was, after all, the nephew of the primary person of interest. And now, I had to admit, Freddy was also the son of someone who might be connected to the alleged crime committed in Unit 4.

Freddy took my silence as an affirmative reply. "That's great, Syl, cause I was calling to ask you if you'd like to join me for a little undercover recon up at Spartina Point this afternoon."

I choked, but made it sound like a tickle in my throat.

"There's a 50th wedding anniversary party being held in the main convention hall," Freddy went on. "I think they're probably holding it on a Monday to get a good deal on the room, or maybe today really is their anniversary date. At any rate, I'm sure Uncle Harry will be in attendance. He likes to put in an appearance at all those special events."

As far as I knew, Freddy was clueless about my trip to the casino with Mercedes last night. *Or was he?* Could Freddy be in on whatever his uncle, and possibly his father, were up to? It sure made sense, but I didn't want to think such scary thoughts, or the huge implications behind them.

Keep your friends close, and your enemies closer, I reminded myself. I didn't know yet exactly which category Freddy fell into, but I thought it was probably a good idea to keep an eye on him.

"What time will you be picking me up?" I said sweetly, glad I'd thought to throw a simple spring dress and matching shoes into my suitcase.

"Who was that?" asked Sheriff Donaldson as soon as I hung up.

"I don't believe it's any of your business, Sheriff, but it just so happens I have a date this afternoon."

"A date?" asked Jimmy, who'd come out from under the table and was now sitting with Priscilla in his lap. "Who knows you're here?"

His question settled around us like a second, though a little less ominous, dark cloud above the dinette set.

Sheriff D abruptly stood and headed once again for the door. "Give Deputy Morgan my regards," he spit out. "And Sylvia—" His expression changed dramatically and he looked at me with genuine concern. "Please, Syl, watch that mouth of yours. I hate to say it, but we don't know for certain yet which side Freddy's on."

I was pretty sure the sheriff would have a conniption if I told him where Freddy and I were headed, so I decided to keep yet another piece of information to myself.

By the time Freddy arrived at 2, I'd had enough time to pull myself together and looked decidedly presentable, if I do say so myself. The professional cleaners had finished working their magic in Unit 4, gathered up their gear and left already, and I was feeling pretty poised and confident, considering I'd been shot at just last night.

Jimmy was having no part of staying there alone with the motel open for business, so he'd added the 'NO' before Vacancy, and pulled the shades down in both the office and living quarters. He put a sign on the door that read, "Closed Due to Family Illness." It was the same sign he'd used when his dearly departed mother had been undergoing chemo treatments a couple years ago.

I met Freddy in the parking lot. He wolf whistled when he saw me and grinned like a Cheshire cat.

"This is not a date," I said adamantly, but took note of how good the guy cleaned up in gray slacks and open-collared shirt. "This is just the two of us checking up on Uncle Harry in the casino convention hall today."

"Uncle Harry," said Freddy, still grinning. "See? Already you're speaking of him as if you were a member of our family."

"You're incorrigible."

"Incorrigible, but cute."

Freddy went around to the passenger side of his red Mazda RX-8. It appeared to be a fairly new car, but, as previously pointed out, I'm not one to know much about car makes and models. If a car gets you where you want to go, that's good enough for me. Reliable transportation is all that matters. Except, of course, in the case of my beloved Mustang.

As we drove slowly down the one-lane driveway, Jimmy pulled the living room curtain back and gave me a big 'thumbs up.' I turned my head so Freddy couldn't see my face and stuck my tongue out at Jimmy.

"So..." I said to Freddy after we'd pulled out onto the highway, "whose 50th anniversary party are we going to?"

"I don't, uh, actually know them," Freddy admitted.

"HHhhmm..." Words failed me.

"I saw the party posted on Facebook," said Freddy, "and it looked to me like it was open to the public."

"I see..."

"Ah, come on, Syl, cut me some slack." He set the cruise control on 50 and shot me a glance. "It's perfect timing. We get to keep an eye on Uncle Harry and I get the additional bonus of getting to keep my eyes on you."

"Good grief and gravy, I can't believe I agreed to this," I said. "We're going to stick out like two sore thumbs."

"Nah," said Freddy, totally unconcerned, "everyone there will just assume we were invited by someone else. Don't worry, we're going to blend right in." Freddy grinned at me, his dimples making him all the more charming.

"Well, okay, if you say so. I guess I can't just sit in the car in the parking lot while you go inside, can I?"

"If you really want to do that," he said amicably, "I'll be sure to crack the window a couple inches for you."

Once again, despite Sheriff Donaldson's warning, I decided to tell Freddy about my adventure with Mercedes at the hotel the previous evening. I chose my words carefully, gauging his reaction to what I was saying.

I consider myself a pretty good judge of character.

Watching his face for subtle clues, I felt nothing but trust. Okay, so maybe I also felt the tiniest bit of lust as well, but I doubted it would cloud my semi-objective assessment of where his loyalties lay.

"That *is* really odd, Sylvia," said Freddy, once I'd paused to take a breath.

"Which part?"

Freddy kept his eyes on the road, but his brow furrowed deeply. "The part you heard about "put on your trunks" and "going swimming.""

"That's the reason Mercedes convinced me to get into the swimming pool." I sighed, remembering my humiliation. "But that turned out to be dead end, too."

Freddy pulled into the resort's main parking lot and drove straight up to the bridge crossing the moat to the main entrance. He got out and handed his keys to the valet.

"Nice to see you again, Mr. Morgan," said the tuxedo-wearing high school student, handing Freddy a claim stub and reaching into the Mazda to place the other half on the dashboard.

I didn't wait for Freddy to come around and open my door. I met him halfway around the back of the car. He looked disappointed. "This is not a date," I hissed. "Do you hear me?"

Nevertheless, he took my elbow and guided me to the mock drawbridge. Halfway across he paused to dig into his pocket for a couple coins to toss into the moat.

"Sturgeon are very interesting fish," he said. "A throw-back to prehistoric times, really. Did you know they can live for hours out of water and still survive if they aren't left out in the sun? They just swim away, like nothing happened."

"Fascinating," I said sarcastically.

Freddy missed the sarcasm and eagerly continued,

"They're bottom feeders, you know, the lowest guys on the totem pole. They'll eat whatever garbage they can find out in the Columbia River."

I attributed Freddy's lengthy sturgeon dissertation on the fact that he might be having second thoughts about us crashing this anniversary party. I reached out and took his hand, a calculated gesture on my part, and led him through the resort doors and straight to the gift shop just inside.

"We can't arrive at the party empty-handed," I explained. "It's not good manners, even if we weren't on the expected guest list."

Freddy bent his arm and lifted his hand, with my hand still grasping his, in front of us. "I am most certainly not arriving empty-handed," he joked.

I did it again; I rolled my eyes. But interestingly enough, I did not pull my hand away.

"There's been a real run on anniversary cards today," said the female high school student running the gift shop cash register.

I peered at her, then bluntly asked, "Shouldn't you still be in school?"

"I'm a senior," she replied, "and I've got early release so I can work the 2 to 10 shift here three days a week."

When she handed me my change, I tucked it into my small clutch bag and asked, "May I borrow your pen?"

I looked at Freddy. "I don't suppose your remember who the party's for."

He grinned again. Damn those dimples! "I don't suppose I do."

'To the Happy Couple' I scrawled across the envelope. Inside I signed, it 'Best Wishes Always, Fredrick and Sylvia.'

"Hey now," said Freddy, reading over my shoulder, "I really like the looks of that. Don't you think our names go well together?"

I softly punched him in the arm without saying anything. Then I returned the pen to the cashier, tucked the card inside the envelope, and we started through the maze of slot machines to the hallway leading to the convention hall.

In the hall we passed yet another high school student, less-than-energetically pushing the carpet sweeper back and forth, back and forth, in an absentminded manner. It was pretty obvious he got paid by the hour.

"What's the matter?" asked Freddy, after we'd walked by the young man. "You look like you've just lost your best friend."

"Oh, I was thinking about something Felicity told me. About how too many of her high school students were making so much money working here at the resort that it's hard to convince them to finish their education."

"HHhhmm..." said Freddy. "I can see how that could happen, all right. The kids get a taste of the almighty paycheck and don't consider their long-term futures."

I was glad Freddy and I were in agreement on that point. It was beginning to feel like we had a lot of important things in common. But I wasn't about to forget our 15 years, give or take, age difference. Nothing was going to get that issue into agreement, and I wondered if it would end up being the ultimate deal-breaker.

We entered the convention room, again hand in hand. I'm not sure how that happened, exactly, but it just felt right.

"See? What did I tell you?" Freddy was pleased as punch with himself. "We blend right in; nobody's giving us a second look."

The room was packed with anniversary well-wishers. I

couldn't help but wonder how many of them had seen the Facebook announcement and had shown up anticipating only the promise of free food.

And that 'free food' was something to behold. This was not your ordinary shoe-leather roast beef buffet. Not by a long shot.

Right in the middle of the room, with easy access on both sides, was a cluster of at least a dozen buffet tables, creating a centerpiece of one of the most extravagant displays of food opulence I'd ever seen. From pickled asparagus to baby shrimp, the platters threatened to overflow the tables, yet each was artfully displayed, and looking almost too good to eat. Almost.

My mouth watered and my stomach rumbled. As if in a hypnotic trance, I was drawn toward the three-tiered chocolate fountain at the far end of the room. I would have been totally distracted from our mission right then and there, had not Freddy's firm grip on my hand pulled me back into the moment.

Gently, he guided me to the 'reception line' along the right-hand wall. I dropped the card, the ink probably still wet, into the bulging basket at the front of the line and proceeded to shake hands with a very nice-looking elderly couple, who politely smiled and nodded and thanked me for coming.

After wishing the anniversary couple our best, Freddy and I worked our way around the outer edges of room, steering clear of the buffet, for now, attempting to pinpoint the whereabouts of Uncle Harry.

Across from the receiving line, on the other side of the buffet, was a small dance floor. Mercedes sat behind her portable keyboard, tinkling the ivories, as she called it. I might have known she'd be here, playing all the old standards for this event. That gal has an extensive musical repertoire going back several decades.

Mercedes' face lit up in a genuine smile, as opposed to her 'I'm just here to entertain' smile, when she saw us. Immediately, she began playing 'If I Knew You Were Coming, I'd Have Baked a Cake' and gave me a big 'thumbs up.' No one seemed to notice she hadn't quite finished the previous song.

She was decked out head to toe in gold sequins. I'm guessing that's her way of acknowledging the 50-year golden anniversary. I briefly wondered if Merc had a similar outfit for every special occasion. I already knew about her black tie, her red, white and blue patriotic ensemble, her Hawaiian luau shimmering green get-up, and her lavender 'breaking and entering' attire.

Silently I mouthed 'it's *not* a date,' but she shook her head and shrugged like she didn't understand me. Then I mouthed 'where's Uncle Harry?' and this time she picked right up on what I was after. I'd call that selective lip-reading.

Momentarily between numbers, Mercedes lifted her hand and waved twice directly at us. Then she held up the two-fingered peace sign.

"Bye-bye and peace be with you?" asked Freddy.

I laughed and Mercedes began playing 'I've Got Friends in Low Places.' She might not ever be as rich or famous as Garth Brooks, but she was one heckuva good undercover partner.

"Uncle Harry's upstairs," I told Freddy. "Room 552, if you want to go visiting."

He shook his head. "You girls and your secret codes. A guy doesn't stand a chance." I was only half-serious about visiting Uncle Harry in his penthouse, but Freddy steered me out of the main room, down the hall, and toward the elevator. He reached out to press the call button, and we simultaneously noticed the elevator starting its way down— from the fifth floor.

"Brace yourself," I said as it made its decent. "The odds are pretty good your uncle's about to make his appearance."

Freddy gnawed on his lower lip.

"You nervous?"

"Well, since I became a deputy, we haven't really seen each other. It's not like I'm still the kid he bounced on his knee, you know."

The bell dinged, signaling the elevator's arrival, before I could reply. As expected, when the doors slid open, out stepped Uncle Harry, a fit 60-something, rather tall gentleman, in what I judged to be a very expensive dark blue suit and striped silk tie. His shoes were polished to a high sheen and it didn't take a jeweler to appreciate his diamond-studded cufflinks.

Clinging to him was his current gal-pal, an over-teased platinum blonde less than half his age wearing an afternoon-inappropriate low-cut emerald green dress. She also wore considerably more makeup than even late-night occasions called for, unless, of course, she was dressed for work and her work demanded she stand under a florescent streetlight for hours at a time.

"Why if it isn't Frederick, my dear nephew!" Harold Rodman the Third clasped Freddy on the shoulder, dislodged his arm from the Miss-of-the-Moment, and rapidly pumped Freddy's hand up and down in a handshake that seemed to go on several beats too long.

"Hello Uncle Harry," said Freddy. "Long time no see."

"Way too long, son, way too long." Uncle Harry seemed genuinely glad to see him, his smile spreading from ear to ear. And then his eyes landed on me.

And let me just say this about that: the elevator wasn't the only thing going up and down today. His eyes gave me the once, and then the twice over, and I felt a little like I imagine a prime piece of meat feels hanging in the butcher's window.

"And who's this gorgeous creature with you?" he asked Freddy, finally completing his lengthy handshake and now quickly taking my hand and pulling it to his lips.

"Harold Rodman, I'd like to present my girlfriend, Sylvia Avery."

Only with extreme help from my personal credo, 'Real CPS workers don't flinch,' was I able to A) keep from yanking my hand back from Uncle Harry's filthy mouth, and B) stop from using that very hand to slap the implied familiarity right off Freddy's smiling face.

The bimbo with Uncle Harry cleared her throat.

"Oh yes," said Uncle Harry. "Yes, of course. I'd also like to present my friend..."

"Deena," the woman supplied after a short, but extremely uncomfortable pause. "Deena Madison."

Freddy inclined his head in her direction. "Nice to meet you, Miss Madison." I noted with pleasure that he did not extend his hand. If he had, I'd have had him use one of the sanitizers in the main casino before I'd touch him again.

"Please! Call me Deena," she gushed at Freddy. Then she purposefully took Uncle Harry's arm again, batting her false eyelashes as she looked up at him. "Shall we go now, darling?"

I didn't know if I should be hurt or relieved that she'd completely ignored me. I decided to go with relieved.

"Frederick! You and Sylvia must join us!" said Uncle Harry. "I insist on it!"

I'd wanted to get close, but definitely not this close, to our primary person of interest. Now I'd just become an unwilling member of a very unlikely foursome. As we turned and headed back to the main reception hall, I wondered what tune Mercedes would be inspired to play next. Probably something like the title song from the once-popular TV show 'Cops.'

I sported a genuine grin as we reentered the hall, silently singing the show's theme song in my head: 'Bad boys, bad boys, whatcha gonna do? Whatcha gonna do when they come for you?'

At least now we were back in the room with that amazing buffet table. I decided to go with the flow and make the best of things. Perhaps I could even learn a little something to share with the sheriff later on.

The anniversary couple had finally abandoned their post at the door and a few uninhibited elderly dancers were hugging and swaying to a slow waltz. Or maybe they were just trying to hold each other up after too many flutes of afternoon champagne—it was hard to tell.

"Frederick," said Uncle Harry, "let's park the ladies here by the chocolate fountain while we men go get us all some champagne."

The good news was that I could finally get my hands on some of that delicious dark liquid heaven. The bad news was that I'd have to make small talk with the Tramp of the Month while I did so.

I considered excusing myself to use the restroom, but I was afraid she'd feel compelled to go with me. Some women were like that, always feeling the urge to pee in twos. So I led with a semi-sincere compliment instead. "My, what great shoes you're wearing! Are they Italian?"

Deena nodded excitedly. "Harry bought them for me.

Genuine Louis Viutton Positano Pumps—monogramed satin." She beamed happily.

"Wow. I'll bet that set him back a pretty penny."

Deena lowered her voice. "They were on sale. Just 900."

"Nine hundred dollars for *shoes*?" I was pretty sure the price of all my footwear combined didn't add up to that much money.

"No, of course not," said Deena, shaking her head. "Nine hundred euros. We ordered them online, so there was an international shipping charge. Harry says next time we'll just go get them ourselves." She giggled.

Granted, math is not my strongest suit, and who knows what the exchange rate is today, but I attempted a quick calculation and whistled under my breath. "Deena—That comes to somewhere over a thousand American dollars."

Deena laughed. "Well, then it's a good thing *I* wasn't paying for them. I don't have a clue when it comes to figuring out metric conversions."

I bit my tongue and didn't say a word.

CHAPTER 11

Mercedes, "the invisible-woman-who-sees-all-from-behind-her-keyboard,' caught sight of Freddy and Uncle Harry while they stood in line for our champagne. She concluded the slow waltz she was playing and jumped right in with a lively instrumental number. I recognized it as 'The Entertainer' and tried to hide a chuckle. Leave it to Merc to make an editorial comment on the situation by playing the movie theme song from 'The Sting.'

Deena didn't seem to be one for initiating much conversation, and an awkward silence fell between us. I decided to use this time to see if she was the stereotypic bimbo blonde, or if she knew anything useful.

"How long have you known Mr. Rodman?" I asked her.

"Oh, Harry says it's the quality, not the quantity, of our time together that counts," she replied.

Her answer sounded rehearsed. I tried another tack. "So how did you two meet?"

"Well, I was dating one of the men who works for him, and one day Harry took me aside and asked me what I saw in my future. He told me to dream big."

HHhhmm... So the boss saw something he wanted and made a play for it. Well, I could see how a guy who could buy Louis Viutton shoes for his lady friend might be slightly more attractive than one of his common henchmen.

"And what did you tell him you dreamed about? I plucked a strawberry off the buffet table, swirled it through the chocolate, and slowly nibbled on it. If I wasn't careful, I might start to enjoy eating fruit.

"Someday I want to be a famous author." Deena sighed and smiled blissfully. "I want to be rich and famous, and Harry says he's going to make it all happen."

"Wow! Deena Madison listed on the New York Times bestseller list." I hoped I could pass off my smirk as a smile. "Mother Madison will be so proud."

"Oh," she confided, "Deena Madison isn't my real name. I just thought it sounded like a name you'd see on the cover of a book."

I suspected those weren't her real boobs, either, but I sure as hell wasn't about to pursue that line of questioning.

"What made you decide to take the name of our fourth president?"

"President?" Deena tried to furrow her brow but the Botox prevented it. "I didn't know we had a president named Deena!"

This was becoming downright painful, but since I *was* a history major, and I love a challenge, I attempted to edify her. "The fourth President of the United States was James Madison."

"Oh! Silly me!" Deena giggled again and raised her shoulders in a shrug not unlike a posture Marilyn Monroe might have taken.

"So you also didn't know his likeness was on the five thousand dollar bill?" I knew I was rubbing it in, but I couldn't help myself.

"Well honestly, no, I didn't," replied Deena. Then she hurried on to say, "but I'm sure Harry must have a wallet full of them."

I didn't have the heart to tell her the five thousand dollar bill had been discontinued in the 1930s. I didn't want to hear her say that even her grandmother hadn't been born by then.

I opted for a more direct approach. "So how *did* you decide on Madison?"

"Oh, I just saw it on a map somewhere."

No way was I going to tell her where she'd seen it. I couldn't imagine playing the straight guy for another one of her Abbott and Costello routines.

Instead, I forged ahead with another socially acceptable follow-up, and highly predictable, question. "So what have you written?"

"Well, nothing yet, but I've been reading about writing and making lots of notes while Harry's otherwise occupied. It's best I stay out of the way while he makes calls and takes meetings and does all his business things."

I wondered what those 'business things' entailed, but if Uncle Harry was as astute as I assumed he was, I didn't think Deena had been privy to any specific details concerning his operation. So instead, I pressed the idea of a wannabe writer who wasn't writing. "Then what is it you're working on?"

Deena, standing there looking like a two-dollar hooker on a Saturday night, could have knocked me over with a feather when she replied, "It's very Biblical."

Where *were* the men with that champagne?! I needed something to wash all this down in the worst way. Trying to wrap my mind around Deena and Biblical in the same thought called for at least another chocolate-dipped piece of fruit.

Deena, not her real name, didn't look a thing like Mother Teresa, and I had to bite my lip to keep from laughing as I suddenly pictured her signing books in a modest black and white nun's habit.

"Tell me more," I prompted.

"Oh, my story has its roots down very deep in the scriptures." She smiled. "But I can't tell you any more than that, or I'll have to kill you." She giggled again. "That's what Harry always says."

I decided it was time to end this line of questioning. "Well, you let me know when the book comes out, won't you?"

"Oh, you'll see it in the front window of all the bookstores," she gushed. "Harry's going to make sure of that. As soon as I write something, he promised he'll use all his connections to get it published and promoted right off." Deena Madison, not her real name, sighed and concluded, "Isn't he just the sweetest man?"

I popped a whole chocolate-covered cherry into my mouth to keep me from giving my honest opinion of Uncle Harry. Unfortunately, I couldn't keep myself from snorting at the same time, and the cherry suddenly stuck tight in my windpipe.

I frantically waved my arms around and pointed to my mouth, trying to convey to Deena the fact that I couldn't breathe. I'm surprised my face turning blue and my eyes bugging out didn't help her realize I was in distress and needed help.

"I'm sorry," she said, shaking her head. I'm sure she tried to furrow her brow again, but not a wrinkle appeared. "I'm not very good at charades."

In a room full of people, no one came to my aid. Maybe they just didn't want to get involved, or maybe they were so wrapped up in their own little worlds that they really didn't notice a blue-faced woman flailing her arms about.

Meanwhile, the edges of *my* world were beginning to turn dark. Then Uncle Harry magically appeared next to me. He quickly handed the two champagne flutes he was carrying to Deena, and wrapped his arms around me from behind.

Uncle Harry squeezed once and nothing happened. Nothing happened if you don't count Deena erupting into a raging fit of very unbiblical jealousy.

"You pig!" She screamed, and threw a glass of champagne in his face, which was also in my face, as he was looking over my left shoulder. "Hitting on Sylvia right in front of me! How dare you!"

Uncle Harry gave me another solid jerk, up and in, just like they show you in first aid class. The cherry abruptly dislodged and flew out of my mouth, smacking Deena squarely on her right breast.

"My dress!" she screamed, and threw the other glass of bubbly. She further saturated Harry, but she missed me this time, as I was bent over double, still gasping for air.

Freddy, meanwhile, had made his way through the crowd and now tried to get between a raging Deena and any further physical assault to either me or Uncle Harry. But Freddy was no match for a woman who considered herself scorned.

"You two-timing lout," she bellowed, and lunged at Harry just as I was straightening back up.

I didn't have time to be impressed by her use of the word "lout." The three of us slammed into the nearest buffet table as if we'd been hit by the middle offensive line of the former Los Angeles Rams. The table hit the floor with a resounding 'bang!" and the chocolate fountain fell across our tangled heap of bodies on the floor.

Merc utilized the full range of her electronic keyboard, stopping in the middle of a tune to break into the Space Cowboy's "Down, down, down, down, down. Everybody's falling down, down, down, down, down."

Deena was on top, Harry on the bottom, and I was sandwiched in between, with warm, fluid chocolate running everywhere. Freddy, in his haste to come to my aid, must have forgotten he was still holding a flute of champagne in each hand. He took a step forward, like he was going to help us up, slipped in the dessert fondue, lost his footing, and sprawled across Deena.

I thought I saw stars, but it turned out it was just the flashing of a dozen digital cameras going off. Chocolate ran into my eyes, but not before I recognized the woman who thinks of herself as the society page reporter asking our names from onlookers. We don't actually have a society page in our little weekly rag, so I was pretty sure we were going to be front page news.

Sheriff Donaldson was going to love this.

Slowly, the four of us managed to disengage ourselves. I rose unsteadily to my feet, checking to see if all my limbs still functioned correctly. None of us seemed any worse for wear, except for the fact that at least three of us had bathed in chocolate. Freddy, who'd landed on Deena's backside, arose without too much of the sticky sweetness on him.

Deena took a tentative step, and one Louis Viutton shoe, her foot still inside, streaked sideways. She landed on the floor a second time, in a rather undignified heap, at Uncle Harry's feet. He bent to help her back up, slipped in the chocolate goo, and he, too, lost his footing, and fell smack on top of her.

I heard Mercedes softly singing Paul Simon's 'Slip Sliding Away' and I somehow managed to refrain from giving her the finger. Instead, I started to giggle. Watching carefully where I stepped, I eased myself over to a less-dangerous patch of floor.

"Are you still thirsty?" Freddy handed me one of the glasses of champagne.

"I thought you'd never ask." Amazingly, both flutes still contained a small amount of liquid in them. He raised his own glass in salute, and we tapped them together. Then we took several quick, albeit tiny, gulps.

Freddy grinned and leaned in close to my ear to whisper, "I'd be happy to lick all that chocolate off you later, in private."

If there'd been any champagne left in my glass, I might have pulled a Deena, and tossed it at him. As it was, it took some doing to look annoyed. Although I'd never admit it, especially to Freddy, the thought of us naked together covered in chocolate *was* kind of appealing, in an exciting, sticky-sick kind of way.

My wicked thoughts were abruptly interrupted by the sudden arrival of Walter Winston. He appeared like a dignified fairy godfather, and he carried a stack of white, hotel hand towels. He handed one to each of us, stoically keeping any caustic remarks to himself. I was grateful for that, as well as for the towel.

The catering staff worked to restore order to the buffet while the four of us wiped as much chocolate as possible from our hands, feet, clothing, hair, and so forth. The gooey stuff was everywhere!

After cleaning up as best they could, Uncle Harry and Deena walked together, arm in arm, toward the elevator. Go figure! I guess Deena wasn't such a dim bulb after all— at least she knew enough to follow the money.

Freddy snagged two more clean towels to protect his car seats, and told one of the wait staff to charge them to his uncle, Harold Rodman. Then we walked out through the casino, Walter trailing along with us.

"You know," Walter spoke loudly over the racket of the slot machines, "this year it would have been my 50th wedding anniversary, too."

I felt genuinely sorry for Walter, but I couldn't think of anything to say at the moment to comfort him. I had my own troubles on my mind.

"I hurried right up here after school," Walter continued, "so I could wish them well, but I was almost sorry I came until all the excitement started." He chuckled. "That was some show."

Outside, we walked back across the mock drawbridge and the men both handed their claim stubs to the valet. Then Freddy turned to Walter.

"Divorce is always a difficult thing," Freddy began. "You think somebody means it when they say 'till death do us part,' and then it turns out there was no real lifetime commitment behind those words." He touched Walter on the arm in a gesture of true compassion.

Apparently, there was more to Freddy than I'd first thought.

"You ever been married, Freddy?" asked Walter.

"Close." He shrugged. "I'm one of those guys who got left standing at the altar."

This had turned into a very private conversation and I felt like an unwilling eavesdropper.

"So you were married almost 50 years?" I asked Walter, in an attempt to remind them I was still here.

"Forty-eight years, five months," Walter said sadly. "And then she ran off with a guy about... well, about Freddy's age, I guess."

Oops. Way to open up old wounds!

Fortunately, Walter's car arrived, and I found a safe subject to talk about, at exactly the same time. "Felicity asked me to remind you to 'hold the bait' on those pizzas tonight."

Walter grinned. "Will do!" He got into his blue, late model Chevy, waved, and drove away.

"Hold the bait?" queried Freddy as his own car pulled up to the covered waiting area. "What's that mean?"

"It means 'no anchovies'."

Freddy laughed and opened the passenger door. He spread a clean towel on the seat, stepped back and held out his hand. "Your chariot awaits, madam."

I grinned, took his hand, and settled myself in. I didn't even think to tell him I could fasten the seatbelt myself, and I also didn't turn my head away when he leaned in to fasten the belt around me, stopping to briefly kiss me on the lips as he did so.

"I'm not even going to ask," said Jimmy when we returned to the Clamshell.

"We decided to bring dessert home," said Freddy with a definite leer in my direction.

"In your dreams," I retorted.

"Yes, always, in my dreams, both waking and sleeping," said Freddy, placing his right hand over his heart and swooning.

"Would you two like to rent a room?" asked Jimmy, grinning and pushing his glasses up on his nose with his middle finger.

"Yes!"

"No!"

Freddy and I replied at exactly the same time. The guy, as I'd noted before, was totally incorrigible. Cute, oh-so-definitely-cute, but undeniably incorrigible.

"I guess not, then," said Freddy. He sighed. "So Syl, we

never did get anything to eat. You wanna get cleaned up and come have dinner with me?"

"Hey, what about me?" asked Jimmy. "My cupboard, not to mention my refrigerator, is bare, thanks in part to you guys, and I haven't eaten all day."

"I thought you didn't want to risk being seen in public," said Freddy, in a rather obvious attempt to ditch the perceived fifth wheel.

"Oh, yeah." Jimmy slumped back down in his recliner. "That's right."

"Why don't we get take-out?" I suggested. I looked at Freddy. "I'll buy if you fly."

"Why me?" he asked.

"You're the least chocolate-coated, and your hair's not bleached bright white."

"Good point."

Jimmy got up and happily retrieved a pink paper menu from the drawer in his desk. "Is Cinco Amigo's Chinese Cuisine okay with you two?"

"Sounds perfect." I handed Freddy two twenty-dollar bills. "Spend any more than that, and you're on your own." I turned to head for the shower.

Mercedes' penchant for apropos musical accompaniment must have rubbed off on me. I started humming "Splish, splash, I was taking a bath..." I stopped at the bathroom door and hollered back over my shoulder. "I'll leave the ordering up to you two. I love everything on the menu."

"Would you love *me* if *I* were on the menu?" Freddy called out.

I chose not to reply.

The hot shower felt so good, I stood there until the water started coming out of the faucet too cool to remain any longer. Blast that small water tank of Jimmy's! But by then, I'd had more than enough time to wash most of my cares way, so I toweled off and pulled on my teal velour sweat suit. I don't know why it's called a sweat suit; it's much too pretty to wear while working up a sweat.

I took a few more minutes to reapply my makeup and fluff my short hair before I reentered the main living area.

Sheriff Donaldson, in full uniform, sat at the kitchen table with Jimmy. "I hope you don't mind," he said. "I gave Freddy another 20 and told him to bring back the family-style dinner for five."

"Five?"

"I know there are only four of us," said Sheriff D, correctly interpreting my expression. "I can count. But with five, you get eggrolls." He grinned happily. "And I just love eggrolls."

The sheriff's laptop was open in front of him, the cord stretching to the outlet next to the refrigerator. I carefully stepped over the cord and took a place at the table.

"We haven't gotten any hits on our APB for the alleged "John Smith" who stayed here Friday night," the sheriff began. "And there's been no sign of the Lincoln Town Car, license plate HR3 003, he registered."

Jimmy stood up and opened the cupboard next to his sink. He got out four plates and some paper napkins and set them on the table. Then he opened a drawer and began counting out forks and serving spoons. "You want chopsticks, Syl? I got a pair of chopsticks in the drawer here somewhere, if you want them."

I smiled. "Of course! Thanks for remembering."

Sheriff D pointed to his screen. "I've been creating a type of spreadsheet, showing us which car was where at what time. Only thing is," he scrunched up his forehead, "we're missing some important details. We don't know exactly which car threatened Jimmy on Friday, or which one shot at you last night."

"So what *do* we know?" I asked him.

"Friday evening, the car with license plate HR3 003, was registered here at the motel by John Smith, a presumed alias.

"About 11 p.m., Jimmy went to get take-out from Cinco Amigos and was threatened by either John Smith and an unnamed partner in the same car, or by two or more occupants of a similar big, black, shiny car."

Jimmy and I both nodded.

"Saturday morning, the same car with the plate HR3 003 dropped off the fish guts. Now, it could have been the same one as threatened Jimmy on Friday night." The sheriff scowled, then continued. "Saturday night, Bob Jones, in HR3 004, spent the night here in Unit 2. On Sunday, HR3 002 was observed up at the Pacific Bluff housing development by Deputy Morgan and yourself, Syl."

"And Felicity," I said. "She was there at Poker Bluff with us. We weren't alone, Carter," I hastened to add.

"And Felicity," echoed the sheriff.

"Then Sunday night, coming home from Spartina Point, you were shot at by an unidentified big, black, shiny car, but you didn't get the license number."

"I did, however," I said indignantly, "manage to come home alive."

Sheriff Donaldson softened his tone. "Yes, Sylvia, and we are all certainly grateful that you did."

I stood and went to retrieve my cell phone. "It probably won't tell us anything we don't already know," I began, "but the cars with plates 1, 2 and 4 were parked at Spartina Point last night when Mercedes and I were there." I showed the sheriff the photos on my phone. "Mercedes confirmed that Number 1 is driven by Uncle Harry."

"Number 3 is the only one we can currently connect to any possible wrongdoings," said the sheriff, more to himself than to Jimmy and me. "And that's the car that just happens to be missing."

"But we don't know which one threatened Jimmy or shot at me," I reminded him. "It could be any one of them."

"True," said Sheriff D, "but so far, there isn't enough for me to get a warrant to search any other of those other big, black cars."

Freddy arrived with the food, coming through the door like a pack mule, overloaded with several bulging restaurant sacks. "Never send a starving man to bring back the food," he said. "I got extra barbecue pork and an order of wontons, and the gal at the counter threw in a dozen fortune cookies." He grinned. "I guess she thought I must be feeding a dozen hungry people."

We ravenously set to eating, and before long, there wasn't all that much left. When we slowed down a little, the sheriff filled Freddy in on what we knew about the status of the individual cars in Rodman's fleet the past couple days.

Chewing and nodding, Freddy took it all in. After awhile, he wiped his mouth with a napkin and said, "It could have been any one of them who shot at Syl, including Uncle Harry himself, or the car previously seen at Poker Bluff, or the one driven by the overly-friendly Mr. Robert Jones."

"Bob would never do such a thing!" Jimmy interjected, blindly defending a man he knew only from his occasional overnight stops at the motel.

"We're not ruling anybody out," said Sheriff Donaldson, pushing himself back from the table. "We don't have enough to draw any conclusions at this time."

Jimmy scowled and started clearing the dishes. Freddy excused himself to use the bathroom, and Sheriff D started boxing up what little was left of our dinner. That left me to do—nothing. It was nice, for a change, to have the men doing domestic duty.

Freddy returned from the bathroom holding my chocolate-stained dress in one hand and laughing. "I found Miss Priss trying to lick the pattern off this," he whispered to me with a smirk. "I told her I'd already offered to do that, but only if you were still wearing it at the time."

Wisely, Jimmy and Sheriff D pretended not to hear. I shattered my well-intentioned eye-rolling moratorium and sighed so heavily I nearly passed out from lack of oxygen.

You give a guy an inch, he'll try to take a mile.

CHAPTER 12

"I'll walk you out," I said to Sheriff Donaldson, seeking to immediately distance myself from both Freddy's suggestive leers and Jimmy's sure-to-follow snide remarks.

Once outside, I asked the sheriff how strongly he'd considered that car number 3, the one that had arrived with the man staying in Unit 4 on Friday, might also be the one that succeeded in scaring the daylights out of Jimmy later that evening.

"Off the record," said Sheriff D, "I'm pretty confident it's the same car, especially after Jimmy told us he was so shook up he couldn't remember if it was still in the parking lot or not when he returned with his food."

"And that's when he heard the answering machine message and called me."

"Right," said the sheriff pointedly, "and nobody bothered to call *me* until after the fish guts were delivered Saturday morning."

I chose not to apologize, since I was pretty sure Sheriff D wouldn't have made Jimmy's call a high priority before something more concrete showed up.

"And Lincoln Number 3 could also be the one carrying the guys who shot at me."

"Yes, that's also a strong possibility," he agreed. "And I happen to hold that opinion myself. But we need to keep an open mind, and since it could still be any of the four, let's not make ourselves dizzy considering all the different car and driver options."

The sheriff put his key into the Interceptor SUV lock and opened the door. "Sylvia," he said, turning to face me, "these guys... Whether there are two, or three, or more involved... these are really bad men." He placed a protective hand on my shoulder. "I want you to promise you'll let me and my department handle all the investigative work from now on."

I looked up into his steel gray eyes and thick, bushy mustache. "Sheriff," I said honestly, "all I can promise is that I'll keep you in the loop. Jimmy called on me to protect him, and that's exactly what I intend to do."

Sheriff D pursed his lips and took a deep breath in through his nose. "That's *my* job," he said, and expelled the air out his mouth in a rush. "And if you insist upon messing around in places you don't belong, you're going to get in the way. And maybe get yourself killed in the process."

I said nothing, touched by his genuine concern.

He caught me off-guard when he bent down and gave me a peck on the cheek. "Just be careful, Syl." Then he quickly got into his rig and pulled the door shut.

I watched until his vehicle merged out onto the highway, then went back into the apartment. Jimmy sat in the living room recliner with Priscilla wedged contentedly between his leg and the arm of the chair. Freddy had taken up a spot on the couch. He patted the seat next to him when I came in.

"We're watching an NCIS marathon," he said. "Join us."

"Yeah," said Jimmy, "I know you've got the hots for Gibbs."

"I do not 'have the hots' for Gibbs," I indignantly informed them both, settling myself on the couch as far away from Freddy as I could get. "But you know I wouldn't kick him out of bed for eating crackers… Tony either, for that matter."

"You leave Tony alone," chided Jimmy. "He's mine."

"Wanna arm wrestle me for him?" I joked, flexing my right bicep.

"Good to know you like 'em both older and younger," said Freddy. "I was beginning to think maybe you'd only seriously consider a much older man. Say, maybe somewhere around the sheriff's age."

"What in the world gave you that impression?" I asked. "I spent the whole afternoon with you today, and now you want to go and get all weirdo on me?"

"I saw you out there at the car with him," Freddy replied. "Be honest, Syl. You got a thing for the old man?"

"As if it's any of your business!"

"Speaking of age differences," interjected Jimmy with one heckuva sloppy segue, "did you know Freddy and I graduated from high school just three years apart?"

"And that's important because…?"

"Well," said Jimmy, "that makes me and Freddy pretty close to the same age."

"Freddy and me," I said automatically. "So what?"

"I guess that depends," said Freddy, "on whether you like young and frisky guys or the older dinosaur types."

"Oh for crying out loud! Would you two drop it, already?" I got up from the couch and headed for the bedroom. "I think I'll call it a day. Good-night, you two."

"Hey, wait a minute!" Freddy called out. "How come Sheriff D gets a good-night kiss and I don't?"

I spun on my heels and glared at him. "Deputy Frederick Morgan, if you're going to spy on me, at least get your Peeping-Tom facts straight. I certainly did *not* kiss the sheriff good-night."

Both Jimmy and Freddy were grinning ear-to-ear. "Well now, my Syllee girl," said Freddy, his eyes twinkling, "that's mighty good to know."

Without another word, I stomped out of the room; I'd been made a fool of one too many times today.

Once inside the bedroom, I flipped the lock on the door. Although fairly confident Freddy wouldn't dare come visit me without an invitation, I thought it best to err on the side of caution. The problem is, I didn't know if I'd be more upset if I left it unlocked and he *didn't* try to join me.

Crawling into bed, I stretched out on the cool sheets and for a moment considered how odd it was that Freddy considered stodgy old Sheriff Donaldson his competition. Imagine what he'd think if he knew his father was more of a rival than his boss!

Smiling at the thought, I quickly drifted into a deep, dream-filled sleep. Dreams that tumbled and wrestled with me all night long. Dreams in which Deena, not her real name, was signing book autographs with chocolate-dipped strawberries.

Early to bed and early to rise, and I awoke Tuesday morning at the very crack of dawn. Sometime during the night, my subconscious had come up with an idea too good to let pass without acting on it. I pulled my teal sweats back on, used the bathroom, brushed my teeth, and ran a quick comb through my hair.

I was relieved to see that Freddy had left sometime during the night. Jimmy was asleep on the couch, but Miss Priss curled herself around my ankles as soon as I entered the kitchen end of the room. I poured her a helping of cat kibbles. "There you go, my sweet girl." I ran my hand along her back and up her tail as she began to eat.

Then I found a pad of paper and pen in the drawer by the phone and wrote a short note for Jimmy: 'Gone for a drive, be back before lunch. S.'

On second thought, I added 'P.S. I'll bring lunch with me' to the bottom of the note. That way I knew for certain he'd stay close to home until I returned.

I pulled out onto the highway and turned north. My stomach started growling before I got to the first cross street. I whipped a U-turn and headed south again, back past the motel and on into Tinkerstown.

The Buoy 10 Bakery opens daily at 4 a.m. It was a couple hours past 4 a.m., but still quite early when I walked through one of the two glass entry doors. My nose was immediately assaulted by the delicious aroma of freshly-made donuts. My mouth watered in eager anticipation as I made my way to the counter.

Glazed or cake donuts? Crullers or maple bars? Apple fritters or bear claws? Decisions, decisions! In the short time it took to be my turn to order, I hadn't narrowed my selection down any.

"May I help you?" asked the woman behind the counter.

"I'll… uh… um… Let's see… I'll, uh… I'll take a half dozen assorted," I finally blurted out. "And a 20 ounce cup of coffee. To go."

"Bag or box? If you want a box, you'll have to order a whole dozen."

I wasn't quite sure if she was making some kind of snide commentary about my non-nutritional breakfast, or if she was just trying to be helpful while a the same time pushing more donut sales. I opted for helpful. "A bag will be fine, thank you."

The smell of fresh bakery goods immediately permeated the air inside my Mustang. Normally, I have a hard and fast rule that my car is not a restaurant on wheels, but dang it all, those pastries smelled so fabulous, I knew I didn't stand a chance of arriving at my destination without breaking into that sweet sack of sugar-laden delight.

I reached over with my right hand and unrolled the top of the bag. Gently removing the first pastry my fingers came into contact with, I brought the ooey-gooey maple bar to my lips. Oh, yum! Yum, yum, yum, *YUM!* But the whole thing disappeared so fast there wasn't nearly enough time to savor it.

The second one out of the bag was a chocolate cake donut with sprinkles. That, too, seemed to evaporate into thin air. As did the cruller.

I quickly did the math. I still had another 10 or 12 miles to get where I was going. Briefly, I considered going back for another half dozen. Damn! Maybe I should have gotten the box instead. I told myself to get a grip and hurriedly rolled the top down on the bag, swearing not to open it again for at least another five miles.

The next 20 minutes I spent sipping my coffee and agonizing over the amazing number of calories I'd mindlessly inhaled. Eater's remorse, I think it's called. I wondered how I could possibly hope to burn off so many calories before they settled on my hips.   Right now I'm what I'd call height-weight proportionate, if you like curvy women.

Lots of men liked curvy women, I mused. And then my mind went someplace unexpected and foreign—and I began to wonder how many calories I could burn off during a session of athletic sex with—

Whoa girl! I was nearing the north end of the peninsula,

and I forced my thoughts to concentrate on the plan that had formed in my head during the night.

Spartina Point Casino and Resort takes up most of the land on the ridge that butts up against the nature preserve at the very tip of the North Beach Peninsula. "The Resort at the End of the World," as it's sometimes aptly referred to.

The casino and hotel dominate the landscape, with the meandering golf course, wound in around natural wetlands, mainly to the east. A few stubborn homeowners had refused to sell out to the Rodman Corporation, and their homes, and accompanying access roads, bordered the resort property on the west side.

I can't say as I blame these residents for not taking the Rodman money and moving on. The west side of the ridge offers spectacular unobstructed panoramic ocean views, the kind of which are becoming quite scarce in other states. What is especially unique is the abundant amount of still-undeveloped property between homes.

Easing my car slowly along the gravel road running just beneath the ridge of houses, I drove until I came to several vacant lots clustered together. Here and there among the scrub pine were what might someday be the driveways of multi-million dollar estates. I pulled off the road and into one such shallow clearing. I parked next to a bright yellow realtor's sign and shut off the car.

I got out and went around to the trunk. The sight of the duct-taped flowers disguising Sunday night's bullet dings reminded me that I'd need to be calling the auto body shop soon to schedule the repair. It also pissed me off just enough that it firmed up my commitment to my plan this morning.

Fortunately, my binoculars were right there where I thought they'd be. I looped the strap over my neck and picked up my holstered Glock. Then I set the gun back down. This was a mission for observation, not confrontation. I doubted too many bad guys were up and about this early anyway. Quietly, I closed the trunk lid.

I've never actually been on a stakeout before, but taking along the pastries seemed like a good idea. If I ended up being out here a long time, I'd need something to eat to keep up my strength. Then I locked the car doors and stuck the keys in my pocket.

A great many lots in this area had been cleared years ago, in preparation for the masses of people expected to relocate here after vacating California during the last governor's term. Apparently, those anticipated masses took up residence elsewhere, and the proposed subdivision fell by the wayside. Only a couple dozen lots of the 50 or 60 that already had utilities in were ever sold, and of those, only a handful now sported a house upon the property.

But nature loves a vacuum, and the scrub pines, salal, scotch broom and blackberry vines had pretty much reclaimed the entire area. Although the soil is predominantly sand, those kinds of plants seem to grow most anywhere.

I worked my way up the gentle hill and along the top of the ridge until I had a clear view of the Spartina Point main parking lot. There were no convenient logs or rocks to sit on, so I took one for the team and sat right down on the damp earth. It had rained during the night, and the remaining moisture immediately wicked into my sweats.

I trained my binoculars on the row of big, black, shiny cars huddled up in the reserved spots near the front casino door. The license plates were much too far away to read, but there were still three cars parked right where they'd been yesterday.

After 15 or 20 minutes with not much to look at, a bread truck pulled into the lot and went on around to the back of the building. I yawned and wiggled my shoulders around to stretch them. My eyes lit upon the donut bag, and I decided it was probably high time for a mid-morning energy snack.

I was just finishing up the apple fritter when I saw movement near the line of big, black, shiny cars. I quickly licked my fingers and put the binoculars back up to my face. Four people, three men and a woman, were standing behind the line of cars.

Harold Rodman the Third shook hands with both of the other men. One of them was the overly-friendly, information-seeking, Mr. Robert Jones. I didn't recognize the other one. Jones and the mystery man got into two separate vehicles, backed out of their parking spaces, and drove away from the casino.

Uncle Harry came around to the passenger side of the remaining car and held the door open for Deena. He patted her butt as she got in, and she smiled up at him adoringly. I thought I might lose my sugary breakfast right then and there.

Uncle Harry walked back around to the driver's side, got in, and they too, left the parking lot. This was the chance I'd been waiting for!

I jumped up and quickly realized my right foot, which had been tucked beneath me the entire time of my surveillance, was sound asleep. Pins and needles shot up my leg when I put any weight on it. Standing on one foot, I tried to brush off my bottom, but the sweats were soaked clear through, and the seat of them stuck uncomfortably to my skin.

Nevertheless, I did my best to hop and stumble, hastily

crashing down through the scrub brush, wincing in pain as the feeling started returning to my right foot. I broke into the narrow clearing near where I'd parked my car and froze in my tracks, my tingling foot forgotten, my heart beating a rapid tattoo in my chest.

Good grief and gravy! A black bear stood between me and my Mustang. I'd heard there was a bear problem here on the north end, but I'd never encountered a live one before, up close and personal, so I wasn't sure if this was a large one or a small one. Size didn't matter at the moment; a bear was a bear!

It sniffed the air all around the car, tilting his, or her, head from side to side, as if testing the wind. Then he, or she, slowly turned and looked straight at me. I prayed this was a nearsighted bear, and remained still as a statue. Unfortunately, the bear began to shuffle in my direction, still with its nose in the air, head waving slowly back and forth, like a cobra swaying to a snake charmer's flute.

I took a tentative step backwards. A downed branch crackled under my foot. The bear lifted its head higher and made a sound something like a cross between a whimpering cocker spaniel and a caterwauling Siamese.

I sorely regretted leaving my gun in the trunk.

All the feeling in my foot had returned by this time, and I decided to make a run for it. I didn't know exactly where I was going to run to, just getting away from there, ASAP, was uppermost on my mind. Not wanting to weigh myself down with extraneous baggage, I lifted my right hand to discard the binoculars.

And that's the precise moment when I suddenly remembered the bag of bakery donuts clutched in my other hand.

The donuts! The bear was after the donuts, not me!

Opening the bag, I examined the remaining contents. One glazed donut, and one bear claw. The irony of the second pastry's name was not totally lost on me, but I didn't stop to dwell on it.

I pulled the donut from the sack and flung it as far as I could, away from me *and* my car. Unfortunately, glazed donuts aren't all that heavy, especially those made fresh this morning at the Buoy10, and it didn't fly far. The bear picked up the scent right away and quickly lumbered over to it, if there's any such thing as lumbering quickly. For the sake of argument I'll call the bear a he, and he lifted the donut in his mouth, tilted his head back, and swallowed the whole thing in not much more than a single gulp.

That left only the bear claw. The good news is, a bear claw is a lot heavier than a glazed donut, so there was a good chance I could sling it far enough from the car to make my escape. The bad new is, that the bear claw looked really tasty, and I'd managed to work up quite an appetite during my stakeout.

The bear chose this moment to lift his head again and utter that indescribable eerie wail. Indecision is quickly cured when encouraged by such ursa major sound effects.

Without further debate, I hurled that pastry for all I was worth, and apparently I was worth a great deal this morning. It flew past the front of the Mustang and into the nearby brush.

"Shoo! Shoo! Go away!" I flailed my arms in an attempt to hasten the bear's departure.

The bear turned toward where the pastry had landed, and with the aid of his capable nose, immediately left the clearing in pursuit of another tasty treat.

I wasted no time in scrambling to the car and unlocking the door, but I did take an extra second to put the empty bakery sack down on my car seat to protect it from my dirty, wet sweats. Then I climbed in and locked the door.

Whew! I took a couple deep breaths, then started up the car and carefully backed into the gravel roadway. The bear reappeared from the pine scrubs right where the car had been, and I couldn't restrain myself. I rolled down the window and bellowed at the top of my lungs, "Glutton!"

Somehow, yelling like that made me feel a whole lot better. I was able to drive sanely back down the gravel road the way I'd come in. At the first intersection, I took a left, and drove less than a half mile to the entrance of Spartina Point Resort.

I proceeded through the first lot to the second, and pulled up beside Mercedes' trailer. It was still relatively early, but I pounded on her door anyway.

"Go away!" she hollered.

"It's me," I hollered back. "It's an emergency!"

Mercedes opened the door a crack. Her sleep mask was pushed up onto the top of her head and she wore no makeup. "It better be good."

I hurriedly climbed the metal steps and pushed my way inside, pulling the door shut behind me. "There's no time to waste!" I said. "Uncle Harry and Deena have left the resort. We've got a window of opportunity here, Merc. Get dressed!"

"Okay, okay," she said, hurrying back down the hallway. "Say hello to Brutus while I pull on some clothes."

I looked around, but didn't see hide nor hair of Brutus until I checked behind the couch. There he cowered, looking quietly up at me with his big, brown eyes. "You big chicken," I muttered, and reached down to gently pet him. His tail thumped against the trailer wall, but he made no move to come out into the room.

Mercedes bustled back down the hallway, dressed in a boldly-flowered Hawaiian muumuu and matching flowered earrings. Variegated dark glasses were perched on top of her head, and flip-flops completed her outfit.

She was obviously going to use the dark glasses to disguise the fact she hadn't taken time to put on makeup, so I said nothing. I even kept quiet about her choice of wardrobe, since I hadn't given her any advance warning of my early visit.

Merc waved the motel's master key card at me. "Would you look at this?" she said with mock surprise. "I plum forgot to return this Sunday night." Then she tucked it securely into her bra.

Merc climbed up on the couch on her knees, reached over, and patted Brutus. "Now you be a good boy and guard the house for me." She stood back up and took two steps to the door. I was right behind her.

"If you were going to arrive at oh-dark-thirty," said Merc, stepping outside into the bright light of morning and pulling her sunglasses down from of the top of her head to shade her eyes, "the least you could have done was bring donuts or something."

CHAPTER 13

Since we didn't have to stop at the front desk to con a key card from the registration clerk, we headed straight for the elevator. Mercedes' enormous dangling earrings swung wildly as she struggled to keep up with my hurried strides.

The elevator car happened to be on the first floor already, and the door slid open as soon as I touched the 'UP' arrow. We stepped inside and I rapidly pressed the button for the fifth floor, then the 'Close Door' button. We had no time to lose.

As soon as the door slid shut, Merc bent over double, heaving noisily for air. "Do you mind me asking," she said between gasps, "how the seat of your sweats got so wet?"

I couldn't think of a single smart remark at the moment, so ended up telling her a short version of the truth. "I was sitting on my butt on the west ridge, keeping an eye on Uncle Harry's Lincolns. That's how I knew when the coast was clear enough for us to do a little more investigating."

"Oh," she replied, nodding. "I thought maybe it was time you got yourself some of those adult diapers," she wheezed out. "Glad that's not the case yet."

Her 'yet' didn't settle well with me, but we arrived at the fifth floor before I could design a good comeback. Blame it on the free-falling crash after a massive sugar rush, but my brain wasn't functioning on full capacity this morning.

Mercedes reached into one of the large external pockets

of her muumuu. "Here." She handed me a pair of purple latex gloves, and began pulling her own pair on. "Bet you thought I forgot these."

Occasionally Merc displays a glimmer of true brilliance, and I'm not just talking about the shine emitted from her various sequined outfits. I thanked her sincerely, and pulled on my 'protection,' as she called them. The door slid open and we padded down the hall to Room 552 with our purple gloves already in place.

Merc hesitated for just a second outside the door, the key card in her left hand, and rapped sharply twice with her left glove-protected knuckles. "Housekeeping!" she called out in a reasonably good impersonation of a hotel housekeeper.

"Nobody's home," I hissed. "I watched both of them leave a half hour ago."

"Doesn't mean he didn't leave one of his henchmen behind," Mercedes whispered back. Receiving no reply from within, she quickly slid the key card in and out of the lock, the light turned green, and we stepped inside.

Uncle Harry's suite was a mirror image of the one we'd previously been in next door, only this one had that homier, lived-in look. The bedcovers were pulled up, but the bed wasn't made, by any stretch of the imagination. A few clothes were strewn about, and sections of a big-city newspaper were stacked helter-skelter on the ottoman of the wing-backed chair. The chair itself was turned to face the flat-screen television mounted inside an enclosed wooden bookcase.

Mercedes went straight for the casino's complementary high-roller fruit basket sitting on the polished office desk and began plucking red grapes from the arrangement, eagerly popping them into her mouth.

"Merc!" I hissed again.

"I can't help it," she said, with her mouth full of fruit. "You got me up before breakfast."

I glowered at her, but said nothing, which I've often found to be the best strategy when I need someone's help. I joined her at the desk and began carefully sifting through the papers strewn on top. Most of them were upscale North Beach restaurant menus.

"You don't think he's going to leave anything incriminating just lying out in the open, do you?" asked Mercedes between grapes.

Good point. I opened the top desk drawer, but it contained only a hotel pen and a few sheets of letterhead notepaper. Briefly, I wondered how many people came to the casino hotel to write their personal correspondence, especially since the hotel advertised free Wi-Fi. The two side drawers on each side of the desk were also empty.

I picked up what I assumed was Uncle Harry's briefcase and carefully set it on the desk chair seat. The metal plate above the handle was engraved 'HR3.' I smacked my forehead with my open palm. "Harold Rodman the Third," I said aloud. "His personalized license plates, his briefcase, I'll bet even his golf clubs, his helicopter, and Deena's butt have HR3 written on them. What an egomaniac!"

Merc shrugged. "For a smart woman, you sure do miss some obvious no-brainers. The guy's got money, and he wants to be sure everybody knows it. I don't see what's so wrong about that."

I made a mental note to keep my future 'ah-ha moments' to myself.

The contents of the briefcase were neatly organized into a couple dozen manila file folders, and inserted into the expanding permanent holder. Naturally, they were alphabetized, printed by hand in bold script.

I flipped open the 'Employees' file. Names, addresses, phone numbers, brief bios and work histories, employment starting/ending dates, and salaries were all included on some kind of modified spreadsheet. I checked for either 'John Smith' or 'Robert Jones.' There was no one listed by those names.

"Mercedes, don't you have a last name?"

She made an attempt to grab the file from me, but I held it just out of her reach. "What's it say about me in there?"

I whistled. "It says you make way more money playing piano a couple nights a week than anyone would guess a woman living in a motorhome in the parking lot was bringing home." I peered at her. "You don't have a gambling problem, do you?"

Merc shook her head. "I'm saving it all up for my retirement. Going to go to the Bahamas." She paused. "You think Brutus will like the Bahamas? Cause if he doesn't, I might have to settle for southern Oregon."

I smiled. "Stop trying to wiggle out of answering my original question. Why don't you have a last name listed in your employment file?"

Mercedes started ticking off a list of one-name entertainers. "Cher, Beyoncé, Sting, Bono, Prince, Enya, Liberace, Madonna." She stopped counting on her fingers, and shook one at me. "You know *any* of their last names?"

I rose to the challenge. "Technically, I think Bono and Sting aren't their real names at all, and Liberace *is* his last name."

"Fine!" Merc indignantly placed her hands akimbo and tried to stomp her foot, but her flip-flops rather ruined the intended effect. "You get my point," she went on. "Professional entertainers don't need two names."

"Yeah, yeah," I said, examining a few of the other files, "your point is that you're not going to tell me, which means you're probably hiding something, but since you've been so kind to help me with this, I'm going to let it go—for now."

My eyes settled on the information inside the 'Discovery Bluff' file. "Looks like Sheriff D is right about the Poker Bluff being a big tax write-off. That housing development is losing money hand over fist."

Mercedes, meanwhile, had gone into the bathroom and I could hear her noisily taking the toilet tank apart.

"Merc! I've been telling you, you watch too much TV!"

She reemerged empty handed. "Nothing." She shrugged. "I guess the bad guys watch television too."

By now I was pretty sure Uncle Harry was too cagey to leave anything even marginally incriminating in an unlocked briefcase, so I closed it and set it back on the floor right where I'd found it. Mercedes had the clothes closet door open and was rifling through Deena's wardrobe.

"I gotta hand it to her," said Merc, holding up a full-length, silver-sequined gown, "the gal's got good fashion sense."

"Come help me here," I said, ignoring her appraisal of Deena's garish dress.

"Hold on a minute!" Mercedes said excitedly. "Would you look at these shoes? I've never seen such expensive, fancy shoes so up close and personal." She excitedly held up a pair of open-toed gold stilettos, one in each hand. "Oh dear gawd— Genuine Manolos!"

"Mercedes—" I said in my official and most authoritative voice, "step away from the shoes."

Reluctantly, she put them back into the closet and joined me near the bed. Together we lifted each corner of the mattress, one by one, but found no hidden stash of secret documents, or drugs, or anything at all.

Mercedes flopped on her back across the end of the bed, feigning exhaustion from our efforts. "Whew! After all this, you're for sure gonna buy me breakfast, right?"

I sat down on the chair at the vanity and shook my head. "Not after I've seen what you make in a single weekend." I stared at her pointedly. "You want breakfast, you're on your own."

"Phooey." Merc sat up and faced me. "Hey, what's that there on the vanity?"

I turned to look where she pointed. "A Bible."

"Yeah, I can see that," she said. "What I meant was, how come it's not tucked way back in some drawer of the bedside table? That's where the Gideons always put them."

I refrained from asking her how she happened to come by that particular piece of information.

"Harrumph," Merc continued, "maybe Uncle Harry's gone and got religion."

I snorted. "Or maybe not..."

I picked up the Bible and noticed a decidedly homemade bookmark in it. Opening to the marked page, which happened to be in Job, I saw the bookmark was nothing more than a sheet of hotel notepaper folded over a couple times. Six or eight verses were written on the place marker in a feminine-looking scrawl.

"Deena..." I said under my breath.

"*Where?!*" said Mercedes, jumping to her feet.

"Deena told me she was going to write a book based on religion," I began, racking my brain to recall the specifics of our one conversation. "At least, I think that's what she said..."

"Oh," said Merc, sitting back down on the end of the bed. "Everybody I know says they're going to write a book someday. No big deal."

I closed my eyes and squinted hard, trying to remember exactly what Deena'd been babbling about at the reception just prior to the chocolate fountain fiasco. "I'm pretty sure she said that what she was writing had its roots deep in the scriptures."

"And your point?"

"Walk through this with me Merc..." I sighed. "Writers write what they know about, right?"

"That sounds like a lot of rights and writers, but I get your drift," said Mercedes, heading back toward the fruit basket. "I'd think it'd be too hard to write about something you didn't know anything about."

"So what does Deena know?" I asked, musing rhetorically.

Mercedes answered me anyway. "She knows shoes, I'll give her that much."

"And even if you did know about something," I continued, ignoring her remark, "and you wanted to write about it, you'd probably have to do at least a little research on it anyway, right?"

"There's that 'right' word again. You used it another two times," said Merc, grinning at me. "So you think Deena knows a lot about the Bible?"

"No, not the Bible itself..."

"Then what are you getting at?" asked Mercedes.

"I'm not sure," I began. "What if, just supposing... What if what Deena 'knows' is something about Uncle Harry's business dealings, or maybe a little about some of his undocumented exploits? And what if she's using the Bible to do her 'research'?"

"I think that's one heckuva stretch," Merc said honestly, "but if she's really thinking about writing a book, then maybe his life might be more interesting to write about than her own."

I laughed. "I'm pretty sure we can count on that."

"Unless she was writing about her shoes, of course." Mercedes was eating a banana, and she spoke with her mouth full.

"Of course." I looked around the room. "There's no laptop here, and no other books or magazines. So except for the daily newspaper, the Bible is the only thing she has to read while Uncle Harry's otherwise occupied."

"I still don't know if you're onto something or not," said Mercedes. "I only know we've been here too long already, and we'd better be getting our butts outta here soon." She stuffed the banana peel into her pocket.

"Merc, what are you doing?"

"Now look," said Miss Hotel-Know-It-All, "hardly nobody ever eats nothing out of the complementary fruit basket, so I know they don't count the grapes or bananas or nothing." She paused, and I wondered if she was waiting for me to correct her grammar.

Not getting even a small rise out of me, she continued, "But if there was to appear a banana peel in their trash, and they realized that neither one of them had eaten a banana, well..."

"Okay. Got it. You're taking your trash out with you." I smirked. "Did you learn that in the Girl Scouts?"

"Carry in, carry out," recited Mercedes, nodding her head. "Yes Ma'am, I done learned the proper way to camp when I was just a little tyke."

She walked over and retrieved the notepad and pen from the office desk and handed them to me. "Now you best get to writing."

"Thanks." I quickly copied down the verse notations,

eight in all, and tore off the top sheet of paper. I put everything back where it belonged and crammed my copied list into the jacket pocket of my sweats. We wasted no more time in exiting the room.

Mercedes pressed the call button at the elevator. "There's no 'UP' arrow on this floor," she said, more to herself than to me. "The only direction from here is down."

"Metaphorically speaking," I hastily interjected.

"You got that right, Sista. You got that right." Merc grinned at me, then watched as the numbers above the door marked the elevator's ascension. I think we were both relieved to be getting out of here before anybody caught us snooping around.

Mercedes was still grinning like a Cheshire cat when the elevator doors slid open. Uncle Harry and Deena, not her real name, stepped out of the car without looking and almost ran right into us. The sight of Uncle Harry, with Deena clinging tightly to his arm, wiped any trace of mirth from either one of our faces.

Harold Rodman the Third scowled, his eyebrows almost touching in the middle. "What are you two doing on this floor?" he barked.

I'll give Mercedes due credit, she recovers much faster in a tight situation than I do. "Ditzy me!" she said breezily, with not a trace of the guilty conscience I felt upon encountering these two. "I pressed the wrong button, and then I didn't even check to see where we were before we got off."

"Oh," said Deena, perkily bubbling as if her roots weren't brunette, "I get confused like that all the time!"

"Must be hard to keep your novel plot straight," I muttered, pushing past them and clambering into the elevator.

Uncle Harry continued to frown, and just stood there staring at us until elevator door closed safely behind us. My knees went weak with relief. Merc pressed the button for level one, and let out the breath she'd been holding. "Hay-soose."

"Hay-soose indeed!" I leaned back against the rear of the elevator and felt my still-wet sweats press against my backside. I vaguely wondered if Uncle Harry had noticed. Even if he had, I was glad he wouldn't have a clue how they had gotten that way.

We returned to Merc's trailer in short order and went inside. "Where's your Bible?" I asked her, anxious to look up my copied list of Deena's verse notations.

"My Bible?" She looked at me as if I were speaking some other language.

Pulling the list from my pocket I waved it at her. "So we can see if there's any connection between the scripture and Uncle Harry's activities, remember?"

"I live in a trailer," Mercedes began, palms up in an innocent 'who me' shrug. "I don't have any extra room here to be carrying around a Bible."

Her totally sincere look kept me from laughing. No Bible? *Seriously?* "Okay, well, I need to get back to the Clamshell pretty soon anyway." I glanced at the clock on her wall. "I promised Jimmy I'd bring lunch with me."

I borrowed a clean dishtowel from her to replace the empty pastry bag on my car seat and headed south. Involuntarily, I shivered as I drove by the spot where I'd been shot at Sunday night. So much had happened in just a couple days, and there were still so many unanswered questions.

Fortunately for me, this trip down the peninsula added no more stress to my already drama-filled life. The weather was marginally nice enough to put the top down, and I enjoyed the ride with the wind in my hair, taking pleasure at seeing the occasional quaint little beach house and then long stretches of tree-lined highway glide by.

I had to drive past the Clamshell to get into town for the best burgers in the county, if not the state. The drapes were still closed at the motel, and the 'No Vacancy' sign was still lit, but I figured Jimmy was just being cautious. Or paranoid. Or both.

At the High Tide, I ordered two loaded mini-tsunami burgers and curly fries. The regular tsunami burger must be ordered a day ahead, and the local legend says it's big enough to feed a party of 15, or one very hungry pregnant woman in her third trimester.

I've always wondered how they'd manage to accommodate that pregnant woman, as most pregnant women I've known had their cravings came on all-of-a-sudden and not 24 hours ahead and I wouldn't have wanted to mess with any of them.

I got a thick chocolate mint shake for me, and a fresh strawberry one for Jimmy. It'd been hours since my breakfast donuts, and I was sure the adrenalin rush of both the encounter with the bear, and then with Uncle Harry, had expended most of the calories.

The High Tide isn't a typical fast food drive-in. All the orders are cooked up fresh, so it takes a little while to get your food. I sat down on the wooden bench in the small waiting space and distracted myself from my grumbling stomach by reading some of the hundreds of business cards tacked to the wall.

"Come here often?" asked a familiar voice behind me.

Even though the voice was familiar, I still jumped like a silver salmon with a hook in its mouth. Then I mustered a weak, and rather insincere smile as I turned around.

"Hello Rich."

He sat down on the bench beside me. "I'm sorry, Syl. I didn't mean to startle you. You must have been lost in thought."

"It's okay. My nerves are just a little shot these days."

"Interesting choice of words," said Rich, his eyes twinkling.

When I didn't show proper enthusiasm for his wordplay, his expression turned serious. "Has the sheriff gotten any leads?"

I shook my head. "They collected brass out there yesterday morning, but it has to be sent out to a lab somewhere." I shrugged. "Most of it's mine, anyway."

Wanting to trust him, but not wanting to give anything away in case it turned out he wasn't on our side, I fell silent. Rich interpreted this as a call for comfort. He reached over and gently gave my hand a squeeze, not letting go afterward.

"Rich..." I began softly, not sure I should open my mouth, but needing to know how he'd answer my question.

"Yes?"

I was pretty sure what the sheriff was going to say about my meddling with his investigation, but I just couldn't help myself. I plunged blindly ahead.

"Sunday night..." I fumbled around in my head for the best words to use. "When you pulled over out there behind me on the highway..." I looked directly into his eyes, hoping by doing so I would know for sure if he lied to me.

"Yes?"

"You said you'd follow me to the Clamshell, but you couldn't stop in because you had an early charter the next morning."

Rich broke into a huge, and for my money, very inappropriate grin. "So you *did* want me to come in with you!"

I jerked my hand away, and went directly back to the questions I desperately wanted answers to. "Salmon season is closed, Rich. Why did you tell me you had a charter trip booked for Monday morning? What was the real reason you didn't want to come in? Were you afraid the sheriff might have some questions for you?"

Rich's eyes narrowed, and for the first time in our acquaintance, I could see the potential for a real mean streak in him. My stomach knotted up tight and I felt what could be a bout of nausea coming on, but I held my ground.

The High Tide's speaker announcement broke the tension between us. "Number 147."

I honestly don't know why the High Tide bothers with a loud speaker. Nobody ever goes back out to their cars, they just sit here on the bench while the food is being prepared. One-forty-seven was my number, but I didn't get right up to retrieve my food order. Not yet.

"Rich?" I maintained eye contact, raised my eyebrows, tilted my head and waited.

"Number 147," bellowed the impatient woman at the counter, this time without the aid of the speaker.

Rich blew out a breath. "I thought we were developing something special between us, Sylvia."

I said nothing.

"But you don't trust me," he icily went on.

"Give me a reason to trust you, Rich."

He sadly shook his head. "Yes, Sylvia, you're right. The spring Chinook season is temporarily closed. Monday morning I was taking a group out to fish for sturgeon."

"One-forty-eight," intoned the woman, having given up

on me ever responding to her call and moving on to the next order.

Rich got up and grabbed the smaller white bag from the counter. Without another word, he slammed out the side door. I sat there with my face flaming hot, too ashamed of myself to call out after him.

CHAPTER 14

"Mini-tsunamis! My favorite!" exclaimed Jimmy, unwrapping his deluxe bacon cheeseburger and biting hungrily into it. He added a couple fries to his mouth, then noisily slurped his strawberry milkshake.

Sitting across the table from him, I picked absentmindedly at my burger, pulling out bits of meat and feeding them to Priscilla, who was sitting up and begging next to my chair. Who says you can't teach cats tricks? Miss Priss had learned to roll over for her cod liver oil hairball treatments and play fetch with a squeaky mouse toy. In my estimation, Jimmy has way too much time on his hands.

"Something the matter with your food?" he asked, coming up for air and noticing my apparent lack of appetite.

"Something's the matter with *me*, more likely," I said. "This whole alleged murder investigation thing has got me jumping at my own shadow." I sighed, and related the story of my encounter with Rich Morgan at the High Tide.

"Gee, Syl, I'm sorry about that," Jimmy said when I finished my tale. "But— well, I was just wondering..."

"Go on, spit it out."

"Well..." Jimmy drew the word out as if it had several syllables. "Well... I thought you had the hots for Freddy, and now you're telling me how sorry you are for insulting his dad like maybe it's him you're interested in."

I stood up and put my barely-touched lunch into the

refrigerator. "Who I have, or have not, got the hots for is not the point," I said. "It's just that it makes me crazy not knowing whom to trust, and I don't like being suspicious of innocent people."

"So you think Rich is innocent?"

"I think he had a reasonable explanation for not walking me to the door Sunday night, so to speak, and it wasn't because Sheriff Donaldson was here." I sat back down. "And, if you'll recall, Sheriff D was the one who first cast doubt on him."

Jimmy nodded, his mouth full of burger.

"It's not that I distrust Sheriff D, mind you," I went on, "but he's apparently got eyes and ears reporting all kinds of things back to him, and some of those eyes and ears may also be working for Uncle Harry."

Jimmy nodded again, and sucked up more of his shake.

"Which makes me wonder if that's a good thing or a bad thing."

Jimmy wrinkled his brow, so I continued. "Sheriff D could be in on whatever's going on, Jimmy, and maybe now he's just trying to throw me off track."

"You mean you think he's a dirty cop?" Jimmy said gruffly. I knew he was trying to do an impersonation of some tough-guy movie actor, but I couldn't place it.

I shook my head. "I just don't know."

"Well, then," he went on, sounding now like a voice-over on a true crime show, "you have to also consider that Officer Freddy, nephew to Uncle Harry, son to Rich, is driving a very expensive car for a guy on a cop's salary."

"Oh, geez..." Again with an involuntary eye roll. I'm going to get a jar to throw quarters in every time I do that—it'd be a good way to finance my next vacation.

"Jimmy," I began, "don't you think that would be a bit

obvious? I mean, don't you think Freddy's smart enough not to be driving around in a flashy car if he obtained the money for it illegally?"

Jimmy shrugged. "I dunno. How smart do you think he is?"

"So I'm back to my original question, Jim. Who can I trust?"

"You can trust me," said Jimmy, setting down the last two bites of his burger to reach over and pat my hand.

"Can I really?"

He scowled. "What's that supposed to mean?"

"What if you know perfectly well what went on in Unit 4 last Friday night, and you're just covering your tracks by feigning fear? What if you're actually the one responsible for something bad happening? What if you planned for the fish guts delivery when you knew I'd be here? What if you wanted to throw suspicion away from yourself by calling the sheriff before Lupé or someone else discovered the crime scene?"

"Oh my gawd, Syl, you're going right over the edge!" Jimmy got up, came around the table, and took me by the shoulders. "Get ahold of yourself, girl! You know me better than that. And you know Sheriff Donaldson is a straight-up guy. And there's no real reason to doubt Freddy's loyalty, regardless of that fancy-schmancy car he's driving. Heck, he's probably gone into debt up to his ears for that car, just to impress the chicks."

I scowled. "What exactly do you mean by 'the chicks'?"

Jimmy laughed. "So I finally got your attention." He released his grasp on my shoulders and started gathering the paper trash from the table. "I'll do the dishes," he said with a grin, "since you cooked."

"You're not dodging me that easily." I got between him

and the kitchen trash can. "You think Freddy's driving that car simply because it's a chick magnet?"

Jimmy laughed. "Oh Syl, what in the world would I know about things like that?" He wiggled his way around me and tossed our lunch waste into the garbage can.

"Fine." I refocused my thoughts. "So then is Rich a good-guy or a bad-guy?"

"That," replied Jimmy, "I cannot tell you. What does your gut say?"

"My gut? *Seriously?*"

"Mom always said you can tell when somebody's lying to you if you just stop and listen to how their words make you feel," Jimmy said sagely. "It's all about feelings. So how does what Rich said today make you feel?"

"Like an idiot for doubting him."

"Then I'd go with that. You're an idiot." Fortunately for him, Jimmy was just out of my reach.

"Thanks a heap."

"Anytime." He flashed a cheesy grin at me, and changed the subject. "So what got you up and out of here so early this morning?"

I pulled the list of Bible verses from my pocket. "May I use your computer?" I considered that a rhetorical question, and moved to sit at the desk in his living room.

Jimmy hovered behind me as I opened a new blank document and carefully copied the Biblical chapter names and verse numbers onto a fresh page. "You suddenly get religion or something?"

Ignoring him, I double-checked my typing against the notepad page, and started to throw the paper away.

"Wait a minute," said Jimmy, taking the 4" by 5 1/2" paper from my hand. He set it on the desk and took a pencil from the top drawer. Rubbing it lightly across the page, it was apparent that whatever had been written on the previous page had left indentations—enough to read at least a portion of what had been previously written there.

"Jimmy, you're a genius!" I said as the individual letters emerged.

"Aren't you gonna tell me I watch too much television?" he said sarcastically.

"Not this time."

Jimmy read the letters and numbers aloud as I read them to myself. "K ST DEL 8 FRI." He shrugged. "You make anything of this?"

"Well, for one thing, I'm relatively sure a man wrote it. Probably Uncle Harry."

"And you surmised that, how, exactly?" asked Jimmy.

I laughed. "I took a handwriting analysis class a couple years ago in order to learn more about the parents of my young clients. Men print in all capital letters more often than women," I explained.

Jimmy pointed to the letterhead on the notepad. "This paper is from the casino hotel. Is that why you think Uncle Harry wrote it?"

"Well, it's also written in the same type of script as the file headings in his briefcase, and I, uh..."

"Sylvia! You mean to tell me you took this paper from Uncle Harry's room? And you were snooping in his briefcase? Are you determined to get yourself *killed*?"

I felt my face flush yet again. Damn that menopause! "It's a long story."

"Ok, I'm gonna let that slide—for now." Jimmy had set the paper back down on his desk and was busily wringing his hands. "Anything else about the handwriting?"

"Normally, printing in all caps also tells us that the person is quite possibly hiding something. I learned it's easier to hide more of your true self when you do that, but since this note is so short, I can't really say for sure."

"HHhhmm..." said Jimmy. "Sheriff Donaldson writes in all caps in his pocket notebook..."

"Sheriff Donaldson wouldn't be able to read his own handwriting if he didn't." I laughed again. "I thought we agreed Carter was one of the good-guys."

"Just sayin'," said Jimmy. "I really didn't mean anything by it."

I typed in the letters and number exactly as they were imprinted underneath my list of Bible verses. I saved the file under 'Investigation,' then pressed 'print.'

"Do you miss your work with Child Protective Services?" asked Jimmy while the paper was rolling through the printer.

"I miss the kids," I said truthfully, "but I don't miss the paperwork."

The printer spit out the list, and I was relieved there was no more time for Jimmy to pry further. I'd left CPS after 30 years in the system, also leaving a never-ending list of suspected child neglectors and abusers to be dealt with by my replacement.

"You got a Bible handy?" I asked.

Jimmy sighed. "Sure. I got a couple dozen of them out in the supply room."

"A couple *dozen*?"

"You wouldn't believe the number of Bibles that disappear from my motel units every year."

"Maybe they think the Bibles are complementary, like the pens and notepads."

"Maybe those so-called religious zealots ought to remember 'Thou shalt not steal,'" Jimmy muttered, heading out the door. Priscilla chose that opportunity to make her rounds outside as well.

While Jimmy was gone, I started working on the possible meaning of the odd notations indented in the notepad.

"K ST DEL 8 FRI." I took the printout to the kitchen table and sat down. "K ST DEL 8 FRI." I started jotting down my thoughts beneath the different 'words.' When Jimmy returned a few minutes later, I had several ideas forming.

He placed the Bible on the table and looked at the paper in front of me. "Whatcha got?"

"Nothing definite," I began tentatively. "But I'm pretty sure '8 FRI' means 8 o'clock on Friday."

"Eight in the morning or eight in the evening?" asked Jimmy. "Last Friday or next Friday?"

I glowered at him. "Who died and elected you technical advisor?"

"It's important that we not assume anything," said Jimmy. "The little details can send us spinning off on the wrong track if we don't consider all possibilities."

"Yeah, yeah, I hear you." I sighed. "And you're right, of course, but first we have to see how much general information we can decipher. So I'm saying '8 FRI' quite possibly means 8 o'clock Friday, okay?"

"Okay," said Jimmy, still standing at my left elbow.

"And quit hovering!"

"Sure, Syl, anything you say." He quickly pulled a chair around from the end of the table and sat down close enough to me to see the writing on the paper.

"ST DEL," I read aloud. "Any ideas?"

"Well, I don't profess to be an expert on the Bible, but I do know quite a bit about it, and I don't believe there's a Saint Del or a Saint Delbert or even a Saint Delilah," Jimmy deadpanned.

I couldn't tell if he was messing with me or not, so I took his comment at face value and continued to study the letters.

"Oh! But look here!" I pointed to the beginning of the message. "K ST." I beamed. "There's a K Street up on the north end."

Jimmy nodded. "Yes there is... So is there a K Street Deli?"

"Hunh-uh. K Street is totally residential."

"Then what about a delivery on K Street?" Jimmy asked. "Think someone was making a K Street delivery at 8 on Friday?"

"Yes! That could be it! Or..." I said, mindful of Jimmy's admonition not to jump too far to conclusions, "at least I think we're getting a lot closer!"

At this point I considered bringing Sheriff Donaldson in on our findings, but I knew if I did, I'd have to explain how I happened to have a page off Uncle Harry's notepad, so I decided it was best to postpone that little story until we'd had a chance to check out some of the Bible verses.

"You're thinking about calling the sheriff, aren't you?" asked Jimmy.

"You into mind reading these days?"

"I could see it on your face," said Jimmy. "That indecisive look of 'should I or shouldn't I' you get every time you're thinking about ordering dessert."

"Oh, really?"

"Yep, and we both know you 'should' get ahold of Sheriff D right away, but we also both know you're going to postpone that call just a little while longer."

"Am I that transparent?"

"Nah," said Jimmy, laughing. "It's just what I'd do."

He opened the Bible and turned to the first verse listed. "You want me to dictate these to you so you can type them into the computer?" he asked. "I promise to read slowly and clearly."

"Good idea," I said, wishing he weren't so accomplished at knowing what I was going to do almost before I did.

I reopened the file labeled Investigation and Jimmy started with the first verse on the list. It was soon easy to spot a common theme emerging among all eight verses.

"They're all about fish," said Jimmy.

And indeed they were.

I printed off a second, up-to-date page, and we pored over the words until they started swimming in front of our eyes. No pun intended.

Why had Deena, not her real name, selected these particular verses to reference? Did they have something to do with 'researching' the book she intended to write, or with Uncle Harry, or both?

"Enough!" I said, throwing up my hands. "Time for a break!" I stood up and stretched my back, rotating my shoulders.

"You need a soda?" asked Jimmy, already standing in front of the open fridge door. "I refilled the fridge from my emergency stock while you were gone this morning, so I've got cold ones."

"What I need," I said, pulling my cell phone out of my pocket, is to check on my house to see if the kids have totally destroyed it by now."

There was no sense in calling Felicity's cell number, due to the notoriously poor reception at home, so I dialed my own home number instead. The phone rang five times, then the answering machine picked up.

"This is Sylvia..." It felt strange to listen to my own

voice telling me I was not at home, and to "please leave a message after the beep."

"Felicity?" I said into the recorder, "it's Sylvia. Are you there? Is everything okay? Please pick up if you can hear me."

There was the distinct sound of the receiver being bobbled around, then a young female voice said, "Hello?"

"Who's this?" I asked. "And what are you doing answering my phone?"

"I'm, uh, one of Ms. Michael's students," she began, apparently unwilling to properly identify herself in case I was going to get mad at her. "And, uh, well, Ms. Michaels said none of us were to touch your phone, and we haven't, but when I heard it was you calling," she rushed on, "I thought it would be okay."

I kept my voice level when I asked, "You've all been listening to my messages?"

"You haven't had any until now."

"Okay, fine." I didn't know if I felt better or worse by her reply. "So exactly where *is* Ms. Michaels?"

"She's outside on the deck cooking chicken on your gas barbecue. You wanna talk to her?" the student sweetly asked.

"That *is* why I called."

More receiver bobbling as my wireless phone was transported to the deck.

"It's for you," I heard the student say.

"Hello?" Felicity said tentatively.

"Nice to know you're still breathing."

"Well, there have been a few challenges..." She chuckled unconvincingly. "But we're doing okay."

"So what's up with cooking chicken on the barbie?"

"You don't have any kindling for your campfire, and

after we burned through the majority of old newspapers you have in your recycling bin, I gave up. The natives get restless when they're hungry."

"But why chicken?" I asked, then continued with just a hint of snide in my voice, "I don't recall anything about Lewis and Clark serving chicken."

It didn't sound like she was smiling when Felicity replied, "I hear it tastes just like grouse."

We lapsed into a short silence while I kept myself from laughing by literally biting my tongue. Jimmy was looking at me like I was having a seizure, but I just shook my head to keep him from coming to my aid.

"So..." I began again. "The kids are all learning a ton by recreating the Corps of Discovery's adventures in the Pacific Northwest, and so far you wouldn't trade it for the world, right?"

"Sarcasm is one of the lowest forms of humor," Felicity said wearily.

"Yeah, I know." I was glad she couldn't see me grin. "Puns are the lowest, cause a lot of times they're just really stupid and not very punny at all."

"Syl—"

"Uh-huh?"

"Syl—" Felicity lowered her voice. "Remind me never to have children of my own."

I snorted. "You're preaching to the choir here, Felix."

"I can't believe how hard it is to keep an eye on them every single minute. The moment my back's turned there's another near-disaster."

"Now, Felix, don't be so hard on yourself." I laughed again. "You've got 20 teenage kids all at once on a five-day sleepover and you're trying to teach them a little something about history at the same time. Mere mortals wouldn't take all that on alone!"

"Nineteen, but thanks for trying to make me feel better."

"Nineteen what?"

"I only have 19 students out here. Kasey's brother Keith never did show up yesterday. I ought to flunk him for that, but frankly Syl, we're all kind of worried. It's really not like him not to let even his parents know where he is."

"His parents?" I was beginning to feel like an echo, but something in my gut, as Jimmy called it, was pushing its way to the surface.

"I called Keith and Kasey's parents on your phone this morning to ask if Keith was home sick, and they said they thought he was with us."

"So you think he's hanging out with his friends, thinking no one will be the wiser?" I suggested.

"I honestly don't know," said Felicity. "Keith is usually pretty responsible."

While Felix had been talking, I'd been idly spinning the original motel note with the rubbing on it around and around on the desk. My eyes suddenly focused on the letters and numbers and my stomach lurched.

"Felix! Where is Kasey right now?"

"Kasey? As far as I know, he's still out trying to get the campfire started." She sighed. "I suppose I ought to go check to make sure he hasn't drained my gas tank to use the fluid for accelerant."

"Felix, listen carefully—I need to know what time Kasey's delivery was supposed to be on Friday."

"You mean the delivery he conned Keith into making for him so he and Lorrie could go out?" Felicity sounded confused.

"Yeah, that one."

"May I ask why?"

I tried to keep my voice calm. "Please, Felix, don't ask questions, just get Kasey on the phone, will you?"

By this time, Jimmy had heard the urgency in my voice and he came to stand by me. I pointed to the note, first tapping the 'K' and mouthing 'Kasey', then to 'DEL 8 FRI.' His eyes got big and round.

"Your home phone signal won't reach out there," said the ever-practical Felicity. "If it's that important, I'll go get him myself and he'll call you right back."

"It's that important, Felix, thanks." I hung up and looked at Jimmy.

"You thinking what I'm thinking?" I asked him.

"Maybe," said Jimmy, "but I don't like where our thoughts could lead."

"Hey now," I said, more to calm myself than reassure him, "who's the one who advised me, not an hour ago, that we can't jump to conclusions before we have all the facts straight?" But my gut feared we were both right.

My cell phone jangled and I quickly flipped it open and pressed it to my ear. "Kasey?"

"Ms. Michaels said you wanted to talk to me," he began. "I swear I don't know how the recliner got broken. Me and Lorrie were just sitting in it together and—"

"Kasey!" I interrupted. "Never mind about the chair—for now," I amended. "I just need to know what time you were supposed to make that delivery to Spartina Point last Friday."

"Oh, that..." Kasey heaved a sigh of relief. "I told Keith that Captain Morgan said for me to get there by 8, but Keith said he might have to work until 9, so I'm not sure when it actually got there. Why? What difference does a couple hours make? It was just one big old ugly fish."

I stared at the note, knowing before I asked the answer to my next question. "What *kind* of fish, Kasey?"

"It was just another old sturgeon for the moat." I could almost see Kasey shrugging it off. "No big deal."

"Thank you, Kasey, now put Ms. Michaels back on."

"So what was that all about?" Felicity immediately asked.

"I'm not sure," I hedged. "I'll call you back as soon as we know something definite. Just trust me, okay?" I paused. "And Felicity..." I hoped she didn't detect the mammoth lump in my throat I was trying to talk around, "you take good care of those kids, you hear me?"

I hung up before she could reply. Picking up the note, I turned to Jimmy. "K ST DEL 8 FRI," I read aloud. "Kasey, sturgeon delivery, 8 p.m. Friday."

Jimmy nodded. "I know," he said softly. "So what do we do now, Syl?"

"Now," I said, my fingers once again on the cell phone keypad. "*Now* we call the sheriff."

CHAPTER 15

I left a message with the dispatcher to have the sheriff contact me right away. "It's urgent that I see him, ASAP," I told him, in what I hoped was an authoritative, but not too pushy, voice. "I have new information he needs to have immediately." He assured me he'd relay the message as soon as we hung up.

I turned back to Jimmy, but he was nowhere in the living room or kitchen. "Jimmy?" I called. "You in the bathroom?"

"Out here!" he hollered from the parking lot.

I joined him at the west edge of the gravel clearing, where he stood next to the dumpster, his hands on his hips, muttering to himself.

"What's up?" I asked.

"I let Priscilla out when I went to get the Bible," he began, "but she hasn't come to the door to get back in."

"And that's unusual?"

"Definitely," said Jimmy. "She's mainly an indoor cat, but she prefers to use the biggest cat box in the world out here rather than the one I have for her inside." He motioned to the expanse of dunes in front of us.

The ocean used to come a lot closer to the motel than it does now. Due to the accretion of sand dumped out the mouth of the Columbia River, the dunes have built up over time. Now about a quarter mile of rolling mounds covered by knee-high dune grass kept us from seeing the water.

"Priscilla knows where her food dish is, Jimmy, and I doubt there are too many mice out on the beach for her to catch. I'm sure she'll be back when she gets good and hungry." I tried to pass it off as just another cat character defect. "Cats aren't like dogs, you know; they pretty much have a mind of their own."

Jimmy called her name a few more times, but there was still no answering meow.

"I don't like this one bit. Miss Priss and I've been roommates for over a decade, and she usually sticks to me like Velcro. In fact, that's probably what I should have named her—Velcro." He gnawed anxiously on his lower lip, scanning the nearby dunes.

"She sticks to you like Velcro?" I replied. "HHhhmm. In that case, is it possible she didn't come out here at all? Maybe she followed you into the supply room."

Jimmy narrowed his eyes, considering my suggestion. "I suppose it's possible," he said slowly. "I had my mind on a few other things when I ducked in there to get the Bible."

Together we walked toward the laundry room, tucked into a narrow space between Units 2 and 3. Jimmy referred to this room as either the supply room or the laundry room, depending on what he was after at the time. It housed one white industrial-sized washer, one similarly gargantuan dryer, and a closet for general cleaning supplies, including miscellaneous motel necessities—like replacement Bibles.

As we crunched across the gravel, Jimmy called her name again, and there was no doubt where Miss Priss had been hiding out. Her plaintive cries rose to a mournful wail and we could hear her scratching frantically to escape her confinement. As Jimmy reached out to turn the doorknob, it sounded like poor Priscilla was hurling herself against the door, thump-bump, thump-bump.

"Something's not right," he said, hesitating. "She's never done anything like that before."

"I'm sure she's just anxious to get out here to be with you, Jimmy."

The door opened inward, so Jimmy gently pushed it open, careful not to bang her nose with it, but Priscilla was now across the small room, cowering by the washer. "Oh my gawd!" he exclaimed. "What's she gotten herself into?" He stepped inside and bent down to investigate. Then he let out a squeal and quickly pulled me inside the room, slamming the door shut behind us.

"Oh my gawd!" he said again. "Just look at her." He clasped his hands to his cheeks and looked about as helpless as a woman on a diet in a room full of chocolate. "Who could have done such a thing to my poor Priscilla?"

It didn't take a college degree to see what was freaking Jimmy out. Around Priscilla's neck, looped through her rhinestone collar, was a dead salmon head, weighing her down, scaring her silly, but not causing any real harm.

"Oh my gawd, oh my gawd, oh my gawd." Jimmy folded his arms in front of him and rocked rapidly back and forth, staying as far away from his beloved cat as possible.

Obviously, it was going to be up to me to remove the slimy salmon snout. I found some rubber gloves among the supplies. They weren't purple, I noted, but they'd have to do. I pulled them on and handed Jimmy a pair.

"I'm not touching it," he said with strong conviction. "No way. You can't make me touch it, Syl. I'm serious. I want nothing to do with this."

"For crying out loud, Jimmy! Think this through. Someone has to hold her still while I remove the fish head. You don't have to touch it. You don't even have to look at it. Just keep her from wriggling away long enough for me to get her collar off."

He reluctantly pulled on the gloves and we bent down together to calm the frightened cat. "Poor Priscilla," he cooed, holding her firmly with a hand on each side of her body, but turning his head away. "My poor, poor, kitty."

"Nice bedside manner," I sniped. "You'd have made one hell of a nurse."

"Just get it off her, Syl. Please? I can't bear to look at her this way. I think I'm gonna be sick."

"You will *not* be sick," I said. "You will be a responsible pet owner and do what needs to be done to help her."

I managed to get the collar unfastened and off the trembling cat. Jimmy continued to hold Miss Priss right where she was while I turned my attention to extracting the collar from the fish head.

I tried to pull it through the head and mouth of the fish, but something was in the way and slowing my progress. "Uh, Jimmy? There's apparently something wadded up in the salmon's mouth."

"Oh my gawd!" said Jimmy. "I don't want to know what it is." He squeezed his eyes shut tight. "I really don't want to know! Don't tell me, Syl, please don't tell me."

"Buck up, you big wussie." I removed a piece of paper and unfolded it. It turned out to be a local gas station receipt with bold writing across on the back.

"On second thought, Jimmy, I don't believe you need to know after all."

Curiosity got the best of him, and he opened one eye. "What is it?"

"Nothing you need to worry your pretty little bleach-blonde head about."

"Sylvia..."

"It's just your plain, old, everyday death threat," I said

nonchalantly.

"Sylvia! What's it say? Tell me! I have a right to know!"

"Really, Jimmy, you need to make up your mind," I said.

He whimpered. "Tell me."

"Fine. But remember you asked for it." I paused. "It says, and I'm quoting now, 'This is your last warning, blondie.'"

"It really says blondie?" Jimmy squeaked out.

"I *said* I was quoting." I cleared my throat. "I'm afraid they've seen through your clever disguise after all."

Jimmy turned loose of Priscilla and bolted through the outer door. "Oh my gawd! It's just like in the Godfather!" he shrieked. He ran past the dumpster and out a short distance on the trail toward the beach, then vomited into the dune grass whatever was left of his undigested tsunami burger and strawberry milkshake.

He was still there, bent over double, heaving his guts out, when Sheriff Donaldson wheeled into the driveway in his Interceptor SUV. I shut Priscilla back up in the laundry room for the time being, and went to meet the sheriff.

For a trained professional observer, Sheriff D was apparently a little off his feed this afternoon. Not only did he miss Jimmy's distressing situation in the dunes, but the fact that I had on rubber gloves and was carrying a cat collar and fish head didn't immediately register with him either.

"Sylvia! You called!" he boomed. He grinned broadly, and his face was all lit up. He moved briskly toward me, arms spread wide, apparently intending to give me a large, unwelcome embrace. "Dispatch said you wanted me!"

I stopped abruptly. "In your dreams, Carter," I hissed. I held the slimy contents of my hands before me as a shield.

"I called you because I think we've had a break in the case, and even before you get here, we've got a second drive-by dead fish bombing on our hands."

Sheriff D dropped his arms to his sides and stood stock-still. "I, uh, sure, Syl. Of course. No problem. I didn't think for a minute you called me about anything else. I was just being, uh, friendly."

"You can save *that* kind of friendly for your *wife*, Carter," I spat out.

Sheriff Donaldson's face puckered up like he'd bitten into something very nasty and bitter. A crimson flush catapulted up his neck. To his credit, though, he didn't try to dodge the issue.

"Yes, Sylvia, you're right," he said softly. "Technically, I'm married." He expelled a deep breath. "But my wife's been in a nursing home with Alzheimer's for several years now." He looked at the ground and scuffed the gravel with his shoe. "She doesn't even know who I am anymore."

I felt genuinely sorry for him, and sorrier still that I'd brought it all up at this particular moment. Mercedes, my key source of information on just about everyone on the peninsula, had been the one to fill me in on Sheriff D's marital status, but she'd unfortunately neglected to mention the state of his wife's health.

"I—I'm sorry," I said softly. "I truly didn't know."

"A guy gets lonely, you know? And I thought maybe you'd understand." He shrugged. "What can I say?"

"Rrrralph!" Jimmy's retching stomach sounds put a screeching halt on our semi-intimate moment and quickly returned us to the problems at hand.

"What have you got there?" asked the sheriff, resorting back to his Official Sheriff Voice, and motioning to the items in my hands.

"Can you get fingerprints off a fish head?" Grateful to be back on safer ground, I was only half-serious about my question, but I had to ask.

"Probably not." He opened the back door of his SUV and produced several evidence collection bags. "But we'll bag and tag, just in case there's something else useful the lab guys can discover."

"Right. Good idea. Like it might be important to know how long the fish has been dead, or what something like that. You just never know."

Jimmy joined us while I was explaining to Sheriff D the circumstances surrounding how we'd come to find Priscilla in the laundry room.

"Feeling better?" I interrupted my event recitation to inquire.

Jimmy nodded. "Musta been something I ate."

Sheriff Donaldson had his notepad out and was scribbling away. He looked up and asked, "Where's that note you said you found in the fish head?"

"I set it on the dryer."

"I'll go get it," said Jimmy, holding up his gloved hands. "I'm still dressed for the occasion." He started across the parking lot without further comment and I was proud of him for being such a good sport.

"But you put in your call to me before you found the cat, is that right?" asked Sheriff D, consulting his notes.

"That's right." I nodded. "I've got more pieces to the puzzle documented inside on Jimmy's computer." I hesitated, but there was going to be no getting around telling him all the sordid details my early morning trip to Spartina Point.

"Sheriff," I began, as he bagged the note Jimmy handed him, "it's a long story, and you're not going to like most of it, but I want you to promise you'll hear me out before you go yelling at me."

Sheriff Donaldson put all the evidence from Priscilla's assault inside a cooler-like container in his vehicle and closed the door. Then he turned and started walking toward Jimmy's living quarters. "Got any coffee?"

While Jimmy started brewing a fresh pot, I showed the sheriff the pencil rubbing we'd done on the notepad from Uncle Harry's room. Although I could tell he was irked as all get-out that Mercedes and I had gone snooping on our own, he kept quiet on that point, at least for now.

"And from this rubbing you conclude that 'K ST DEL 8 FRI' means that Kasey was to deliver a sturgeon to Spartina Point at 8 p.m.?"

"I talked to Kasey just an hour ago. All the pieces seem to fit."

Sheriff D pulled his notebook back out of his breast pocket and sighed. "Kasey's what? Seventeen?"

"Yeah, about that, why?"

"Is there anyone legal age, and totally above reproach, that you can produce to collaborate your conversation with him?"

"Uh-huh." I nodded. "Felicity Michaels was standing right there the entire time I spoke with him."

"Can you get her on the phone now?" asked Sheriff Donaldson.

I called Felicity again. She must have been standing right next to the phone, waiting for me to call back. She answered as soon as my cell number showed up on the landline's Caller ID.

"Syl, what's going on?" I could hear the tension in her voice.

"How are the kids doing, Felix?"

"They're fine, but you're scaring the heck out of me, Sylvia."

"Felicity, I need you to go into my bedroom, alone, and close the door. Then call me back on the Clamshell office number so I can put you on the speaker here. I need you to be able to verify a few things so we can figure out exactly what *is* going on."

I hung up, and the motel phone rang seconds later. I pressed "Speaker" and said, "Felicity, Sheriff Donaldson and Jimmy are both here with me. We're going to have to ask you some questions about Kasey's conversations with me, both on the phone a little while ago and when we were there in my kitchen with him yesterday."

"Okay," came the small voice out of the machine.

"I'm taking notes," said Sheriff D, "so I may ask you to repeat a few things. We're just trying to establish an accurate timeline here, Ms. Michaels."

I imagined Felix was nodding, so I continued.

"Last Friday evening," I began, "Kasey picked up a sturgeon from Captain Morgan down at the port to deliver to Spartina Point. Correct?"

"Correct," said Felicity. "And then he stopped by the market where Keith works just north of Unity and talked him into making the run to the resort for him so he and Lorrie could get to the movie on time."

"So they traded vehicles a little after 7 o'clock?" asked Sheriff D.

"Yes."

"Does anyone know what time Keith got off work that night?" he continued.

"I called the store looking for him when he didn't show up for our campout," said Felix. "I thought he might have been at work, making money instead of attending class, and

I asked him about that."

"And?" said the sheriff and Jimmy at the same time.

"The manager on duty last Friday night said Keith left in Kasey's red pickup about 9:30 Friday and he hadn't seen him since."

Sheriff Donaldson sat at the dinette table, his brow furrowed, furiously writing in his little spiral-bound notebook. Jimmy had retrieved Miss Priss from the storeroom and was gently washing her all over with baby shampoo in the kitchen sink.

"When we spoke earlier," I said to Felix, "Kasey said he was supposed to deliver the sturgeon by 8 o'clock."

"That's right. But Kasey figured an hour or two wouldn't make any difference since sturgeon are practically invincible, and the fish was in water in a big, covered tote, so he asked Keith to make the run for him."

"And Kasey has delivered live sturgeon to the casino before?" broke in Sheriff Donaldson.

"Sure," said Felicity, "lots of times. Probably three or four times a month over the past couple months. He's just paid to unload them directly into the moat."

"Wow. When it says 'fresh fish' on the menu, I guess they mean it," said Jimmy, unwittingly echoing Felicity's earlier supposition.

"They don't eat these fish," I corrected him, "they put them in the moat cause Uncle Harry wants the moat to be realistic, and alligators are against the county rules."

"You get that information from Freddy?" asked Sheriff D, without a trace of jealousy or other inappropriate emotion.

"Yes," I admitted. "Freddy says sturgeon can live for over a hundred years. They're tough-skinned and... HHhhmm... Well, he told me a bunch of other stuff about them, but, hhmm... I just can't seem to remember it all right now. I think it was something about their feeding habits."

"Hold everything," said the sheriff, lightly tapping his pencil on his notepad while he thought things through. "If Kasey's been delivering these sturgeon to the moat at the rate of three or four a month for at least the past three months, and they allegedly live for darn near ever, isn't it getting a little crowded in there?"

The sheriff's question hung in the air like an ominous storm cloud over the ocean.

Jimmy finished rinsing the shampoo off Priscilla. He fluffed her up with a towel before setting her on the floor. She's obviously been through this routine before and immediately went and stood expectantly by the outer door.

"You guys still there?" asked Felicity from the phone speaker.

"Yeah," I said. "We're still here, Felix. You got any thoughts about how many mature sturgeon that moat can hold?"

"Not a clue," Felicity admitted. "So what's all this have to do with Keith's disappearance?"

"Maybe nothing," Sheriff D quickly interjected. "Right now we're just fact gathering. If we have any further questions for you, Ms. Michaels, we'll be in touch." The sheriff made eye contact with me and ran his index finger across his throat in a 'cut' motion.

"Gotta go, Felix. Thanks!" Again, I hung up before she could say another word.

"So what do you think, sheriff?" I said as soon as the line disconnected.

"I think we need more information," said Sheriff Donaldson. "Freddy's not on duty right now; do you happen to have his home number handy?"

I unsuccessfully tried to fight down that all-to-familiar flush creeping into my face as I flipped open my cell phone and pressed the button to call Freddy. When I told him we were sorting through some new information on the case and needed his expertise, he said he'd be right over.

Meanwhile, Priscilla was urgently scratching at the back door.

"Would you look at that?" said Sheriff Donaldson. "That cat goes to the door and scratches to get out, just like a dog would do."

Jimmy scowled. "I wish she'd just use her cat box today. I don't like the idea of letting her out there again right now."

I walked over and put my hand on his shoulder. "They didn't hurt her, Jimmy. And besides, with the sheriff's rig parked in the lot, they wouldn't dare try anything else."

"I guess you're right." Jimmy opened the door and Miss Priss eagerly bounded for the dunes. Jimmy laughed. "Guess she's really got to go."

Together, we stepped out on the steps to keep an eye on her. Once Priscilla got to the edge of the parking lot to the sand by the dumpster, she wasn't in all that big a hurry. She sniffed here and there, taking a tentative scratch or two, not quite satisfied with any particular location.

"Maybe she needs a little privacy," I suggested. "We're both staring at her, after all."

Jimmy harrumphed. "She's never been that discriminate about where she does her business. One night she even used the bathtub instead of the cat box right next to it.

"Would you hurry up, already?" he called out.

The sheriff came out the door behind us. "You think

yelling at her's going to speed her up, Jimmy?" He chuckled.

"At least she didn't make a beeline for the place you tossed your cookies a little while ago," I teased.

It was nice to think about something other than the case for a few minutes. I felt an odd sense of equilibrium, almost peace, descend over the three of us, just standing there companionably, watching as the cat dug in the sand.

Jimmy started out across the parking lot after her. "So help me, Miss Priss, if you don't hurry up, you're going to have to come back in and hold it."

The sheriff and I had a good laugh. "Good luck with that," Carter said under his breath.

But apparently Priscilla took Jimmy's admonition to hurry it up, and his rapid approach, quite seriously. She suddenly began to dig in earnest, the sand literally flying up around her.

Jimmy stopped in his tracks a half dozen feet from her. His face had no color in it when he turned back around to face us. "Sheriff," he called out, "come quick. And bring another one of those evidence bags."

I previously had not thought the sheriff capable of moving so fast. He grabbed the evidence collection bags and tools from the Interceptor and bolted across the parking lot before the possible implications of Jimmy's words even registered with me.

Then, inexplicably, like the passersby who cannot turn their eyes away from a horrible car wreck, I was drawn to the spot where Jimmy stood, now holding Priscilla tightly in his arms.

Sheriff Donaldson knelt down with what looked like a large pair of tweezers, and began to extract a dark blue Mariner's baseball cap from the sand. The underside of the bill was exposed, and written there in heavy black letters was the name 'K Walker.'

"Oh no—" I put my hand over my mouth. My stomach lurched violently, and I was glad I hadn't eaten much of my lunch.

Sheriff D carefully placed the hat into one of the bags and sealed it. He looked up at me and pushed his hat back on his head. "Looks like there might be a spot or two of blood on it."

A small whimper escaped Jimmy, but there was so much cotton in my mouth I couldn't utter a sound.

"And since we know where Kasey is at the moment, we'll have to assume, at least for the time being, that this hat belongs to Keith."

Jimmy whimpered louder, and hugged Priscilla so hard to his chest that she emitted her own little pitiful sound of pain.

The sheriff stood up and tapped the radio button on his collar. "Dispatch," he said into the receiver, "looks like we're going to be needing those dogs again."

CHAPTER 16

Without waiting to ask Sheriff Donaldson for permission, I went inside to get my cell phone and called Felicity. "Send the kids home and get over here," I told her.

"I can't do that," Felix whispered into the phone. "I've pretty much put two and two together, and if it turns out as bad as I think it could, this might be my students' last few days of normalcy for awhile."

When I didn't say anything to confirm or deny her comments, she continued, "I'm not willing to ruin their wilderness adventure on top of everything else."

I considered telling her that staying at my comfortable house, complete with electric heat and indoor plumbing, hardly qualified as a 'wilderness adventure,' but decided not to chide her for her word choice at the moment.

"It's serious, Felix. You gotta get over here. If you're not willing to send the kids home right now, how about calling Walter or somebody else to cover for you?"

"Well, yeah, I guess I could do that... But what excuse will I use?"

"For Walter or the kids?"

"Either. Both. I dunno, Syl. I'm pretty sick to my stomach right now. Maybe I'll just tell them all I'm not feeling well. At least it would be some form of the truth."

"Tell Walter you're having 'female problems' or something like that. Men always cower and rush to acquiesce to anything a woman wants at the mere mention of anything remotely related to a woman claiming it's that time of the month. You're still young enough to get away with that."

Felix fell silent for a moment. I was pretty sure I knew what she wanted to ask, but I refused to offer up any information unless she specifically requested it.

I got to hand it to her, the gal has guts. It only took a few seconds of quiet contemplation before she felt brave enough to ask, "Sylvia, do you know something you're not telling me about Keith's disappearance?"

I'd already decided this would be one time where honesty was absolutely the best policy. "We believe we found Keith's hat buried in the sand out by the dumpster next to Unit 4. That's all I know for sure."

"Oh... my..." I could tell she was fighting to keep from getting emotional while she was still in charge of her students. "Okay. Thank you for telling me. I'll call Walter now. See you in a few."

Freddy, Felicity, and the van containing the Search and Rescue dogs, all arrived at pretty much the same time. They parked wherever they could find enough room behind my Mustang and the Sheriff's Interceptor, since we'd restrung "Do Not Cross" yellow crime-scene tape across the far end of the parking lot again.

Sheriff Donaldson, Jimmy and I had then gone back inside to wait. Now Sheriff D stood up and cleared his throat. "Now that the K-9 Unit is here, I don't want to see *any* of you out there unless I call you to come out. And that includes the cat." He motioned to Priscilla, napping unconcerned in her favorite spot, perched on the back of Jimmy's recliner. "You got that?"

"Got it, yes sir!" Jimmy quickly replied. "No people and

no cats outside this room until further notice. Yes, sir, I got it! Loud and clear, sir! No problem!"

Sheriff D looked at me pointedly. "You got it too, Sylvia?"

"Yes, I got it too." I shook my head. "I'm not a child, Carter."

"Good. Then we're all clear."

The outer door dinged and Freddy and Felicity came through the office and into the living quarters just as the sheriff was about to go out. Both Felix and Freddy were wearing jeans, pullover sweaters, and grim expressions.

"Deputy Morgan," said Sheriff D, with a great deal more official tone to his voice than was absolutely necessary, "regardless of your lack of uniform, you're on duty now. Please keep everyone inside while the dogs go over the grounds one more time."

"Yes, sir." Freddy replied.

For one horrifying moment, I thought he might snottily salute. As though reading my mind, Freddy clandestinely winked in my direction.

"And see what you can add to our knowledge of sturgeon." Sheriff D inclined his head toward me. "Ms. Avery there needs some help filling in the blanks."

Then the sheriff politely tipped his hat to Felicity and stomped on outside.

"My," said Felicity, coming around to my side of the table, "the sheriff's certainly in a foul mood today."

"I suspect you'd be pretty grumpy too, if your S and R dogs missed finding a vital piece of evidence the first time they worked over a suspected crime scene," I replied.

"Is that what he's got stuck in his craw?" asked Freddy. Without asking if anyone else wanted some, he opened the cupboard, took down a cup, and poured himself what was left of the coffee.

I was pretty certain Sheriff Donaldson was still reeling over the fact that I'd viciously thrown his legal marital status in his face, but I kept quiet on that point. I figured it was best to keep that conversation between the two of us. No need to make the information public unless there was some need for it.

But I also figured Carter thought the fact that he already had a wife was only the thing making me reject him as a potential suitor. If it ever came up again, and I sincerely hoped it wouldn't, I'd have to be sure to set him straight: *Not interested!*

Felicity rescued me from contemplating the reasons behind Sheriff D's foul mood by remarking, "The last time the K-9 Unit was here, I had to coax Priscilla out of the tree with a can of tuna, remember?"

"You fed Priss my good tuna?!" Jimmy asked incredulously. "I wondered what happened to that can of primo albacore I was saving! You know how expensive that stuff is these days?"

Freddy cleared his throat. "I doubt the presence of Priscilla distracted the dogs all that much," he said, getting back to the point. "They're trained better than that."

"So maybe..." I considered my words carefully. "Maybe the hat didn't have the same scent on it as the one they picked up in Unit 4. Maybe the baseball cap isn't related to what went on in there at all."

"You know you don't believe that, Syl," said Felicity softly. "None of us do."

Freddy nodded. "I doubt, however, that there's anything more to find out in the dunes. The dogs might have missed the scent from the cap simply because the scent from the garbage bin next to it overpowered all other smells."

"It does get rather odiferous out there sometimes," agreed Jimmy.

"I'm sorry to say this," continued Freddy, "but it's likely the hat was left behind when... someone... was put into the trunk of the car with the HR3 003 license plate."

It's pretty much we were all thinking, but hearing it said aloud had a nauseating effect on most of us. We fell silent, lost in our own disturbing thoughts, until Jimmy suddenly remembered the list of scriptures.

I got Freddy and Felicity caught up on just enough about my early morning trip to Spartina Point to raise both pairs of their eyebrows into a high arch. Then I printed off four fresh lists of the Bible verses I'd entered into the database earlier and handed each person a copy and a pen.

We eagerly gathered around the kitchen table, and I, for one, was grateful for something to do while we waited for the K-9 Unit to finish their search.

"So what is it we're supposed to be looking for?" asked Felix.

"Clues," I replied. "We know that Deena, not her real name, told me she was 'researching' a book she was going to write. We also know that writers often write about things that are close to home."

"Write what you know," Jimmy chimed in. "That's what they always say."

"Makes sense," agreed Freddy.

"And we also already know that every one of these Bible verses mentions something about fish." I looked at my three friends sitting around the table and shrugged. "But we don't know why."

"So you figure if we brainstorm together, we might come up with something," said Felicity.

"Exactly!" interjected Jimmy once again. "Four brains are better than one."

"Have you shared any of this information with Sheriff Donaldson yet?" asked Freddy. "I think we need to follow protocol and honor the chain of command here."

"Uh... well..." I stammered.

"I take it that's a 'no'," said Freddy.

"Everything's been happening so fast, there just hasn't been time," I defended myself. "It's not like we're holding out on him on purpose."

Freddy scowled and sat thoughtfully for a moment. "Okay," he finally said, "I guess it won't hurt anything to take a look at these verses before he knows about them. We'll just make sure he knows the moment we suspect we've found anything."

"Right," said Jimmy, "just doing a little investigative research. No harm in that."

Felicity was already putting on her teacher's thinking cap. "Is this list written in the same order as they were on the bookmark you copied them from?" she asked.

"Yes it is," I replied. "Apparently Deena, not her real name, went straight through the Old Testament to the New, jotting them down in this exact order."

"Then I guess we'll just take it from the top," said Freddy, now serious about Sheriff D's directive to take charge in here while he was outside. "Genesis, Chapter One, Verses 20 and 21."

"Shall we just read the part about fish?" asked Felix.

"That's what they all have in common," Jimmy said, rather unnecessarily.

Freddy considered this for a moment. "Yes, let's start with just the lines or phrases referring to 'fish' and see what we come up with. We can go back to gather more information from the rest of the passages later, if we need to."

"Genesis 1:20-21," Felicity began, "God created the great creatures of the sea."

"'Great creatures of the sea' isn't specifically about fish," I said, "but this verse was written first on the bookmark."

Freddy nodded. "Ok, then maybe Deena was just warming up, or maybe we're talking about great big fish creatures." He smiled, and made a notation on his paper. "The second one is Genesis 1:26-31."

"The only specific fish phrase in that one is 'let them rule over the fish of the sea'," said Jimmy, without consulting the list in front of him.

"Jimmy!" I said, "don't tell me you were able to memorize all eight verses and phrases!"

"Geez, Syl— This is from one of the best parts in the Bible. God's creating the heaven and the earth and—" he stopped abruptly. His face, which had been unnaturally pale all afternoon, turned a light, healthy pink.

I grinned. "Jimmy, you constantly surprise me."

"I don't just put the Bibles in the motel rooms, you know," he replied. "I've actually read clear through the book several times."

Freddy cleared his throat. "Theological discussions will have to wait. We're now on Exodus 7:18."

"The fish in the Nile will die, and the river will stink," Felix read from the paper.

"Those fish guts last Saturday morning sure stunk," I said.

"And so did the fish head tied to Priscilla's collar a little while ago," added Jimmy with a shudder.

Freddy made another brief notation. "Might be nothing, might be something," he said. "We'll sort it all out later." Consulting his list, he continued, "Job 12:7-10."

"Or let the fish of the sea inform you," read Felicity. "Sounds like it might be a line in some kind of 'Finding Nemo' spy movie."

Nobody commented further on that, not even Jimmy.

Freddy went on. "Job 41:7."

"Can you fill his hide with harpoons or his head with fishing spears?"

Jimmy brightened at this and bounced up and down in his chair. "Speaking of fishy movies, this one sounds just like *Moby Dick*! You think maybe Melville got his inspiration from these verses? You think maybe Deena is writing an epic story like *Moby Dick*? Like maybe a sequel or something?"

I thought it was blasphemous to use the name 'Deena' and the word 'epic' in the same sentence, but again, I managed to keep my comments to myself. And there are people who say I have no self-control! I may end up biting my tongue in half with the effort, but I wouldn't be the first one to make disparaging remarks about Deena's writing, even though I found Jimmy's idea totally ludicrous.

Freddy dutifully jotted Jimmy's idea down.

"The next one is in Hosea," said Felicity. "Chapter 4, verses one through three. It ends with 'the fish of the sea are dying'."

"Could refer to a red tide or something like that killing them off," suggested Freddy. "Poisoned waters, maybe an environmental statement about pollution."

"Assuming these verses are about a book she's working on, we don't even know the setting where it all takes place," I said. "Could be anywhere, like about the oil spills in the gulf."

"Good point," said Freddy. He made another notation.

"The next one's from Matthew," said Felicity.

"The first book in the New Testament," supplied Jimmy, "if that makes a difference."

"At this point, we're not sure what makes a difference," said Freddy. "So I'm writing down every single thing we come up with that might have even the tiniest significance. True brainstorming has no edit or filter."

"Matthew 4:10," continued Felix, "Come with me..."

"And I will make you fishers of men," finished Jimmy, dramatically.

"Show off," I muttered.

Freddy chuckled, and I made a face at him.

"Fishers of men," said Freddy. "Anybody got anything on that?"

"The Fighting Fishermen are the high school's mascot," offered Felicity, "but then, I doubt either Deena or Uncle Harry would actually know that."

"I'll write it down anyway," said Freddy. "You never know."

"So that brings us to number eight," I said. "Matthew 7:10. "Or if he ask for a fish, shall we give him a serpent?"

"Hey," said Jimmy, "you know that old saying, 'give a man a fish, and he'll eat for a day, but teach a man to fish and he'll eat for a lifetime'? Maybe that's somehow connected, too."

"The way Mr. X told that story," I said, disdainfully referring to my former spouse, "it ends with 'teach a man to fish, and he'll sit out in the boat all day drinking beer'."

I don't talk about Mr. X very often, and I think my mention of him now made all three of my companions a little uncomfortable. Another silence fell on the table like an old-growth fir tree.

"Ok now," said Freddy at last, "let's see what we've got."

He consulted his notes. "First, let me read straight through this once without interruption." He made a couple more quick marks on the paper.

"By putting it all together in this order, we have: God created great sea creatures. Men rule over the fish of the sea. The fish in the Nile die and the river stinks. Let the fish inform you. Can you fill his hide with harpoons or his head with fishing spears? The fish of the sea are dying. I will make you fishers of men, and finally, if he ask for a fish, shall we give him a serpent?"

Freddy's eyes met the eyes of each of us. "Well?" He focused on Jimmy. "Mr. Bible Know-it-all Guy, what do you make of it?"

Jimmy shrugged. "I've already put in my two cents worth."

The rest of us mulled it around for a few moments and still came up empty-handed.

"I'll read it again," said Freddy, "slower this time."

When he finished, we were still sitting there like the Biblical pillars of salt.

Finally, Felicity broke our silence. "What if we looked for a secondary theme?" asked our favorite schoolteacher.

"Ok," Freddy readily agreed, happy to have someone with something to contribute. "So, uh, just how do we do that?"

"Beyond the mention of 'fish' in each verse, what else do these selections point to?" She looked at our blank faces and smiled. "Let's all read the verses again, to ourselves. Then quickly write down the first three impressions you get from the piece. Just anything that pops into your mind."

It only took a couple seconds for me to complete the assignment. I wrote 'death, water, creatures.' Then I looked across the table at Jimmy's list. Even upside down, I could read 'dying, sea, serpents.' Jimmy had playfully connected the 'seas' and 'serpents' with a hyphen, to make 'sea-serpents'.

Next to me, Freddy had 'river' and 'die' and no third word. He looked over onto my page, and then to Jimmy's and nodded. "Oh, I see..."

Jimmy raised his head in time to catch Freddy looking at his three words. "Ms. Michaels!" he whined, "Freddy's cheating! He's copying my answers!"

I snorted, and tried to cover it with an admittedly phony-sounding cough. I looked at Freddy, who was able to maintain a much better poker face than I could.

Felix scowled in my direction, then patiently said, "He's not cheating, Jimmy—we're working together on this." She stood at the end of the table, looking for all the world like she was instructing a class of high school students.

"Let's pool our answers now and do a little more brainstorming."

In no time at all we collaboratively came up with some variation of 'dead fish in the water', the 'water's full of dead fish', or maybe 'the dead water is full of fish'.

"Hey... I just thought of something..." I wrestled my thoughts, trying to make sense of a foggy niggling in the back of my brain. "Sunday night... Mercedes and I accidentally overheard Uncle Harry talking, and he said something to someone about putting on your trunks and going swimming."

"And where were you when you accidentally overheard this?" Freddy asked.

I ignored the question and continued. "We thought somebody was going to be drowned in the casino pool, so I went in there to prevent anything bad from happening, but nobody showed up."

"Let me get this straight," said Freddy. "You were wearing a bathing suit in the pool at Spartina Point, the one with the aquarium-like viewing area in the bar, and I missed it?" He leered at me like a horny Cheshire cat; he seemed to do that a lot. "How come everybody got to see that sexy water show but me?"

"Just for the sake of argument," I said loudly, returning everyone's attention to the subject at hand, "let's assume Deena's notes do reflect something she's been privy to during her association with Uncle Harry."

"I thought we'd already decided to take that as an educated hypothesis," said Felicity.

"Yes, we did," I agreed. "But to continue expanding on that premise, what do we have in these notes that could possibly connect us to Keith's disappearance?"

"Keith was transporting a sturgeon—" Freddy began.

"Wait!" interrupted Jimmy. "Does a sturgeon qualify as a 'creature of the sea'?"

"I don't see why not," I said. "They're a pretty prehistoric-looking creature, if you ask me."

"HHhhmm..." said Freddy. "The fish in the Nile will die and the river will stink."

"Are the sturgeon in the Columbia River dying out for some reason?" asked Felicity.

"Not that I'm aware of," I answered. "Not in any large numbers. I do know that the Department of Fisheries is imposing a one-fish limit, though." I hoped Freddy wouldn't figure out where I'd gotten my information.

"Sylvia," asked Freddy, taking us in another direction, "do you remember exactly where the bookmark was placed in Deena's Bible?"

"Uh-huh." I nodded. "It was in the book of Job, at the page of the second reference."

Freddy consulted the list of verses. "Can you fill his hide with harpoons or his head with fishing spears?" He raised his eyebrows.

"Freddy..." I began, "remember when we crossed the casino moat yesterday afternoon? What was it you were telling me about the feeding habits of sturgeon?"

Freddy wrinkled his brow in thought. "I told you that sturgeon are bottom feeders. That they'll suck up any old garbage they can find on the bottom of the Columbia River. Why?"

"They'll eat *anything*?" I wanted to be absolutely sure of this point before I offered my hypothesis.

"Yep. Smelt, anchovies, herring and sand shrimp are probably their food of choice, but they're not picky. The stinkier the better." He grinned. "I always spray anise oil or WD-40 on my bait to attract them to it."

"So..." I took a deep breath and jumped on in. "What if someone 'filled his hide with harpoons'?"

"I'm afraid I don't follow you," said Freddy.

"Filled his hide," I repeated. "What if that refers to force-feeding a sturgeon?"

"With harpoons?" asked Jimmy, pushing his glasses up again.

"With drugs," answered Felicity, piecing together what I'd been trying to say. "What if Uncle Harry was smuggling drugs by force-feeding the sturgeon some type of, you know, zip-lock bags or something like that, full of cocaine or heroin or methamphetamine or some other street drug?"

"Then that would mean Kasey, and Keith, have been running drugs from the port to the casino," said Freddy.

"Unknowingly," said Felix. "Remember, we must give them the benefit of the doubt. It's innocent *unless* proven guilty, not always *until*."

"Don't rule out the possibility that Kasey's extra cash came from his silence, as much as his service," I said to her, putting a hand on her forearm. "Best not to have blinders on about this, Ms. Michaels."

"We better let Sheriff D in on what we think we've discovered," said Freddy, rising to his feet.

"And maybe," said Sheriff Donaldson, his booming voice startling us from the doorway, "maybe you've known all along what fishy business your uncle and your father were in on, Freddy."

"Carter!" I didn't want to believe my ears. "Just what are you implying?"

Sheriff Donaldson stepped into the room and held out his hand to Freddy. "I hope I'm wrong, but I have to ask you to hand over your cell phone, son."

CHAPTER 17

Freddy didn't hesitate; he immediately complied with the sheriff's request. All he said was, "Would you like me to relinquish my badge and service pistol, too?"

"No need," replied Sheriff Donaldson. "I don't think we're in any danger of being mass murdered at the moment."

"If that's an attempt at humor," I said darkly, "it falls way short."

The sheriff flipped open Freddy's cell phone and checked the recently called numbers while the rest of us just sat there, aghast. "Look, I'd be remiss if I didn't cover all the bases," he said. "I just want to be one-hundred percent sure Freddy hasn't been tipping anybody off about our investigation."

Freddy had called the motel phone when he'd asked me to attend the anniversary party with him yesterday, so when I heard the sheriff read the Clamshell's number aloud, it came as no surprise.

"That's the motel's number," said Jimmy without hesitation.

"Oh, that's right," replied Sheriff D. "I remember now." He'd been sitting here at the table with Jimmy and me when the call came in, so he was well-aware of the reason for that call. The sheriff's eyes met mine. "That was when he called here to ask you out."

"It was *not* a date!" I shrieked.

"It wasn't?" asked Freddy, leering at me again. "So you go wrestling around in chocolate with just anybody these days?"

"How come you never told me you two were dating?" Felix asked me.

"Cause Freddy and I are almost the same age," Jimmy answered Felix, "and Syl's all wigged out about it."

"I am most certainly *not* wigged out about it!" I punched him in the arm for emphasis.

"Oh, then we *are* dating." Freddy continued to smirk.

I looked at his eyes twinkling and his dimples deepening, and my mind went to mush. I could think of absolutely nothing to flip back at him to prove his statement false. All I wanted at that moment was to wrap myself safely in his arms, chocolate or no chocolate.

Sheriff Donaldson snorted and flipped to the main directory of phone numbers. "I see he's got both of your numbers in here," he said to me.

"What business is that of yours?" I snapped.

Then I turned my ire on Freddy. "My home phone is listed in the phone book. How'd you get my cell phone number? I don't recall ever giving that to you."

"I'm a trained investigator," he said without remorse. "And since we're dating and all, I thought you'd want me to have it."

If there'd been not quite so many witnesses, I might have punched him in the arm a second time, but he'd have probably misconstrued it as foreplay.

"I hate to interrupt your lovers' quarrel," said Sheriff Donaldson to Freddy. "But
how come there's no listing for Harold Rodman? You got your uncle in here under a code name or something?"

Freddy guffawed. "As I'm sure I've mentioned before,

we're not that close."

His boisterous laughter, and the way he sat there, so totally at ease with the sheriff's invasion of his privacy, apparently satisfied his boss. I know it worked for me. Either Freddy had absolutely nothing to hide, or the man was a very talented actor. My Gibbs' gut intuition, as Jimmy called it, told me Freddy was totally trustworthy.

Sheriff Donaldson handed the phone back to Freddy. "Sorry about that, son."

"No problem. I'd have done the same thing myself," Freddy graciously replied with a half-hearted shrug. "Don't worry about it." He clipped the phone back to his belt.

"Sheriff Donaldson..." Felicity broke the uncomfortable silence in the kitchen. "Have... have the dogs found anything else out there?" She inclined her head slightly toward the door.

Sheriff D shook his head. "I'm afraid not."

Felicity blew out a sigh of relief. "I suppose that's bad news for you, but it's good news for me." She shuddered. "I can't imagine being the one to have to identify a body or anything."

"I doubt we'll ever find a body," said the sheriff. "Too many places around here to hide things. The whole county is dotted with massive wooded areas, and with the peninsula being surrounded on three sides by water, well..." He sighed. "It's real tough to get closure on people reported missing."

"What about the baseball cap?" asked Freddy.

"I'm sure Kasey wasn't wearing his cap this morning," Felicity said. "Some of the kids were wearing their hats inside the house, and I've been trying to teach my students better manners than that, so I reminded them, for like the bazillionth time, that when a roof covers your head you really needn't wear a cap to keep the weather off, since there's no rain or sun indoors, and Kasey stood there grinning like crazy cause he wasn't guilty—this time—and I told the boys—" she abruptly stopped talking.

"You finally run out of air?" laughed Jimmy.

"I'm sorry," said Felix, "I ramble when I'm nervous."

"It's understandable," said Sheriff D. "And for the record, I commend you on your attempt to teach them hat etiquette."

Sheriff Donaldson chuckled, then he turned somber. "But both boys' names begin with the letter 'K'," he began, "and the name on the cap says 'K Walker.' So we don't know for sure if it was Keith's or Kasey's, or even when or how it got here."

"We're left with still more questions than answers," I said. "Even if the hat belonged to Kasey, Keith could have been wearing it."

Felicity smiled. "In my experience, girl twins share everything; boy twins not so much. I doubt the boys ever traded hats."

"What about DNA, then?" asked Freddy. "Wouldn't that tell us if Keith had been here?"

"Unfortunately, DNA in identical twins is almost always identical," said the sheriff. "Almost always," he repeated for emphasis.

"Unless the genes mutated after separation in the womb," supplied Jimmy, matter-of-factly.

We all turned and stared at him.

Oblivious to our collective surprise over him having this bit of pertinent information tucked away in that incredible brain of his, he continued, "But it's a very small, very tiny percentage, and not likely to show up with regular testing anyway."

"Thank you, Professor Einstein," said Sheriff D, a bit testily. "I was just about to mention that."

"However," said Freddy, "They will be able to match the DNA on the cap to the DNA left in Unit 4, right Sheriff?"

"I was just about to mention *that* too," said the sheriff. "I handed all today's evidence— the fish head, cat collar, gas receipt and all—over to the K-9 guys, who will deliver it to the lab techs. We should know something definitive in a day or two."

Sheriff Donaldson paused briefly, and looked out the window toward the dunes in quiet thought. Then he turned and said, "Now you know as much as I do about what's going on out there. So tell me, what've you four been up to in here?"

We all began talking at once. The sheriff threw his hands up in a 'stop' gesture, and we immediately complied, but as soon as he put his hands back down, we all started talking at the same time again.

"Whoa! And *stay* whoaed!" Sheriff D bellowed.

Instantly, we shut our mouths. I was pretty sure Felix disapproved of his classroom management techniques, but it was certainly effective, and she wisely chose not to voice her opinion about it right now.

"Deputy Morgan, what do you have to report?" asked Sheriff D.

Freddy, with a little help from the rest of us, quickly related our findings, and/or our suspicions, to the sheriff. While Freddy reviewed his notes aloud, the sheriff nodded sagely and stroked his mustache, but to his credit, did not once interrupt.

"So that's when we decided to come get you," finished Freddy, "but you were already standing in the doorway."

"Yes, well, I can see how you've come to your

conclusions," said Sheriff D. "And you may be right about drugs being transported in the sturgeon bellies." He continued to nod thoughtfully while he spoke. "Whether either of the twins, or both of them, knew anything about it will come out in the wash... eventually."

"Kasey might have known, but if Keith knew, I doubt we'd have found his baseball cap here," said Freddy.

"How do you figure?" asked Sheriff Donaldson.

"From what we've been piecing together," said Freddy, "Kasey picked up the sturgeon at the port at 7 o'clock, and was to have the fish to the casino by 8 p.m."

"That's right," said the sheriff, still tugging on his mustache and nodding like a bobble-head doll. "Go on."

Felicity supplied the next piece. "But since he didn't get off work until 9:30, he was already an hour and a half behind schedule.

"Now let's suppose someone was anxiously watching for this 'delivery.' They wait an hour. Nobody shows. They know what to look for—a red pickup truck."

"They might even have had the license plate number," interjected Jimmy.

"Very true," continued Freddy. "So let's say they drive south from Spartina point looking for Kasey," said Freddy, "and they locate his truck parked behind the market."

"And they lay in wait," said Felix, putting in her two cents worth, "and when they see Keith come out of the store, they inadvertently kidnap him instead."

"Or maybe, since the guys registered in Unit 4 were already checked in," added Jimmy, "someone called them to go locate the missing delivery."

I'd been quiet throughout this discussion, but now I jumped in with a thought of my own. "Hold on a minute!" I turned to the sheriff. "Did you put out an APB on Kasey's truck?"

Sheriff Donaldson looked at me with—I don't know what—in his eyes. "Sylvia," he said, "I know my job. I reported Keith missing yesterday afternoon. I put out a tri-state AMBER Alert when you returned from your house and said he hadn't shown up at the high school campout."

"An Amber Alert?" asked Felicity.

Jimmy piped right up. "AMBER Alerts began in 1996, originally named for 9-year-old Amber Hagerman. Then they made it a backronym for 'America's Missing: Broadcasting Emergency Response'."

By now we were all getting used to Jimmy's encyclopedic brain.

"But isn't that just used for younger children?" ask Felicity.

Felicity has been a high school teacher her entire career. In my former line of work, it was, unfortunately, important to know the abduction guidelines. "It's used for children up to age 17," I said.

"Waiting 24 hours before filing a Missing Persons report is customary," supplied Freddy, "but not mandatory. Especially when the missing person is a minor. With younger children it's urgent that you not wait at all, but with teenagers it's a judgment call."

"Right," said Sheriff D. "And when I put out the AMBER for Keith, I also
put out a BOLO on Kasey's truck at the same time."

"BOLO?" asked Felix.

"Be on the lookout." Jimmy, Freddy and I all answered her at the same time. I guess Felicity is the only one of us who doesn't watch too much television.

Meanwhile, my respect for Sheriff Donaldson had gone back up a couple notches. Carter had formulated his own theories and quietly acted on them. He was the right man for this job, his personal indiscretions notwithstanding.

"So did you find the truck?" asked Jimmy, getting us roughly back to the point.

"I cannot comment on an ongoing investigation," said Sheriff D, not meeting anyone's eyes as he spoke.

I think most of us instinctively knew from his body language and carefully chosen words that he knew exactly where the truck was, and that it was not good news.

"Hey!" said Jimmy indignantly, "you have to tell us! Nobody here's going to go ratting to the press or anything."

"Sheriff Donaldson," said Felicity, begging him with her eyes, "please tell us what you know."

Sheriff D looked out the window and over across the dunes again and sighed. "Ok," he finally said, but it goes no further."

"You have our word," said Felicity.

The sheriff spoke slowly and carefully. "A late-model Nissan pickup truck was located six or seven miles off a north county logging road this morning by some mushroom hunters."

"What color was it?" asked Felix.

"We can't be sure," said the sheriff.

"You can't be sure what color the truck was?" Jimmy's eyebrows met his hairline. "Why not?"

Sheriff Donaldson exhaled slowly while he chose his words. "The license plates had been removed and the truck was burned beyond any hope of color recognition. Whoever torched it must have used gallons of accelerant. We do know, that it was burned a couple days ago."

"Like maybe last Saturday morning?" I asked.

"Saturday morning..." Felicity squeezed her eyes shut and took a deep breath. "I'm almost sorry I asked."

Sheriff D awkwardly patted her shoulder. "I know this won't be much of a consolation, Ms. Michaels, but no human remains were found in, or around, the truck."

He was right—it was no consolation. Felicity turned and threw her arms around him, clinging tightly, sobbing uncontrollably into his shirtfront.

"Ms. Michaels—" Sheriff D tried to extract her, but with no success. Pleadingly, he looked at me.

"Felix," I said gently. I put my arm around her waist and gently but firmly turned her toward me. "Come—sit down."

Jimmy handed her a kitchen hand towel, the best he could do at the moment, and Felicity immediately blew her nose on it.

"Let's go back to the sturgeon," said Sheriff Donaldson, helping us all regain some semblance of composure. "The sturgeon are placed directly into the moat, right?" He looked around for confirmation, and got a room full of head nodding. "So who takes them out of the moat?"

It was time for me to come clean to Sheriff D about my first trip to Spartina Point with Mercedes Sunday night. He knew we'd gone into the casino to spy on Uncle Harry, but when he first chastised me on the subject, I'd merely told him we hadn't learned anything important, and sidestepped the details.

The sheriff didn't know anything about Mercedes and the magical key card, and I was afraid full disclosure now might get one or both of us thrown in jail.

"Sheriff," I began, "what's the statute of limitations on breaking and entering?"

"Oh boy." Sheriff D grimaced. "Sylvia, what have you done?"

Trying my best to make it sound as non-law breaking as

possible, I told him how we'd placed water glasses against the wall in the suite adjoining Uncle Harry's and related as much as I could remember about the conversation we'd heard.

When I finished, Sheriff D stared at me with an indescribable expression. I braced myself for the tirade I knew I deserved.

He took yet another deep breath. Slowly, softly, he said, "Didn't I tell you not to go getting in the way of our investigation?"

"Technically, Carter, you didn't tell me that until after Merc and I had already gone eavesdropping."

"Funny you didn't mention anything before now about your B & E during that Sunday night rendezvous with Mercedes."

"Breaking and entering," three of us said simultaneously to Felicity.

"I knew that one," she replied.

"Sylvia?" said Sheriff D.

"It's all water under the bridge, now, isn't it?" I stood with my fists grinding into my hips, glaring at him.

"And speaking of water," Freddy thankfully interrupted our stare down with a rather sloppy segue, "when you thought someone was going to be drowned, Sylvia, you assumed it would be in the casino pool, right?"

"Of course." I nodded.

"The fish in the dead water will die," Jimmy softly transposed a few words in the phrase we'd all been playing with earlier. "A moat's water is stagnant, isn't it?"

"Yes," said Felicity. "And stagnant and dead are pretty much the same thing."

Sheriff D's radio cackled and he stepped outside. The rest of us remained silent as we struggled individually to process the information.

When he came back through the inner door, the sheriff was almost smiling. "We just caught us a break," he said. "You know that note in the fish head—the one that was written on the back of a gas receipt?"

"How could I forget," said Jimmy, shuddering for emphasis.

"Well, it turns out the gas was paid for with a credit card, and the printouts display the last four digits," continued Sheriff Donaldson.

"And they didn't use a stolen credit card?" asked Freddy.

"Apparently the fish head episode wasn't premeditated," said the sheriff. "Which is good news for us. The lab guys were able to match the last four digits to a credit card issued to Rodman Enterprises."

"Which means what, exactly?" I asked.

"Which means there's 'just cause' to bring Uncle Harry and associates in for questioning," answered Freddy.

"But what about the sturgeon in the moat?" asked Jimmy. "Wouldn't it be better if drugs were found in the fish before you grabbed the guy?"

"Well," said Felix with renewed verve, "I think it's certainly time for all of us to take a little field trip up north, don't you, Sheriff Donaldson?"

"Not all of us," said the sheriff authoritatively, "just Freddy and me."

"Hey!" said Jimmy. "It's a free country! If Syl and Felix and I want to go gambling up at the Spartina Point casino right now, you can't stop us!"

Sheriff Donaldson rolled his eyes and conceded defeat. "Just stay out of our way. All of you." He called dispatch and arranged for both other deputies on duty to meet him at the drawbridge of the casino right away. "Tell them to use the lights and sirens only until they get past Ocean Crest. I need them there as soon as possible, but I don't want to announce our arrival."

Freddy and Sheriff D ran to the parking lot and climbed into the Sheriff's SUV. Jimmy made sure Priscilla was tucked safely inside, then he, Felix and I hurried to my flower-powered Mustang.

"Shotgun!" yelled Jimmy, clambering into the front passenger seat. The top was still down from my earlier trip, and I was grateful he opened the door to get in and not try to pull some 'Dukes of Hazard' vault over the side. I stopped to hold my car seat forward so Felix could climb into the back.

The sheriff pulled from the lot a few seconds ahead of us, leaving a spray of gravel behind him in his haste.

"Son of a bitch!" I yelled. "There goes the paint job on my hood!"

"You can sue the county later!" hollered Jimmy, pounding on the dashboard like he was whipping a horse. "Just don't let them get away!"

Felicity, meanwhile, was still struggling to get her seatbelt fastened in the back seat. I looked at her in the rearview mirror, her eyes red and puffy and her face distorted by a combination of grief and fear.

I stepped on the accelerator and the needle moved quickly up to 50 miles per hour, the legal limit for the highway. The sheriff's Interceptor, lights flashing, was leaving us far behind.

"Step on it!" hollered Jimmy again. "They're getting away! We're going to miss all the good stuff!" He made a noise like a police siren.

I pressed a little harder on the gas pedal. When we got

up to 70, I held it steady.

"Jesus, Syl, won't this thing go any faster?" asked Jimmy.

I raised my eyes to the mirror to look again at Felicity in the back seat. Her shoulder-length hair was in motion all over her head, much like Medusa's mythological snakes.

She met my gaze in the mirror. "I'm—pretty—sure—nobody's—going to—stop to—give you—a ticket," she fought the wind to force the words out.

Afraid to watch the speedometer, I firmly pressed my foot to the floorboard, and was rewarded by seeing the gap close slightly between the two speeding vehicles. Wind whipped through the car, literally taking our breaths away.

Jimmy sat up straight in his seat and stretched to raise his head slightly above the windshield. The skin on his face rippled and rumpled like my hands did in one of those newfangled public restroom blow dryers. I thought then, and again now, that the effect was straight out of some horror movie.

Jimmy opened his mouth and I thought his head might be ripped right off. "Wheeeeeeee!" he screamed as if he were on some kind of roller coaster ride at Disneyland. His spiked blonde hair plastered back flat against his skull.

Felicity reached forward and yanked on the back of Jimmy's shirt. Thankfully, he hunkered back down and turned to face me. His eyes were watering from the force of the wind, while I prayed my contacts wouldn't dry out and affix permanently to my eyeballs.

"Cowabunga!" hollered Jimmy.

Cowabunga, indeed! I took a quick peek at the dashboard dials and continued to white-knuckle the steering wheel. I didn't know at what point we'd blow a head gasket, or throw a rod, or whatever else might happen, but figured if the sheriff's vehicle could go that fast, so could my Mustang.

Felicity sat forward and she pushed her head between the bucket seats. "Good thing there's not much traffic tonight. At least none going north."

"They're all pulling off the road for the sheriff to go by," I hollered back. "And I've got my emergency flashers going, so they're not about to pull out in front of us!"

"Hey!" Jimmy said again. "Anybody want to have dinner in the casino restaurant later? It's all-you-can-eat Taco Tuesday."

I would have given him a dirty look, but I was afraid to take my eyes off the road long enough to make my point. Mario Andretti, I'm not, but I was determined to get us there in one piece, and I made good on that just a few short minutes later. With genuine, wet-armpit relief, I wheeled into the Spartina Point Casino and Resort main parking lot at a much slower pace.

The sheriff's rig was parked by the moat, next to a squad car. Since the cruiser hadn't passed us on the way here, I assumed they'd either come up the back road of the peninsula, or were already north of us when dispatch called them out. Both vehicles still had their whirling blues going. It wasn't quite dark enough yet for the casino's parking lot lights to come on.

I didn't want to call any more attention to the fact we'd arrived so quickly, so I pulled my car into an available lined parking space several cars down from the action taking place at the moat.

Jimmy immediately popped out of the car and joined the officers' conversation. Sheriff D, Freddy, and two deputies stood in a small huddled cluster, apparently strategizing.

The sheriff talked animatedly, gesturing with his hands. Freddy was nodding in understanding, while one deputy was adamantly shaking his head, and the other's distorted expression could definitely frighten small children.

This ought to be good.

CHAPTER 18

I extracted myself from the car and was pleasantly surprised my knees didn't buckle as Felicity and I walked toward the men.

"Hey! Wait up! What's going on over here?"

I turned to see Mercedes hustling her sequined self across the parking lot from her motorhome. Even her shoes and matching handbag were sparkling in the evening light. *Honestly!* The woman could keep several dozen Asian children gainfully employed making all the sparkling beads and bangles for her wardrobe alone.

"How come nobody tells me when somethin' big's comin' down?" Merc arrived beside Felicity and me and bent over double, gasping for air. She really did need to put in some time at the gym, but at the moment I chose not to mention it again.

"Looks like an episode of 'Cops', she choked out. "What's with all the flashing lights?"

Merc straightened up, and I put a finger to my lips, shaking my head. There'd be plenty of time for explanations later. Right now I wanted to be able to hear what Sheriff Donaldson was planning to do without being told I didn't belong here.

Mercedes made a motion of zipping her lips and the three of us women edged just close enough to hear the sheriff's orders to his deputies.

"...but you better leave your shoes on. Might be broken

glass on the bottom," Sheriff D was saying. "And you definitely will need your heavy-duty gloves."

"Definitely," Freddy chimed in. "The ridges of spines along their backs are extremely sharp, and you won't be able to grab them without industrial protection."

"But Sheriff," whined the taller of the two deputies, "I don't wanna ruin my uniform. My wife'll kill me if I have to buy a new uni. It's just not in our budget this month, or next month either. What if the water makes it shrink?"

"That material is wash and wear," Jimmy said with a snort. "To keep it from shrinking, maybe you shouldn't eat so many donuts."

The sheriff glared at Jimmy, then continued to the officers, "Just get in there, will you? We can sort all this all out later—uniforms, shoes, gloves—the works."

The two young deputies hustled to their vehicle and removed their wallets and everything else from their pockets. Then they began dragging their feet, taking their sweet time, carefully placing their utility vests, along with their personal items, on the driver's car seat.

Meanwhile, Sheriff Donaldson was chomping at the bit. He paced back and forth along the edge of the moat. "Bill! Bob! Would you two hurry it up? We're losing the natural light out here. Get a move-on, will you?"

They reluctantly came back to the moat, pulling on their all-weather, Kevlar-lined, cowhide gloves and began working their way down the steep embankment, hanging onto each other for support and muttering unintelligibly. Bill lost his footing and slipped the final foot or so, sending water splashing up on Bob.

Bob's outburst was now anything but unintelligible. "Holy Mother of Mrs. McGillicuddy! What the hell did you splash me for?"

"Don't blame me," said Bill. "It was you who let go." He wiped his face with his sleeve. "Just watch what you're doing when you step down. It's slippery."

Bob stepped down into the water beside Bill and both men stood just about knee-deep. They bent over to peer into the muddy water.

"Lotsa coins been tossed in here," said Bill.

"Yeah, I'll bet there's over a hundred bucks or better right here by the bridge," said Bob.

"Gamblers," said Freddy, smiling. "They're a superstitious lot."

"I guess since there's no fountain, the moat is the next best thing," said Bill.

"Think any of them actually improved their luck by tossing coins in the moat?" asked Bob.

"What I think," said Sheriff D, "is that you two better hurry up and corral one of those fish or you're going to be needing all those coins to supplement your unemployment."

Bill took a tentative step toward the center of the trough. "How deep is this thing, anyway?"

"It's only supposed to four and a half feet in the center," answered Freddy without hesitation. "It was built shallow so the patrons could see the fish when they walked across the bridge."

"And you know this, how?" asked Sheriff Donaldson.

Freddy shrugged. "I worked with the construction crew here last summer during my days off."

Sheriff D scowled. "I thought you said you and your uncle weren't close."

"We're not."

"So why'd he hire you for just two days a week?"

Freddy sighed. "Uncle Harry didn't do the hiring, and

the foreman was in such a hurry to get this place up and running, he didn't care if his employees were full or part time. And since I was usually available mid-week, it worked out great."

The sheriff considered this statement, and said nothing more.

Meanwhile, Bill and Bob were both more than waist deep in the water.

"I'm only 5 foot 8," said Bob, using one hand on the footbridge to balance himself. "If it's four and a half feet deep, that doesn't leave much room."

Mercedes couldn't contain herself. "Whaddya wanna bet he wrote 5 foot 10 on his job application?" she whispered. "Never met a man under six feet yet who didn't lie about his height—*among other things!*"

I contained a snort, then elbowed her to keep quiet.

"Well," said Freddy, "I doubt the guy sitting on the backhoe actually got out a tape measure while he was digging. Let's say it's five feet, tops."

"Just grab one of those fish, throw it up here, and you can both get out and get yourselves dried off," said Sheriff Donaldson.

The men tentatively moved toward one of the six or eight sturgeon we could see lurking on the bottom near the bridge. The 5-foot fish lazily waggled his tail and moved just out of reach.

"It's not going to hold still for you, you know," said the sheriff. "One of you needs to get on each side, so it can't get away."

Bill eased back away from Bob and started working his way around the fish nearest his friend. The sturgeon saw him coming and decided it was a good time to swim under the bridge to the other side of the mock moat.

"How 'bout that one?" asked Bob, pointing to a lunker now resting close to the embankment.

Bill took a step forward and his foot slipped on the silt-covered bottom.

Kersplash!

Bill emerged spitting and sputtering, and the first thing he saw was Bob laughing his head off. He took two quick steps and dunked Bob's head under water.

"Hey!" yelled Bob when he reemerged. "Whaddya do that for?"

"Now we're even," said Bill, "and we don't have to worry about getting any wetter. Let's just get ahold of one of these damn fish and get out of here."

The next few minutes were nothing less than a scene right out of the Keystone Cops. The two totally incompetent, bumbling men, flopped, floundered, and flailed in the water until exhaustion threatened to overtake them.

While the deputies were busy putting on a show, I used the opportunity to quietly introduce Mercedes to Felicity and bring her up to speed on the missing student and the possible drug trafficking connection.

"Hay-soose!" she whispered. "Didn't I tell you Uncle Harry was bad guy? I just didn't know how bad." She turned to Felix. "Any chance the missing kid ran away from home? Kids that age do that sometimes."

Felicity shook her head. "Not this one."

The men stopped their futile escapades and leaned against the bridge support to steady themselves, heaving for air.

Sheriff Donaldson sighed and looked at Freddy. "Care to join them?"

Before Freddy could answer, two uniformed men

arrived from inside the casino.

"What took you so long?" barked Sheriff D. "We've been out here almost 20 minutes. Don't you monitor those security cameras better than that?"

The men stole an uncomfortable look at each other before one of them replied. "Rodman's got us watching the tables, not the parking lot. It was a hotel guest who saw your lights out here from her window and called the desk to ask what was going on."

Sheriff D looked up at the building, where there were faces peering out from numerous windows, but none yet from the fifth floor. Then he looked at the sole big, black, shiny Lincoln parked in the reserved space nearby. "Have you informed Rodman of our presence?"

The same security guard spoke again. "No, sir. Not yet. He doesn't like to be bothered with our day-to-day activities. He's only to be disturbed for the big things."

"And we weren't sure yet if this was a big thing," chimed in the second guard, happy to have something to contribute.

Sheriff Donaldson nodded. "I'd appreciate it if you both went back inside, and didn't bother to tell Rodman about this. It's a police matter, and we've got it handled."

"Yes sir," said the first guard.

"Be happy to do that sir," said the second one.

The men turned as one and quickly reentered the casino.

Sheriff D turned again to Freddy. "I take it your uncle also hires part-time security guards?"

"It's cheaper not to have to pay full-time employee benefits," said Freddy. "But don't you worry," he continued, "one uniform is enough for me. I haven't moonlighted here since the general construction was finished."

"Well, son," said the sheriff, "that's certainly good to know." He paused. "Now, how about hopping in there with these two clowns and getting us one of these fish to take a closer look at?"

Freddy hesitated. "Sir," he began, "with all due respect, sir, since you're probably planning on slitting the belly of one of these sturgeon anyway, I don't think we have to haul them out alive." He beamed. "So why don't you just shoot one of them, Sheriff?"

I'm pretty sure Felicity, Mercedes, Jimmy and I all held our breath.

Sheriff Donaldson clapped Freddy on the shoulder. "Son," he said, "that's a right fine idea. And the restaurant can just make it their special tonight."

"Again, sir, with all due respect," said Freddy, pushing his luck, "if we find what we think we're going to find, won't we need the entire fish for evidence?"

Sheriff D chuckled. "Wouldn't that be something to take to the guys in the evidence locker?" Then he turned somber. "But you've got a point, Freddy, and we do need to document the chain of evidence."

"Sylvia! Before it gets any darker, would you please get the camera out of my Interceptor and bring it here?"

"No need, Sheriff!" piped up Mercedes. "I been taking pictures ever since I got here." She held up her smart phone. "Got all the pictures we need, right here. Could even use the video option if you want me to."

Sheriff Donaldson cleared his throat. "Sylvia? The camera?" Then he turned to Mercedes. "Don't you go selling any of those pictures to the media, and if you even *consider* posting them on YouTube, Facebook, or Twitter, I'll arrest you for obstructing justice."

Merc, bless her heart, stood her ground. "I ain't

obstructing nothin'," she said, going toe to toe with the sheriff. "I'm just an interested citizen, checking up on how my tax dollars are being spent."

"Listen here," said Sheriff D, "I could give you a half dozen logical reasons why it wouldn't be good idea for you to broadcast or podcast or whatever it's called, when we're just here doing some preliminary investigating." He paused and then added, "But I'd prefer you just stop recording *because I said so.*"

Sheriff Donaldson towered over Merc by a good foot. She's not one to be easily intimidated, so I think maybe she was hoping to have some bargaining power if she ever ended up in the local court. She wisely tucked her phone back into her bra.

I retrieved the camera with the large 'For Official Use Only' sticker from the sheriff's rig and took it over to him. "Want me to take the photos?"

"Sorry," he said, shaking his head, "a deputized officer must be the one to document the custody of evidence. I want to take no chances that another smart aleck attorney could get Rodman off on a technicality again. "

"I totally understand," I said, and handed the camera to Freddy.

Freddy grinned lecherously, then immediately took a photo of me. "For my scrapbook," he whispered. Then he quickly took several of the casino sign next to the bridge, the men in the water, and the police cars in front of the building.

"Okay, Sheriff," he said, "I got the establishment shots. And the correct date and time are already set, so fire at will."

"Whoa! Whoa! Whoa! Just hold on!" Bill frantically waved his arms in the air above his head.

Freddy couldn't help but chuckle. "I said 'fire at will,' not 'fire at Bill'."

"Will and Bill are both short for William," said Felicity.

Mercedes started to giggle. I do that sometimes too when I'm tickled by something funny, or when I'm really nervous. At the moment it could be either scenario, and I didn't dare look at Merc for fear of losing all control.

Sheriff Donaldson pulled his revolver from the holster. "I'm not going to shoot either one of you, no matter what your name is." He paused, then quietly said under his breath, "Too many witnesses."

"Wait a sec!" yelled Bill again. "What if the bullet ricochets off the water?"

Bob positioned himself slightly behind Bill. "Yeah, what if one of us gets hit?"

"Then your widows will collect on your county life insurance," said Sheriff D without a trace of a smile behind his mustache. He looked straight down into the water and took careful aim.

Felicity and Jimmy both put their hands over their ears, squeezed their eyes shut tight and grimaced, anticipating the next sound.

Ka-pow! Ka-pow! The sheriff fired twice at point-blank range while Freddy documented his actions with pictures.

Bill and Bob stopped cowering and waded over to retrieve the sacrificed sturgeon.

Freddy handed me the camera to hold. The waterlogged deputies grunted and strained, and finally managed to hoist the fish up high enough so he could grab it by the tail and drag it out onto the edge of the parking lot. Then Freddy gave the guys a hand up before taking the camera back and snapping a few more shots.

"You weren't kidding about those sharp spines," said

Bill. "Even with the gloves on, I could feel 'em tryin' to stick me."

"Yeah," said Bob, "how'd you manage to pull it up without gloves on?"

"I grabbed it by the tail," said Freddy, shrugging. "There aren't any spines on the tail."

Mercedes was busy digging in her clutch purse again. "Here!" she said, coming up with a four-inch pearl-handled knife. "You can use this to cut it open!"

Sheriff Donaldson's eyebrows went up a notch. "What else you got in that bag?" he growled. "You don't have any other concealed weapons in there, do you?" His eyes narrowed as he peered at her.

"This here knife's for protection," Merc growled right back at him. "A girl's entitled to carry protection."

Before the sheriff could reply, Freddy reached out and took the knife from her. "Protection?" He whistled softly. "This is a genuine Smith and Wesson S.W.A.T. automatic knife." He pressed a hidden button and the blade shot forward.

"A switchblade?" Jimmy squealed and jumped back. He knocked into Felicity, who grabbed his shoulders to steady them both.

"Where'd you get a knife like this?" asked Sheriff Donaldson.

"I dated a cop for awhile when I lived in the city," said Merc. She shrugged. "I wanted to get something out of the relationship, so I took the knife when I left."

I knew she'd taken purple latex gloves from a doctor, and now a S.W.A.T. knife from a cop. I wondered what trophy she'd claim if she'd ever dated a stripper.

"You stole his knife?" asked the sheriff incredulously.

"You wanna use it or not?" Mercedes put her fists

against her hips.

I knew she was employing all the bravado she could muster to distract the sheriff from looking into her sequined handbag. No doubt she was carrying her unregistered pink .22 in there too. And probably a generous supply of condoms.

"Yeah," said Freddy, "this'll do fine." He handed the camera to the sheriff. "If you don't mind, sir, I think there's just enough daylight left to record this." He stooped over and began to slit the belly of the sturgeon open as the sheriff photographed him. The rest of us gathered as close as we could to watch.

To no one's surprise, the fish's guts were filled with heavy-duty plastic pouches, sealed tight. There were also numerous bright shiny coins that had been ingested since the fish arrived in the moat.

"Hay-soose," muttered Mercedes again, "this here fish's sucked up more change than I made in tips last weekend."

Freddy carefully cut into a corner of one pouch and handed it to the sheriff. "It looks like either cocaine or heroin, Boss."

Sheriff Donaldson turned to Bill and Bob. "I think it's time you two made a little visit to the penthouse to collect our suspect."

"But—we're all wet," said Bill.

"Yeah," said Bob, adjusting the crotch of his pants. "I need to get home and change before I chaff."

Sheriff D shrugged. "I just thought you two'd want to be the ones to apprehend Harold Rodman the Third on suspicion of drug trafficking, that's all. I can go get him myself, if neither one of you want to go on record as the arresting officer."

I smiled. Carter was throwing Bill and Bob a bone as

their reward for going into the moat, and it was darn nice of him to do so.

Both young men perked right up.

"Yes sir," said Bill. "Right away, sir." He immediately started for the casino door, Bob hot on his heels.

"Deputies!" bellowed Sheriff Donaldson, emphasizing his words by pointing to their vehicle. "While I hope you don't need your weapons, you *are* going to need your cuffs!"

The men sheepishly returned to their squad car, put their utility vests back on, and zipped them up. Together they strode with heads held high, across the drawbridge and through the large, glass casino doors.

Freddy got a battery-powered handheld spotlight from the back of the Interceptor. He and Sheriff D started counting the number of sturgeon in the moat, estimating the cash value of the drugs.

"Largest drug bust ever in this county," said Sheriff Donaldson. "Too bad it's not an election year."

Freddy grinned. "Oh, I'm sure you'll get enough publicity to garner up a commendation or two, maybe even one from the DEA and one from the governor. Then you can trot the clippings out when it's time to run again."

The flashing lights of both vehicles were still going full-tilt, and a small crowd had gathered around us in the parking lot.

"Nothing to see. Nothing to see." Sheriff D motioned with his hands for the looky-loos to go on inside. "Show's over."

But the show was far from over.

The sound of Uncle Harry's helicopter starting up on the helipad behind the hotel instantly claimed our attention.

"Damn it all!" exclaimed Sheriff Donaldson. He drew his weapon from the holster for the second time. "We can't let him get away!"

We heard the chopper lift off, and just as it crested the building, Sheriff D fired two warning shots straight up into the air. As if on cue, the floodlights of the casino came blazing on.

Those high-powered floodlights, combined with the flashing blues of both police vehicles, must have been momentarily blinded the pilot. He miscalculated the height and location of the massive flagpole sporting the Rodman family crest on the east corner of the building and flew right into it.

The chopper rotated almost clear around the pole, and for just a moment, I thought the pilot might regain control. Then the helicopter catapulted in slow motion, end over end, and crashed just out of our line of vision inside the overflow parking lot, apparently exploding on impact.

The noise of shrieking metal, the flash of fire extending up over the short line of golf course trees, the full blossoming mushroom, was too much for Felicity. She screamed and buried her eyes in Jimmy's chest.

Sheriff Donaldson slid his gun back into the holster and he and Freddy started running toward the scene, the sheriff calling for an ambulance into his radio as he ran.

Mercedes and I took off after them, our reaction time just a little slower.

"Hay-soose!" Mercedes puffed as we ran. "I hope they didn't hit my motorhome. All I own is in that trailer! If they hurt one little hair on Brutus' sweet little head, somebody's damn sure gonna pay. You don't go messing with me or my dog without serious repercussions, you can bet your sweet ass on that!"

I figured Merc's motorhome, with or without Brutus, wasn't in anyone's thoughts but hers right about now. The fireball from the wreckage had produced enough heat to peel the paint off a few of the employee's cars parked out there.

We caught up with Freddy and the sheriff as they stood at a respectable distance from the crash sight. "Cancel that ambulance," Sheriff D said into his radio. "Just send out the meat wagon, the fire department, and the lab techs."

Freddy reached out to put a protective arm around me. There was nothing anybody could do but watch the blaze as it burned itself out.

"There's irony for you," said Sheriff Donaldson. "Rodman installed those flagpoles with banners advertising his family crest just to piss off the commissioners who told him he couldn't build more than five stories high." He shook his head sadly. "He was done in by his own ego."

We stood in silence until we heard the fire trucks careen into the main parking lot. In a few minutes, reporters would be swarming in for the story. Sheriff D turned to head back to the slain sturgeon to finish collecting the evidence.

Debris from the explosion littered the area. Mercedes walked over between two unscathed cars and picked up one Louis Vuitton, gold lamé shoe.

"Don't anybody move!" she yelled, turning back toward us, waving the footwear in her hand. "Y'all have to help me find the other one of these shoes. They're just my size!"

CHAPTER 19

It was well after midnight by the time Jimmy, Felicity, and I returned to the Clamshell. The trip south took considerably longer than the trip north had, despite the fact we knew the exact location of the entire North Beach Peninsula police force.

Walter was sitting in his car in the parking lot waiting for us when we pulled in.

"My kids!" exclaimed Felicity, pushing me out of the way to scramble out of the backseat of my car. "Who's watching my kids?"

Walter walked over and placed his hands on Felix's shoulders. "Kasey's parents showed up a couple hours ago and spilled the beans." He pulled her to him and she collapsed against his chest, sobbing. "I'm so sorry."

"What about the other students?" I asked.

"As soon as they heard, the rest of the kids packed up and took off for home." Walter managed a weak grin. "They said they'd be back to clean your place later."

Right that minute I couldn't have cared less.

"I'll put on some coffee," said Jimmy, unlocking the motel office door. "Decaf." He made eye contact with me and softly smiled. "Please, everyone, come inside."

The four of us gathered around the kitchen table and filled Walter in on the sobering evening's events at Spartina Point. When we finished, Walter just sat there, his mouth opening and closing like a guppy, looking from one to the other of us.

"You all could have been..." he began. "I had no idea the extent of..." His voice cracked. "I'm just so glad you're all alright."

"We're fine," I assured him. "And I'm sorry we didn't check in with you before now. I just thought you'd still be at my house with the kids."

"The kids..." Felicity said quietly. "My kids." Tears started rolling softly down her cheeks again. "Our kids."

I reached over to take her hand. Walter, sitting on the other side of her, did the same. Jimmy walked around the table and put his hands gently on Felicity's shoulders and we paused for a moment, each in our own thoughts.

"Poor Keith. Poor Kasey." Felix shook her head. "Kasey's going to feel guilty about this forever."

"He's not responsible," I said, unnecessarily. "He couldn't have known he was being used to run drugs up the peninsula or he wouldn't have been so cavalier about handing off his delivery job to Keith. I don't think either of them had any idea what was going on, if that's makes you feel any better."

"In a way, it does," said Felix. "I'd like to think it was merely a tragic chain of events that got Keith killed. But I'm not sure Kasey will ever forgive himself."

"Twins are always so close." Jimmy added his two cents.

"Yes, they are," I agreed, "but this is going to impact everybody at the high school to some degree, students and staff alike."

"Speaking of the high school," Walter interjected, "Principal Anderson has already called me to request my assistance. I'm going to be coming in for a few days to help with the grief counseling."

Felicity nodded. "Even without a body, there'll have to

be some kind of service for Keith. It'll probably be held in the gym. Everyone will want to be there."

"But none of us are going to be very useful if we don't try to get some sleep," I said, standing up and placing my coffee cup into the sink. "I've a feeling the next few days are going to be long ones."

Walter and Felicity declined Jimmy's offers to give them both rooms at the motel, wisely deciding they wanted to sleep in their own beds at home. I wanted that, too, but Jimmy was not about to let me leave.

"We still don't know where those other guys are in their big, black, shiny cars," he said, digging his fingernails into my forearm. "You have to stay, Sylvia; they might still be after me."

Reluctantly, I agreed to spend what was left of the night at the Clamshell. I hated to admit it, but Jimmy was right about his life being in danger. Somebody, somewhere, still thought he was witness to a murder, and Jimmy was a loose end.

"Don't worry," said Jimmy, "everything will look better in the morning."

I wanted to slug him when he said that, but instead I went quietly into his bedroom and shut the door without further comment. I knew I only had a few hours to try to make peace with his mattress.

Oddly enough, I slept, and when I awoke, the day did seem brighter. The fact that it was after 10 a.m. and the sunshine was streaming through the window probably had a lot to do with my improved disposition.

I pulled on Jimmy's bathrobe, used the bathroom, and headed for the kitchen, where I could smell what I hoped was fresh coffee, and not last night's reheated decaf stuff.

"Good morning, beautiful," said Freddy, sitting

comfortably on the couch. He was dressed in his full deputy's uniform. Priscilla was curled in next to him. "Join me in a cup?" He lifted his coffee mug in salute without getting up.

"Only if I can drown you in it," I growled.

"Oooohh, I see someone's not a morning person."

I ignored his remark, fished my previous night's coffee cup out of the sink, rinsed it out, and poured myself some of the steaming brew. "Where's Jimmy?"

"Sheriff D dropped me off here and took Jimmy to the station so Bill or Bob can take his formal statement."

"Carter's not going to take it himself?" I sat in the recliner next to the couch and modestly pulled the hem of the bathrobe over my knees.

"The sheriff has his hands pretty darn full this morning," said Freddy, chuckling. "Three news crews arrived from Portland, two from Seattle, and he's doing everything he can to make the most of it."

"Getting his 15 minutes of fame, is he?"

Freddy chuckled. "I suspect he'll be putting a video link on his resume next time he runs for office."

We sat sipping our coffee in companionable silence for a few minutes, and I was almost able to forget my hair was a mess and I had no makeup on. Almost.

"So why are you here this morning?" I asked, pulling Jimmy's robe a little tighter about me.

"This is big, Syl," Freddy began somberly. "The DEA guys are swarming all over the place. Right now they're at both the casino on the north end and the port down south in Unity." He stopped talking and thoughtfully scratched behind Priscilla's ears.

"Oh, geez... Freddy... Your dad..."

"Yeah," said Freddy softly, "my dad." He took another

large swig of coffee, draining his cup. "They don't know for sure what his involvement is in all this, but Sheriff D told me to lie low today and let the Feds do their job."

"Sounds like good advice." I got up to get us both a little more coffee. "But why are you *here*, exactly?" I asked, leaning over to refill his mug.

Freddy grinned, showing his dimples again. "Because the sheriff wants to be sure *you* stay out of the way, too."

"*What?!*" I nearly poured coffee in his lap. "Carter sent you to keep an eye on me? The nerve of that guy! I mean, I could understand when he thought I needed a bodyguard, but a babysitter? *Seriously?!*"

"I dunno," said Freddy, smirking, "I thought I pulled a pretty darn good duty this shift, all things considered."

I left him sitting there with that stupid smirk on his face while I went in to shower and dress. If Sheriff Donaldson thought I was just going to sit idly by and do nothing today, he had another thought coming.

But for some strange reason, I took a little extra care and time making myself presentable this morning. I returned to the kitchen dressed in navy slacks and cream-colored blouse. Two men in black coveralls with white letters on the back proclaiming 'DEA' were parked at the kitchen table with Freddy.

"Good news, sweetheart," said Freddy, looking at me with an impish grin.

I made a mental note to chastise him for so loosely using the word 'sweetheart' at a more private time.

"Dad's been arrested, his boat's been confiscated, and these nice gentlemen want to know if you can provide an alibi for him for last Saturday night."

I failed to see how any of this was 'good news,' but I kept my opinion to myself. Obviously, Freddy was under a bit of a strain.

"Ms. Avery," said the agent closest to me, "Richard Morgan claims he had dinner with you last Saturday. Can you collaborate this?"

"Can I..." I wrinkled my brow, painfully aware that I was speeding toward the need for Botox injections to smooth it back out. "Saturday night? Don't you mean he needs an alibi for *Friday* night?"

The agent sighed. "Please, just answer the question. Mr. Richard Morgan, a.k.a. Captain Morgan, says he had dinner with you last Saturday evening at the Rusty Rudder. Is that a true statement?"

Freddy made eye contact with me and tilted his head, waiting attentively for my reply. I couldn't tell if my answer was going to make him feel relieved or piss him off.

"Technically, that's correct," I said slowly, measuring my words. "I had an early supper at the Rusty Rudder and I shared a table with Rich. We were together from about 4:30 until just after 6 p.m. Why?"

"We'll ask the questions, ma'am," said the smartass seated closest to the door.

"If I'm providing someone with an alibi, the least you can do is tell me why he needs one for that particular day and time." I just barely refrained from finishing my statement with 'you little control-freak punk.'

"I'm sorry," said the agent who'd asked me the first question, "but we cannot comment on an ongoing investigation."

I'd heard the very same statement from Sheriff D just a day ago. The standard company line, the end-all, be-all phrase to absolve any type of law enforcement officers from telling you what's really going on.

"Fine," I replied, marching to the door and dramatically

swinging it open. I motioned with my index finger for them to leave. "Then have a nice day."

The two men stood, shook hands with Freddy, and nodded to me on their way out.

"Well?" said Freddy, after the outer door shut.

"Well, what?"

"When were you going to tell me you're dating my father?"

I walked to the refrigerator and stood there holding the door open, both to cool me down and to search in vain for something that might pass for a reasonable breakfast. All I saw were the cartons of Jimmy's leftover Chinese food from last Friday night, and I was afraid of what I might discover growing in there if I peeked inside.

"Sylvia?" Freddy obviously did not know when it was prudent to back off.

I closed the door, turned around, and sighed. "I'm not 'dating' your father, Freddy. If you want to get technical about it, I'm not dating you, either, so don't get so... so... *whatever* with me."

He quickly clasped his hands to his chest and grimaced. "Ouch! You sure know how to hurt a guy, Syl."

"Look," I said, softening a little, "I didn't even meet you until Sunday morning, and although you bought breakfast for both Felicity and me at the Sea Biscuit, we've never had a real date."

Freddy scowled. "So what do you call our trip to the anniversary party at the casino on Monday?"

"It was *not* a date!" I stomped my foot for emphasis.

"We were all dressed up," countered Freddy.

"We were there on an Uncle Harry reconnaissance mission, and nothing more."

His scowl turned into a sly grin. "We took an intimate

chocolate bath together just two days ago, and still you deny me?"

I tossed a dishtowel at him; he was lucky the first thing I laid my hands on wasn't a cast iron frying pan.

Thankfully, the bell on the outer office door dinged, sparing me from any further reflection on Freddy's perception of our relationship. *Relationship?* I honestly didn't know how I felt about him, or his father Rich, for that matter, who is only five years older than me, not 15 years younger.

Sheriff Donaldson strode into the room without knocking, and went straight to the fridge. "You got any soda?" he asked. "I'm about all coffeed out." He helped himself to a can of diet cola, popped the tab, and sat down at the table.

"Those DEA guys don't mess around," he said. "They've just been waiting for a chance to shake down some of the independent fishermen around here. Wish they'd let me know what they were up to before now." He took a swig of his soda. "I feel kinda foolish about all this." He stared down into his pop can.

"About all what?" I prompted, anxious for him to continue.

"Let me guess," said Freddy. "The port in Unity is the hub of a major drug ring that begins in Mexico and works its way north from port to port a lot like a modern-day Underground Railroad."

"Only the drugs are boat-hopped by otherwise honest fishermen who aren't catching enough fish to make their boat payments and are looking to score some quick cash."

Sheriff D peered at Freddy. "How did you know?"

"Yeah, how *did* you know?" I echoed.

Freddy shrugged. "Dad's known something wasn't quite

right with some of the independent guys for some time. He suspected what was going on, but with his own boat to run, he didn't have the time or opportunity to investigate."

"And now it looks like he's been caught right smack dab in the middle of it," said the sheriff.

"You think he knew the sturgeon he sent to the casino were stuffed with contraband?" I asked.

"No way!" said Freddy, "I'd bet my life on it. Dad's always been as straight an arrow as they come."

Sheriff Donaldson tilted his head, considering. "Your faith in your father is admirable, son," he said. "And I hope you're right about him."

"But how is it possible he didn't know?" I stubbornly pursed my lips. "Wasn't he the least bit suspicious when he was asked to provide a delivery boy for these other fishermen?"

"Everybody down there used Dad's delivery network," said Freddy. "He got some kind of a commission whenever another boat used his high school kids to run fresh seafood to any of the peninsula restaurants."

My eyebrows shot skyward. "So your dad's a delivery pimp?"

"Ba-ha-ha-ha!" laughed Sheriff Donaldson. "I'll have to remember to repeat that one to the boys at the DEA."

"You'll do no such thing." Freddy scowled at him. "Dad's just a regular guy, trying to make a decent living."

I put my hand over Freddy's. "I'm sure he is," I whispered just to him. Then I turned to Sheriff Donaldson. "So— Do we know anything concerning the whereabouts of HR3 003, John Smith, Robert Jones, or any of the other... uh... 'associates' of Uncle Harry?"

Sheriff D nodded. "The 003 Lincoln was abandoned in a rock quarry up near Quilcene. Apparently, either the occupants or the local gun enthusiasts used it for target practice. It's totally pock-marked. No telling how many of your shots hit the mark, Syl."

"Isn't that area a part of the Olympic National Forest?" I asked.

"I don't think that was much of a concern for them. The way I figure it, Quilcene is about as far as they could drive under the cover of darkness. They must have gotten somebody to follow them up there to give them a lift back. If they'd driven during the daylight hours, the car would have been seen and reported right off."

"So what about those accomplices?" asked Freddy.

In the trunk of HR3 001, we found Rodman's personal laptop." Sheriff Donaldson smiled. "The guy didn't even bother with passwords."

"Don't tell me that all his business dealings, including names and numbers were listed in his laptop unprotected," said Freddy.

"Ok," said the sheriff, smiling slyly, "I won't tell you."

"Fabulous news!" said Freddy, perking right up. "This is great! It will totally clear my father of any wrongdoings!"

"We all hope that, son," said Sheriff D, nodding. "The DEA is going over those files with a fine-tooth comb even as we speak."

"That *is* excellent news," I said. "As soon as everyone's rounded up, then Jimmy can get back to sleeping with both eyes closed." I chuckled, then sighed. "Although I do feel sorry for Deena, not her real name."

"Why so?" asked Freddy.

"The poor woman just wanted to be a writer. She thought Uncle Harry was going to be her E-ticket to the publishing world."

Freddy nodded. "And the only thing she ever wrote was

a list of Bible verses..."

"And technically, that's what got her killed," I finished for him.

Sheriff Donaldson took his last sip of cola and crushed the can in his hand. "That reminds me. The memorial service for Keith is tomorrow afternoon," he said. "It's in the paper today. Two o'clock at the high school."

And on that somber note, he stood up, tossed the soda can into Jimmy's recycling bin, tipped his hat to us both, and let himself out.

"So," said Freddy, as we watched the sheriff pull out of the driveway, looks like tomorrow's going to be a pretty emotional day on the North Beach Peninsula."

"I don't even want to think about it," I replied. "High school kids shouldn't be dealing with death and grief. They should be planning their proms and looking toward the future with hope and happiness."

Freddy reached over and placed his hand on my arm. "You want something really good to look forward to, Syl? Something beyond tomorrow's memorial?"

I stood up and got a paper towel so I could blow my nose. It was either that or go to the bathroom for some toilet paper. Jimmy lived frugally; he didn't believe in spending money on tissues, and I wasn't even sure he'd washed the kitchen hand towel Felicity had blown her own nose on yesterday.

"What do you have in mind?" I asked Freddy.

"On Friday," he said, "the Memorial Service will be behind us and things will slowly begin to get back to normal." He paused, making sure he had my attention. "So how about you and I go out on a *real* date?"

I froze with the paper towel pressed against my nose. I lowered it so I could speak. "A date? You're asking me to go out, like to dinner or something, on Friday?" I know I sounded ridiculous, paraphrasing his words like that, but I was stalling for time to think this through.

"Yep." Freddy nodded. "I thought we'd keep it simple and go to Cinco Amigos. I know we both like the food that place puts out. And you do have to eat, you know."

I finished blowing my nose and threw the paper towel in the trash under Jimmy's sink. "I do enjoy the food there," I said tentatively. "I could eat it every day."

Freddy took it as a good sign that I hadn't immediately said no. "I can pick you up at your place, or meet you there, whichever you prefer."

I know I surprised him when I offered no argument. "Thank you, Freddy. I'd prefer to meet you there. Will 6:30 work for you?"

At 6:30 on Friday, Freddy stood next to the restaurant door under the porch roof overhang, trying to avoid another one of our chilly, all-day spring drizzles. He was holding a single red rose in his hand when I pulled my Mustang into the parking lot.

Right behind me came Jimmy in his Pinto, Felicity in her Camry, and Walter in his blue nondescript Chevy sedan. The front lot was nearly full, so we parked one, two, three, four, all in a row at the far side of the building. Freddy looked a little sheepish as we bailed out of our cars and approached the front door.

"They have to eat too," I told him.

Refusing to be intimidated, Freddy presented me the rose. "I didn't bring a flower for anyone but you," he said, gallantly holding the door as we all traipsed inside.

"Not a problem," said Jimmy, "we can all share Syl's rose. We'll just stick it in a water glass on the table for a centerpiece."

Freddy chuckled good-naturedly and said he thought that was a fine idea.

"Me gustaria una mesa para cinco personas, por favor," said Felicity to the host waiting to seat us.

"Table for five," said Jimmy.

"She just said that," said Walter as we followed the maitre d' through the restaurant to a larger table in the back. "Mesa means table and cinco means five."

"Oh, right," said Jimmy, as we all took our seats. He cagily tried to position himself between Freddy and me, but Freddy was too quick for him.

"Look you guys," said Freddy when we were all seated. "I get that Syl was too uncomfortable to have dinner here with me alone, and that's fine. I have no problem with three chaperones."

I opened my mouth to protest, but he held up his hand to keep me from speaking. "We can even order a big family-style meal," he went on. "But I simply must draw the line at paying for all of you. I'm going to have to insist upon splitting the check, got it?"

"Got it," Jimmy replied, nodding happily. "And I'll even spring for the barbecued pork appetizer myself."

Pedro, our waiter, came and poured hot oolong tea for each of us. When he left with our order, Walter lifted his teacup in a toast, and we all followed suit. "To good friends!" he said.

"To very, very, good friends," I amended, looking fondly at each one of them sitting around the table. "Where would we be without them?"

With his free hand, Freddy reached over and squeezed my knee. He winked at me and smiled.

"And here's to the DEA for locking up all Uncle Harry's

henchmen and throwing away the key!" added Jimmy.

"And here's to Keith," said Felicity softly. "May he rest in peace."

Walter looked at Freddy. "Would you like to add something to the toast?" he asked him.

But before Freddy could reply, his cell phone rang.

CHAPTER 20

Freddy looked at the number on the display and frowned. "Sorry," he said, "I have to take this. It's Sheriff Donaldson."

He got up to leave the table. Walter motioned for him to stay seated. "You may as well talk right here, Freddy. We're going to ask you all about it as soon as you finish the conversation anyway."

Freddy smiled, shrugged and sat back down. He swiped his finger across the screen. "Hello?"

Not one of us could keep from leaning in to eavesdrop.

"Yes. Uh-huh. Of course. Yes sir. That's right. Sylvia, Felicity, Jimmy and Walter are all right here with me." He covered the mouthpiece and whispered, "He wanted to know if I could fill everybody in, and I told him we were all here together."

"Well, duh," said Jimmy, busily running both sides of a piece of barbecued pork through the hot mustard before popping it into his mouth.

Freddy took his hand off the receiver and put it back against his ear. He listened intently for several minutes. "Yes sir. That *is* a relief."

He put his hand over the mouthpiece again, as if that would do any good. "Dad's going to get off with probation and community service. It's not going to trial. The DEA held a preliminary hearing this morning and made several recommendations to the county prosecutor. The judge agreed not to be too harsh on Dad for wanting to trust his half-brother. They released his boat since there was no evidence Dad had knowledge of any crimes."

We all smiled and nodded knowingly. The judicial system on the North Beach Peninsula was well known for coloring just a little outside customary lines.

Freddy listened without comment for a few more moments, his eyes getting bigger and bigger. "Is that so?" he finally said. The color seemed to drain from his face. "Well, yes, I guess that's true."

"What's true?" Jimmy impatiently blurted. "You're listening too long without telling us what he's saying."

I used my chopsticks to poke Jimmy in the ribs. "Shhhhh..."

Freddy was totally focused on the phone call, staring down into his empty plate. "Okay. Uh-huh. I'll do that." He nodded while he spoke. "First thing Monday morning. Uh-huh. And Sir—thank you very much for calling, Sir. I appreciate it being you who gave me the news." He hit the hang up button and sat in silence.

"Well?" said Jimmy.

But before Freddy could answer, Pedro arrived with numerous platters heaping with sweet and sour chicken, pork chow mein, egg foo yung, tempura shrimp, crab puffs and egg rolls. All conversation came to a halt as we hungrily dished up our plates and began devouring the food.

When Jimmy finally came up for air, he queried Freddy again. "Well?"

"Well," said Freddy. He swallowed and set his fork down while the rest of us continued eating. "It looks like I'm buying dinner tonight for everyone after all."

"You are?" asked Jimmy. "Then I'm going to order one of their chocolate ginger sundaes for dessert," he said happily.

"How will you have any room left for dessert?" asked Felicity.

Walter and I exchanged glances. "Freddy," I said slowly, "what did the sheriff have to tell you?"

"Did you get a raise?" asked Walter. "You certainly deserve one, with all the extra hours you put in."

"No." Freddy shook his head. "No raise." His eyes began to twinkle. "Sheriff Donaldson just informed me that Uncle Harry's private attorney spoke up for Dad at the hearing this afternoon."

"Good for him!" said Walter. "I'm so glad!"

"The DEA plans to confiscate the entire Pacific Bluff development," continued Freddy, "but apparently dear old Uncle Harry left me a little something in a special codicil that the DEA agrees I'll be able to keep."

"I thought you weren't all that close," I said.

"Uncle Harry didn't have any children of his own—not that he admits to, anyway—so I'm it. The favorite nephew."

"How little a something?" Felicity asked.

"Did he leave you one of his big, black, shiny cars?" asked Jimmy. "'Cause if he did, you have to promise me you'll have it painted right away. If I never see another one of those cars drive by, it'll be too soon!"

The twinkle expanded, and soon Freddy's dimples took over.

"Felicity," he said slowly, "from now on, I guarantee you that no one without a high school diploma will ever again be hired at the Spartina Point Casino and Resort. Not as even as a part-time valet, housekeeper, kitchen help, golf caddy, or gift shop clerk. Anyone seeking employment there will have to finish their high school education first."

"How do you know that?" Felicity's brow furrowed.

"How can you control who works there?"

"Good grief and gravy!" My hand flew to my mouth. "Are you saying what I think you're saying?"

"Spartina Point is one of the major employers on the North Beach Peninsula," Freddy began. "No jobs, no tourists, no taxes collected—the economy of the entire county could collapse if the casino closed."

"I know Mercedes would be hurting," I said. "Her entire income revolves around keeping those doors open. Not to mention everyone else who works there."

"So..." Freddy continued, "the Powers That Be decided after Dad's hearing this afternoon that there'd be no sense in the DEA shutting the place down. It would be a lose/lose situation."

"I'm not arguing with common sense," said Walter, but how can they justify not taking every single one of Rodman's assets?"

"Apparently, there's a loophole."

"Must be big enough to drive a truck through," I suggested.

Freddy grinned. "According to the certified historical documents, the original Shallowater Reservation boundaries crossed the mouth of the bay and included Spartina Point."

"So the casino is actually on reservation lands?" asked Felix.

"Uh-huh," Freddy replied.

"And that means to be legal, it must be owned and operated by a Native American, is that correct?" asked Walter.

"Right," said Freddy, "and since Uncle Harry had no native blood in him, the casino, in fact, was operating illegally." He couldn't help himself, his grin lit up his whole face. "That is, until now."

"Fred the Red!" I exclaimed.

"*Who the what?!*" asked Jimmy. He started to push his glasses up on his nose with his middle finger, caught me scowling at him, checked himself, and used his index finger instead.

"Uncle Harry and my dad have the same mother, but not the same father," explained Freddy. "My grandfather on my father's side was half Cherokee. My father is a quarter, and I'm a card-carrying one-eighth Native American. Enough to satisfy the legal requirements for ownership of buildings on tribal lands."

"Then at the meeting after the hearing..." began Felicity.

"Turns out the DEA can do just about anything they want to," said Freddy, "so they've decided to grant the resort a special dispensation, of sorts, to keep the county's economy going."

He paused, reached over and squeezed my hand. "So, my Syllee girl— how would you feel about dating a guy who owns a casino, a hotel, and a golf course?"

The food nearly forgotten, we all turned to stare at Deputy Frederick Morgan, sole heir and new owner of the Resort at the End of the World.

"Holy crap!" exclaimed Jimmy, bouncing up and down in his chair. "Holy mother of all craps!"

I couldn't have said it better myself.

ABOUT THE AUTHOR

Long Beach, Washington, author Jan Bono has had five collections of humorous personal experience stories published, as well as two poetry chapbooks, one book of short romance, nine one-act plays, and a full-length dinner theater play. She's written for numerous magazines ranging from Guidepost to Star to Woman's World and has had more than 30 stories included in the Chicken Soup for the Soul series in the last five years. Jan was Grand Prize winner in the Coast Weekend serial mystery chapter contest in 2012. Her Sylvia Avery Mystery Series is set on the southwest Washington coast.

See more of Jan's work, and follow her blog:

www.JanBonoBooks.com
www.JanBonoBooks.com/blog